Praise for other works by Dustin Stevens:

Stevens has ratcheted-up the suspense level in this 2nd in a series book to the point where I crave a 3rd book to be written by this fine author! – Amazon Reviewer

A suspense thriller par excellence, and a must-read for fans of this genre. – Kindle Purchaser

I've read both of the Reed and Billie series, and I loved them. The relationship between the two is developing. Enough twists and action to make this another great read from Mr. Stevens. I'm really looking forward to your next installment--I'm hooked on this dynamic duo. – Verified Reader

Loved this second book in the series- who can resist watching the relationship evolve for this man and his canine partner (who are both mourning the loss of their partners). Terrific characters and suspense. More, More, More!!! – Kindle Reviewer

Must love dogs. Great story and great characters. I hope there will be many more about Reed and Billie. It took a while for me to figure out the why, but I like a good mystery and this is one. Thanks again Mr. Stevens. I look forward to reading the next one. – Amazon Customer

Thrillers are some of my favorite reads because I love to be pulled into a story and through intense situations, all in the safety of my own home. I've read some pretty good ones lately and can now add to that list author Dustin Stevens' "The Boat Man". The story of Detective Reed Mattox, who is attempting to lay low after the death of his partner, yet is pulled into a pretty intense serial murder investigation. The killer is called The Boat Man and is name after Charon from Greek mythology, who carries souls across the rivers Styx into the world of the dead. This is essentially a story of vigilante justice and the mystery involved is a very good one. I found the read to be both intense and very enjoyable. Would definitely recommend and I now plan on checking out some of this author's other novels. - Top 500 Amazon Reviewer

One of the best books I have read since getting my Kindle. The book is very suspenseful while dealing with a subject that has generated a great deal of controversy through the years. While reading the book there is a definite struggle between your heart and your brain over how you should be reacting to the events in the book. I wish every book I read was close to the quality I found in this book. - Kindle Customer

Best book I've read in a long time and I read for hours every night. It was so good to read a police thriller without the main character being "saved" from himself by some hot woman. Fantastic character development and being a dog lover, loved that he is K-9 cop. The book held my attention and I didn't figure out what was going on until the end. I read so much that I rarely leave reviews but I want the author to know how much I enjoyed his work. I highly recommend this book. - Amazon Customer

It certainly was a Thriller. I was intrigued by the complexity of sub-plots, the difficulties experienced by Maddox just trying to do his job; trying to do the right thing. Because doing the right thing is all we have to define our character once the cards are dealt. And in what was left of The Boat Man's mind he believed in his cause, too. First exposure to this author's excellent, engrossing work of art. - Amazon Reviewer

3

Other works by Dustin Stevens:
The Debt
Going Viral
Quarterback
Scars and Stars
Catastrophic
21 Hours
Ohana
Twelve
Liberation Day
Just a Game
Ink
Four

The Zoo Crew Novels:
Moonblink
The Glue Guy
Tracer
Dead Peasants
The Zoo Crew

The Hawk Tate Novels:
Fire and Ice
Cover Fire
Cold Fire

The Reed & Billie Novels:
The Partnership
The Kid
The Good Son
The Boat Man

Works Written as T.R. Kohler:
Shoot to Wound

One Last Day

Dustin Stevens

For Melissa

The strongest person in the world is
the grieving mother that wakes up and
keeps going every day.
– Tara Watkins Anderson

Section 1. The terms of the President and Vice
President shall end at noon on the 20th day of
January, and the terms of Senators and
Representatives at noon on the 3d day of January,
of the years in which such terms would have ended if
this article had not been ratified; and the terms of
their successors shall then begin.
- 20th Amendment, United States Constitution

The feel of the weapon sent a jolt of electricity the length of his arm before muscle memory kicked in, pulling him back to what felt like a different lifetime.

Only six weeks had passed since he last held a weapon, a beautifully restored Remington 870 Wingmaster pump shotgun. Bought for the specific use of hunting pheasants, it was the maiden voyage for the man and his new toy, the duo going on a Thanksgiving hunt that had netted six birds, two of which made it onto his table for dinner later that same day.

Before that he had owned countless rifles and handguns, a Wyoming man through and through, enjoying a weekend hunt as much as the occasional round of target practice out in the acreage behind his home.

Despite all that conglomerated history, not one of those instances were what came to mind as he gripped the 9mm semi-automatic in his right hand and raised it to shoulder height. Feeling the energy it possessed, the feelings it evoked, his entire being was transported back in time, every nerve ending in his body tingling with sensation, allowing him to ignore the burning in his front deltoids from keeping the weapon extended before him.

Back to a different continent, in a time when he wore another type of uniform, but was still very much in the employment of the United States government.

Back to a place where the world existed only in black and white rather than infinite shades of gray.

"Who the hell are you?"

The man across him from said nothing, merely standing and staring, a single tendril of blood snaking down out of his left nostril.

"Who sent you?"

Still there was no response, heavy breaths lifting the man's shoulders, sweat streaming down either side of his face, the defiant glare making it clear that he had no intention of answering, the malevolence in his eyes stating he would love nothing more than to be holding the gun, would not hesitate to use it if given the chance.

Seeing that very thing, recognizing it instantly, the only possible recourse was to shift his aim slightly to the side, the barrel moving from the center of the man's chest to the fleshy part of his upper thigh.

"Remember, it didn't have to be this way."

Chapter One

The bottom hem of Senator Jackson Ridge's suit legs pulled up just slightly as he leaned back in his chair and propped his feet on the edge of his desk, revealing a few extra inches of his caramel-colored calfskin boots. With both legs stretched out to full length before him, he avoided the urge to cross them at the ankle, keeping them side by side instead and rotating his toes in unison to either side.

Extending his neck up a few inches, he peered down the length of his nose, inspecting what he saw.

"I tell you, Susie, that new polish guy we have around here is one gifted sumbitch," he deadpanned, his gaze still aimed at his feet. "Any way we can talk him into heading back to Wyoming at the end of the week?"

Seated on the opposite side of the desk, Susan Beckwith, his Chief of Staff for the last sixteen years, forced the corners of her mouth up into a faint smile, glancing once to the senator's feet before looking him full in the face.

"Good morning to you as well, Senator Ridge," she replied. "And I'm not sure if Armando is looking to relocate, but we can certainly ask him."

Having done some variation of the same dance a hundred times over, Ridge let out a low snort, a smile creasing the soft skin on either side of his mouth.

"It's called sarcasm, Susie. Can you imagine what life would be like for an immigrant from Haiti back in Cheyenne?"

Not expecting an answer in the slightest, knowing none would be coming even if he were, Ridge rotated his focus across the desk and said, "And for literally the last time, would you please call me Jack?"

This time the smile that crossed Beckwith's features was a bit more sincere, revealing a thin sliver of teeth beneath her muted pink lipstick. "Not for one more day, sir."

To that, Ridge could do nothing but sigh, allowing his head to rest back on the leather chair he was seated on, the new position bringing his gaze up toward the ceiling. In his periphery he could see the long, familiar trappings of the space that had been his second home for more than a third of his life, all of it prepared with a painstaking attention to detail, fully acknowledging his home state of Wyoming.

On the wall above him was a four-by-five elk that he had harvested a lifetime before, the cape still as soft and shiny as the day it was shot. Around the edges of the room were stuffed grouse and sage hens, all either taken by his own hand or donated from a visiting constituent.

Behind him, a pair of flags hung limply on their poles, the folds of the American stars and stripes and the red-and-blue bison of Wyoming aligned with perfect precision.

Jackson Ridge had first arrived in Washington, D.C. thirty-six years prior, only five years removed from his service in Vietnam, three more than that from college at the state university, the surprising victor of an emergency election to fill a seat vacated by the sudden fatal heart attack of the longest-tenured congressman in the country.

At the time, the decision to run had been something more akin to a dare than an actual plan of any sort, the type of thing only a young man armed with arrogance and the feeling of invincibility would do. A C-student through college, the entirety of his first twenty-five years had been spent in either Wyoming or Vietnam, which, for his liking, was one place too many.

As one of just a few democrats in the entire state, the choice to run was aided considerably by the fact that he wouldn't need to appear in a primary, his only intention at the time being to give himself a bit of extra time to make a final decision on the matter.

How he had somehow managed to turn that into a narrow victory to become the sole representative from Wyoming was something that still boggled his mind, the sort of thing government classes all over the country were still dissecting.

Perhaps even more surprising was the fact that he had managed to turn the shocking upset into five more successful runs in the House before jumping over to the Senate, securing four straight terms there as well.

What had started as a crapshoot, a longshot wager that sounded like it might be interesting, had turned into more than three-and-a-half decades, the youthful exuberance that he had arrived in town with now long gone, beaten away by time and reality.

What was left in its wake was something Ridge still wasn't quite certain of, less sure if he even wanted to know.

"One more day," Ridge intoned, repeating Beckwith's words. "Thirty-six years, and we're down to one last day."

To that Beckwith again remained silent, just as he suspected she might.

Moving slowly, Ridge pulled his feet back from the corner of his desk, setting them down one at a time on the floor, the heels of the boots echoing out on contact. At sixty-six years of age, he was slowing down for sure, though he liked to believe he was doing a might bit better than most of his colleagues.

Still hanging on to most of his hair, the strawberry-blonde color of his youth had ceded to silver, cut short and pushed to the side. A matching mustache graced his upper lip and drooped down

along either side of his mouth, stopping just short of his jawline, clipped to a uniform length.

Standing an inch above six feet in height, he weighed only eight more pounds than he had the day he first showed up at the Capitol, his very first suit still tucked away in the corner of his closet, changing fashion styles being the only thing keeping it from being a mainstay in his rotation.

Shifting around to face forward, Ridge laced his fingers atop the desk before him, regarding his Chief of Staff fully for the first time that morning.

More than twenty years his junior, everything about her gave off the impression that she was the eldest in the room, from the frumpy style of her business attire to the straight brown hair that was forever pulled up high on her head. Donning the same pointed glasses she'd worn since the day she was hired, the effect was to make her eyes look two sizes larger than normal, seeming as if she were perpetually boring her gaze into him.

"So, what's on the agenda for today?"

The question seemed to be exactly what Beckwith was waiting for as a spark of energy moved through her, putting her into motion. Dropping her attention down to her lap, she flipped open the faded leather organizer she was never without, going directly to the red ribbon tucked down along the top to mark her place.

"January 2nd," she began, just as she had every morning for years, pausing only long enough to clear her throat. "First thing this morning we have a media event with some of your constituents."

Making no effort to mask the small groan as it rolled out of him, Ridge allowed his head to drop, his focus on the bare desk before him, his thoughts on the topic clear.

"Those jackals couldn't leave me alone for one more damn day?"

Brushing past the comment without acknowledgment, Beckwith continued, "These are people that happened to be in town visiting from Wyoming, folks that voted for you in the last election. Shouldn't be much more than saying thank you and asking a few softball questions. Each of the attendees has already been vetted completely."

Reading between the lines, Ridge knew that his Chief was telling him to quit complaining and suck it up, this sort of thing being just another of the hundreds he had already performed, some things simply unavoidable when ascending to a post such as his.

"And after that?" he asked.

"After that, you are having lunch with the majority caucus to discuss final transition plans."

"Final transition," Ridge repeated, the words bitter on his tongue, allowing his face to relay how he felt about the situation, the new reality still a long way from having completely settled in.

If it ever would.

"Are we still getting bombarded by that peckerwood wanting to get in here to redecorate?"

Pausing long enough to look up at him, her mouth partially open, a look of disapproval on her face, Beckwith said, "Yes, Senator-elect Hodges has again requested to gain admittance to the office so they can begin making plans for move-in tomorrow, if that's what you mean."

It was exactly what he meant, just as they both knew it was, the backhanded comment a perfect summation of Beckwith's masterful use of passive-aggression.

Moving past it, Ridge waved a hand before him. "No, absolutely not. I am still Senator until noon on the 3rd of January. He can wait until then like everybody else."

"Sir-" Beckwith began, barely getting the word out before Ridge again waved his hand her way, cutting her off.

"And you can tell the *Senator-Elect* that if he has a problem with that he can take it up with the United States Constitution."

"But-"

"Amendment Twenty."

"May-"

"Section One," Ridge said, cutting her off for the third time before settling back in his seat, his mustache twitching just slightly as he fought to hold back the smile that threatened to burst forth from him.

Tormenting Susie was truly one of the things he was going to miss in the coming months.

"With all due respect, sir," Beckwith countered, pushing the words out slowly, as if waiting for him to jump in again at any moment, "*everybody else* has allowed their successors to begin making plans."

"Yeah, well, everybody else hasn't been in the same office for twenty-four years only to get thrown out on their ass by an ungrateful populace."

Her face neutral, giving away nothing in response, Beckwith stared at him a moment before closing the book on her lap. Rising from her seat, she pressed the planner against her torso, folding both arms across it, and slowly stepped around to the backside of the chair she had been seated on.

"Yes, well, the media will be arriving here shortly, sir. I'd suggest not saying anything like that while they are here."

Chapter Two

The only thing that still looked even vaguely familiar from an hour before was the desk Jackson Ridge was seated behind and the assortment of God's creatures arranged along the walls, everything else in the room having taken on a massive overhaul.

Gone was the single chair positioned in front of him, replaced with a trio of matching seats, each one with thick wooden legs and brightly colored cloth stretched over padded cushions. In each one sat someone from the local Wyoming constituency, their collective faces relaying that they had not signed up for the situation they now found themselves in and would love nothing more than to turn and bolt from the room.

Looks that Ridge empathized and even sympathized with, the same feeling permeating his body.

Behind them most of the remaining space in the room was consumed by no less than a dozen members of the media, their respective brands plastered across the microphones and cameras they held, indicating an equal split between local stations tucked away in the Rockies and brands much closer to where they were now seated.

With each passing moment, they seemed to push in a little tighter, a constant battle of jockeying for position, each wanting to get the best vantage for any potential newsworthy item that might come to pass.

What they thought they might possibly be able to glean from such a staged presentation Ridge couldn't pretend to have any idea, well past the point of caring.

"Senator Ridge, what do you think you'll miss most about being here in D.C.?" a middle-aged woman with thick red hair asked. Seated in the far right chair, her voice was deep and low, her body wrapped in a heavy woolen sweater and a long denim skirt.

Acutely aware of the mass of humanity crammed into the back half of the room, Ridge opted to bypass the first response that came to mind, doing the same for the second and third choices as well.

Flicking his gaze to the side, he could see Beckwith pressed against the wall, her mouth drawn into a tight line, a barely perceptible twist of the head displaying she felt the same way.

More than a handful of such instances where he hadn't exercised such restraint could be easily found on YouTube or a number of other sources. There was no need to add to the collection on his way out the door, no matter how much he wanted to.

A fact Ridge liked to believe was a sign of something known as personal growth.

"About D.C.?" he asked, raising his eyebrows slightly, feigning sincerity, playing the part. "The traffic, of course. Do you know how much I'm able to get done going from one place to another in this town?"

On cue, a bit of scattered laughter rang up from around the room, the woman offering a polite smile in response.

Doubling down on his attempt at levity, Ridge added, "I mean, we come from Wyoming, where a traffic jam is considered four cars at an intersection."

To that the laughter rose just a bit, the woman's smile thawing slightly as she added, "And usually a cow or two."

Again more laughter could be heard, the woman's crack bringing about more amusement than both of the Senator's combined.

For a moment, Ridge let it go, allowing the woman the floor before the smile began to fade from his face. "No, but seriously, it will undoubtedly be the people. Not necessarily my colleagues here in Congress, but the people I've been able to work with every day."

There he paused, again glancing to Beckwith and pressing his lips together, nodding just slightly, hearing the clicking of cameras in the background as he did so.

"And just as much, I'll miss the constituents," he continued, turning back to face the woman. "People like yourselves, that take the time and effort to stop by in their journeys, or even in some cases, making this their destination, just to come see us.

"I can't begin to tell you how many quality folks from Wyoming I've encountered here that I otherwise wouldn't have, and how much they have meant to me."

Seemingly content with the response, the woman's cheeks flushed, her complexion fast approaching the same hue as her hair. Sliding her hands down the front of her thighs, her face bunched up tight in a smile, a small nod of thanks was her only response.

Matching the look for an instant, Ridge shifted his focus a few feet to the right, staring at the man seated straight across from him.

Wearing Levi's and a pressed pearl snap shirt, the man was rail thin, his long frame contorted slightly to the side. In his hands was a light tan cowboy hat, Ridge unable to see the label on the inside, but reasoning that it looked a lot like the Stetson he had back at home in his closet.

Just a few more days and a ring of mashed hair around his head would be as clear as the one now worn by the man seated before him.

"Good morning," Ridge said, nodding to the man, unspoken permission granted for him to speak.

"Morning," the man said, pausing to clear his throat, using the gesture to glance back over his shoulder at the reporters standing within arm's reach of him.

"Oh, now, don't worry about them," Ridge said, one corner of his mouth curling back slightly. "The only person in this room they'll bite is me."

Again, a small round of laughter could be heard, the comment drawing a bit of relief from the man, tension visibly fleeing him as he smiled, his shoulders sagging slightly.

"Senator Ridge, I guess I have more of a statement than a question for you here this morning."

Feeling a tiny pinprick in the pit of his stomach, not sure where the man's next words might be headed, Ridge kept his face neutral. Over the years he had faced more than his share of situations that began in such a manner, someone cloaking a backhanded stab with a thinly veiled compliment, or even worse, arriving under false pretenses only to use their ten seconds to accomplish some sort of deep-seated vendetta.

Casting his gaze over to Beckwith, he saw her standing without reaction, again hearing her words from just a short time earlier guaranteeing him that everybody present had already been vetted.

"By all means," he said, using his right hand and motioning toward himself, indicating for the man to continue.

"Well, as you can probably tell, I earn a living as a rancher in the Big Horns," the man began.

There would have been no rightly way to know where the man called home, though the first part of his statement was indeed true enough.

"You're right," Ridge replied. "My daddy was a rancher all his life. You have a similar look."

Stopping there, he waited for the man to continue, not bothering to go any further.

Years before, he might have pressed the matter, even going as far as to offer thanks to the man or launching into a lengthy diatribe about how vital his vocation was to the state, and even the country as a whole.

Through time he had come to discover that such words often came out as pandering, the media seizing on them, using every opportunity they could to undermine his credibility and integrity.

"I didn't know that," the man replied, "but it makes sense, given that you were one of the leaders to spearhead getting the gray wolf removed from the Endangered Species List. I can't begin to tell you what a difference it has made for people like me to be able to protect our herds."

Feeling the previous bit of apprehension evaporate from within, Ridge smiled. Working to de-list the wolves was at the top of the list of accomplishments he felt most proud of from his career, the move managing to simultaneously help people like the man before him and piss off a lot of tree huggers and media types in the process.

Leaning back, he shifted his gaze down for a moment, allowing his eyes to glaze over, letting every person in the room wait while he seemed to process the statement.

"You know," he began, "as a Democrat, I knew my efforts were going to alienate and infuriate a lot of people, but I wasn't about to let that stop me."

Moving his attention back up, he continued, "Like I said before, my father was a rancher, and a great many of my voters – people like yourself – are ranchers, so I've seen and heard firsthand for years what a concern wolves posed to that way of life.

"It may not have been popular, as many of the people behind you can attest, but I thought it was the right thing to do then, and I still do now. I'm just glad it helped."

"It did," the man replied, nodding in earnest before retreating back into himself, his attention again moving to the hat in his hands.

Taking an extra moment to drive home the words he'd just said, Ridge waited until just short of the brink of the room becoming uncomfortable before turning to the final chair in order.

Seated in it was a woman that looked to be nudging fifty, her face heavily lined from exposure to years of the Wyoming elements, her hair an equal mix of sandy brown and silver. Dressed in khaki slacks, her top half was swallowed by a burgundy jacket zipped to the throat, her fingers twisted together in her lap, displaying obvious nervousness.

"Hello, how are you?" Ridge asked, dipping the top of his head just slightly.

For a moment there was no response, the woman simply meeting his gaze, before she too nodded. "Hi."

Pursing her lips slightly, she continued to stare at him, seeming to be debating something internally, before saying, "Senator Ridge, I'm here to ask a favor of you."

Despite her stare, her ramrod-straight posture, her words were soft and clipped, bearing a clear amount of uncertainty in what she was doing.

Fighting to ensure there was no external response, nothing that seemed to not be completely planned, Ridge looked back at her. "Well, I'm only Senator Ridge for another twenty-five hours, but I'll be happy to see what I can do."

Despite the smile on his face, the handful of chuckles around them, the woman's features betrayed nothing, her nostrils flaring just slightly.

"Senator, when you were a member of the Senate Armed Services Committee, you voted to send soldiers into Afghanistan."

A palpable shift in the room occurred the moment the words were out, Ridge almost sensing the hyenas along the back pressing in, the pair of constituents that had already had their turn shrinking back.

His own insides clenching tight, he refused to glance toward Beckwith, making sure his aim was on the woman and her alone.

"Yes, that's right."

"One of those soldiers that went over was my son," she said, a few red lines creeping into the whites of her eyes. "And the favor I'm here to ask you today is, can you tell me if his death meant anything at all?"

Chapter Three

General Arnold Ames was the first to arrive, just as he usually was. A military man to the core, his mind was built to automatically subtract seven minutes from every appointment, the tedium of having to wait a few extra moments minor compared to his extreme distaste for ever arriving late.

The bright winter sun was blotted from view by the dark tinted glass of the front doors as he stepped inside the restaurant, the unmistakable aroma of charred meat hanging in the air, the low din of conversation and utensils scratching against porcelain just audible.

"Good afternoon, General," a young hostess with a white Oxford shirt and even whiter teeth greeted him as he entered, her lower half blocked from view by a wooden podium. "How are you today?"

"Very well, thank you," Ames replied, striding across the black marble floor and pulling up just short of her. Having no interest in how she was, or to continue the conversation a moment longer, he said, "I have a reservation for two at noon."

"Certainly," the girl replied, her mega-watt smile failing to dim in the slightest. "Would you like to be seated now, or wait for your guest to join you?"

The man he was scheduled to dine with was certainly not a guest, though Ames didn't feel the need to make the correction. "Seated, please."

Nodding once, the hostess led him down a narrow corridor, small dining rooms visible to either side, most of them already more than half full. Without glancing in either direction, not particularly caring who was present, even less who saw him, he kept his gaze aimed straight ahead, his focus just above the top of the girl's dark brown hair.

Moving in lockstep, they bypassed the majority of the building, going nearly to the far back wall, most of the ambient noise around them falling away, before hooking a left and entering a small private room. Consisting of just three tables in an even row, only the center one was set up for dining, already bearing water glasses and cutlery, a basket of bread waiting.

To either side, the adjoining tables were barren, their chairs removed.

Just as Ames had requested.

"Here you are, General," the girl replied, "your server will be along in a moment to collect your order, I will be sure to bring your guest back as soon as they arrive."

"Hmm," Ames replied, nodding stiffly, waiting until the girl had departed before stepping forward. Grabbing the table by either side, he twisted it ninety degrees so that the place settings were arranged front-to-back with the door instead of perpendicular to it.

Moving quickly, he slid each of the chairs into position before the respective plates, taking the seat on the far side of the table, his back effectively to the wall, enabling him to see everything that came or went.

The Char House was certainly a far cry from some of the more posh and trendy restaurants in D.C., the place chosen because it allowed for the sort of privacy that Ames so craved. Never did he have to worry about the prying eyes or ears of some Washington insider, able to conduct business that was best handled far from the public sphere.

Which for a man of his position, was pretty much all business.

A regular for more than a decade, the House was grateful enough for his business to cater to every request he made, knowing that the back room was the only acceptable place for him to be seated, that no other guests were to join while he was present.

Ninety seconds after the general took his seat, a young man with blue-black hair slicked flat to his head and a matching bowtie around his neck entered, bowing slightly at the waist in greeting. "Good afternoon, General. A pleasure as always."

"Hello, Richard," the general replied, refusing to ever employ the man's given name of Ricardo, "I'll have three fingers of Lagavulin, water on the side, no ice."

"Very well, sir," Ricardo answered, again bowing slightly and retreating as quickly as he had arrived.

With both feet planted on the floor, Ames kept his attention on the door, the agitation he felt hidden behind a mask that was decades in the making, the kind of thing forged through some of the worst conditions the world had to offer.

The call had come in less than an hour before, requesting an appointment he had not planned, did not in the slightest want to take. Knowing it would throw off the schedule he had put together for the day, pushing back his departure at the end of it, he had balked at first.

If he had his way, the man he was set to dine with would no longer exist, let alone be able to call him out of the blue.

The fact that he'd had no choice but to accept the meeting rankled him even further, the situation one that he had hoped would be long over by now, though each time he allowed himself to believe that, something else seemed to arise.

With his bottom flush against the seat and his spine full against the backrest, Ames sat ramrod straight and waited, a pair of countdowns moving in tandem through his mind.

The first one ended after two minutes, Ricardo arriving with a cloth napkin and his drink, setting the items down and retreating without a sound.

The second took an additional six minutes, the hostess again appearing, a tall man with receding hair and a few days of growth on his cheeks in her wake.

"Here you are, sir," the hostess said, employing the same sing-song cadence she had used on Ames.

"Thank you," the man replied, pausing inside the doorway long enough for the hostess to gather the insinuation and melt from view before taking a step forward.

Ames had first met Leopold Donner twelve years earlier in Iraq, Donner part of a contract group that the CIA had brought in to help assist with security for key personnel in the region. A former Navy SEAL, he had been not long removed from service at the time, the low man on the proverbial totem pole, still getting his legs under him on the civilian side.

It was that fact alone that had enabled Ames to deal with him, the ways of the military still very much present in the young man, his conditioning impeccable, his haircut tight, his respect for rank and authority without question.

In the time since all three had slipped to varying degrees, the freedoms of the outside world bringing about changes that Ames didn't particularly care for.

"Always with the cloak and dagger," Donner said, striding to the table and leaning across it, extending a hand toward Ames.

Rising from his seat, the general accepted the shake, squeezing tighter than necessary, letting Donner know that the comment was neither needed nor appreciated.

"A man doesn't ascend-"

"To your position," Donner inserted, cutting the older man off. "Yeah, yeah, I got it."

Feeling the acrimony within rising, a flash of warmth hitting the small of his back, Ames released the shake and lowered himself back into his chair.

"Your time since the service seems to be getting longer every time we meet."

Grabbing the back of the chair before him, Donner jerked it over to the side of the table, placing himself so he could see the door and Ames both in his periphery. "And your time in seems to get longer every time we meet. You thinking of hanging it up anytime soon?"

Already feeling a strong dislike for the man beside him, not particularly caring for the new seating arrangement or the line of questioning that was occurring, Ames fixed a glare on Donner.

"I assume you did have some purpose in calling and asking to meet here today?"

Eschewing the question, Donner raised his chin a few inches, pushing his voice up several decibels, and said, "Hey, Ricky! Can a fella get a beer in here?"

Appearing an instant later, as if teleported into the room, Ricardo stood in the doorway, his hands again clasped behind his back, his body stooped forward just slightly at the waist.

"Of course, sir. What would you like?"

"Anything in a bottle," Donner replied. "None of that on-tap stuff for me."

"Certainly," Ricardo said, again disappearing as quickly as he had arrived, much in the same manner as he had with Ames.

Watching the sequence with a look of bemusement on his face, Donner kept his attention on the door, Ames feeling his aggravation grow with each passing moment.

"Again I ask, you did have some purpose in calling and inviting me here today, correct?"

Aware that he was being baited, the general watched as Donner took his time twisting his attention back to the table, the same half-smile still in place.

"Relax, you're a government employee. There's nothing that can't wait a few extra minutes."

More heat flashed to Ames's face, his upper lip growing moist, his features hardening.

The lunch outing was not something he had planned, a perfectly decent salad and sandwich both still stowed in the lunch sack in the bottom drawer of his desk.

Donner had one minute to start making sense, or he would leave the still untouched scotch on the table and stick his cohort with the bill.

Seeming to sense the line of thought that was playing out beside him, or at the very least having the common sense to realize when he was in danger of overplaying his hand, Donner raised both his hands in concession, the smile falling away from his features.

There he remained, silent, as Ricardo delivered his beer, paying the bottle no mind as they waited for the room to be theirs again.

"Have you seen the news this morning?" Donner asked, dropping his tone slightly, for the first time giving Ames the impression that there was some actual reason for their meeting.

"Not since breakfast," Ames replied, leaving any response at that.

Shifting onto his left haunch, Donner pulled a smartphone from the side pocket of his cargo pants and placed it on the table between them. Tapping at the screen a few quick times in sequence, he twisted the item so it was facing the general.

"This just went live a little over an hour ago."

Ignoring the handful of questions that instantly came to mind, Ames slid his attention from Donner to the phone, a video display consuming the entire screen.

The angle of the image was from on high looking down, the camera work a bit shaky, the color a tad distorted as if being shot beneath bad lighting. In the center of the screen was a middle-aged woman with sharp cheekbones and a burgundy coat, graying hair pulled back behind her head.

Never before had Ames seen her in his life.

A moment later sound became audible, starting with basic background noise before the woman started to speak, her voice low, just barely perceptible.

"Senator, when you were a member of the Senate Armed Services Committee, you voted to send soldiers into Afghanistan."

Feeling his breath draw in sharply, Ames flicked his gaze to the doorway, seeing nobody, before glancing back to the phone. Still far too early to know what he was seeing or why it was brought to him, he couldn't deny the palpitations running over his scalp, making his steel-grey flattop itch.

Once the question was asked, the camera shifted slightly, moving from the woman across a wide desk, finally coming to rest on a man that Ames was infinitely more familiar with.

"Yes, that's right," the man replied.

Again the camera tilted away, this time returning to the woman. "One of those soldiers that went over was my son, and the favor I'm here to ask you today is, can you tell me if his death meant anything at all?"

Abandoning his position against the back of the chair, Ames leaned forward, folding his arms before him and resting his weight on his elbows. Only vaguely aware of Donner beside him, or even the restaurant they were now seated in, he kept his entire focus on the screen, awaiting the response.

"I...I..." the man began, his voice breaking just slightly, before finishing, "I don't know."

The video ended less than a second later, the sharp jerk of the angle making it appear that whoever was doing the recording had just been cut off, a staffer stepping in to save their charge.

Waiting another moment, Ames stared at the phone, making sure the video was complete, before raising his gaze to Donner.

"This was taken this morning?"

"That's right," Donner said. "And unless I'm mistaken, that was Senator Jackson Ridge."

Using his forearms for leverage, Ames resumed his previous position. "I know who it was."

Raising his eyebrows slightly, Donner retrieved his phone, pocketing it away. "And then you also know-"

"That the man was a tremendous pain in the ass," Ames said. "Yes, I remember that as well."

Hooking one arm over the back of his chair, Donner extended the other and grabbed his beer, grasping it by the neck. "This video is going viral. I thought you might want to take a look."

While his first response was, as always, disgust – at the man sitting before him and the situation as a whole – Ames couldn't rightly argue that it was wrong for him to have called.

In situations such as this, erring on the side of caution was always the better approach.

"Going viral," Ames said. "Meaning?"

"Meaning it will be everywhere in time for the evening news," Donner replied. "Maybe even enough to cause the old fart to start rattling some cages, stirring up a lot of trouble for us."

Mulling the information over for a moment, Ames replied, "You are aware that as of right now he has less than a day left in office, right?"

"I am," Donner answered.

Nodding grimly, Ames fell silent, continuing to process the information. For as much as he wanted to lash out at Donner, to tell him that this entire meeting was nothing more than a fool's errand, paranoia from perpetually covering their back trail, there was a certain kernel of logic to what the younger man was saying.

At the very least, the situation would be worth monitoring for a couple of days.

"Jackson Ridge hasn't been much of a factor for years now."

"Right," Donner said, "not since his parents passed. Just the same, with this being his last day, he might try to turn this into something. Go out with a bang and all that."

Again Ames forced himself not to scowl, hating the use of clichés, but knowing they did sometimes serve a purpose, this being a prime example of such an instance.

"Who's the woman?" he asked.

"Dunno yet," Donner replied. "I figured I would run this by you before I started having anybody dig into it."

Looking away from Donner, Ames shifted his attention to the door, allowing his focus to blur as he chewed on the new information.

"Don't just use anybody. Do it yourself, report back to me every two hours until we know this has passed."

Chapter Four

"I am so, so sorry," Susan Beckwith said, the fourth such apology since they'd left the office. "We were told that she was here to comment on some state park that you had helped secure funding for. Where in the hell she got that-"

Pulling up abruptly in the middle of the hall, the stop so sudden Beckwith nearly collided into him, Jackson Ridge turned to face her, his body parallel to the wide hallway spread to either side.

"She got that," Ridge said, "because I *was* on that committee and I *did* vote to send troops to Afghanistan. Her tactics might have been off, and her approach less than sincere, but all things considered, I'd say we could cut her some slack, don't you?"

Shifting slightly, he took another step down the hallway.

"Yes, but sir," Beckwith began, starting alongside him as well.

Pulling up a second time in as many minutes, Ridge smiled slightly and said, "And while you're at it, cutting yourself some wouldn't be a bad idea either, Susie.

"The woman lied to gain access. You did your job, you had no way of knowing that would happen."

Reaching out, he patted her lightly on the arm, the long ago accepted signal that he was releasing her from his side for the time being, and turned back down the hall.

The Senate Dirksen building was considered by some to be the lesser of the two structures housing the offices of Senators, most sitting members squirreled away in the newer, more posh Senate Hart building right next door.

To Ridge, it had always been more of a badge of honor, the aging brick and dark color schemes much more in line for an old soldier like him, certainly a better representation of the people of Wyoming.

Pushing his hands into the front pockets of his slacks, he put his feet along the seam in the tile floor running through the middle of the expansive hallway, the events of the previous hour running through his mind.

To say that he had been dreading the ordeal would be an understatement. Many sitting congressmen viewed dealing with the media as something approaching a sport, a back-and-forth affair that they derived no small amount of pleasure from.

Ridge had never had such a view on the matter, a stance that was more than matched by the opposing side. Each armed with a healthy amount of wariness, the two worked with each other when they must, avoided when they could, always with a large dose of wariness.

Never, ever was the slightest molecule of trust present.

For Ridge, that belief had been earned a lifetime ago, having been on the front lines in Vietnam, returning home to find the story that had been shared with the public was a far cry from what was actually occurring.

Since arriving in D.C., his thoughts had only become stronger, having witnessed decades of hyperbole and spin, the ways in which much of what occurred in the country each day was now dictated more by the court of public opinion than any actual meritocracy that might exist.

Despite that, he had rather enjoyed the event up until that question was lobbed his way. The red-haired woman was nice enough, placing a question out there for him that allowed poking a bit of fun at his transplanted home, even allowing her to get in on the action with a nod to the place he would soon be returning.

The rancher was even better, setting him up to remind everybody of his roots, his very reason for getting involved in politics to begin with.

Things had turned south with the third woman, though, of that there was no doubt. The question was one he was not prepared for, certainly not the sort of thing Beckwith or his staff would have ever allowed inside the door.

Even so, he couldn't bring himself to harbor the slightest bit of ill will toward the woman, respecting her for asking the question, finding it hard not to believe that if he were in her position he wouldn't be doing the exact same thing.

The problem, as always, was with the pack of jackals standing behind her, catching every word of the interaction on tape, taking the opportunity to start firing questions his way as well, each more pointed than the one before.

"Afternoon, Jack," a voice said, pulling Ridge from his thoughts, causing his pace to slow as he strolled forward. "Heading in the same direction I am, I'm guessing?"

To his right, the owner of the voice stepped out into the hallway, a man in his mid-forties with a blonde flattop and fleshy face, his prodigious midsection extended nearly four full inches over her belt. Bypassing a suit for khakis and a sport coat, he extended a hand as he stepped from his office, closing the gap between them.

"Hello, Thomas," Ridge replied, addressing Senator Tom Macon from South Dakota. "Funny how we all seem to line up like cows at the trough come feeding time, isn't it?"

A smile crossed Macon's face as the two men moved forward, the reaction in response to Ridge's comment, an inside joke they always shared, finding some way to incorporate a nod to their respective western states.

"That it is," Macon replied, assuming the same stance as Ridge, the two ambling through the open hallway and pulling up short of the elevators. Reaching out, he pressed the button to call the lift their way, waiting as the doors slid open before extending a hand inward. "Please, age before beauty."

Feeling the corners of his mustache shift upward, Ridge wagged a single finger at his friend, stepping inside the elevator. "This once, I'm going to give it to you. Just this once, though."

"Much obliged," Macon replied, following Ridge inside, the doors closing and slowly lowering them to the basement cafeteria. "So, how's it feel to be a short-timer?"

Feeling his back molars clamp down tight, Ridge fought any urge to let Macon hear them grind, not wanting to make a single sound, give off the slightest impression that the comment had even registered.

If left to his own devices, he would have slid out of office days before, avoiding any press junkets like the one that morning, bypassing any awkward elevator conversation, eschewing having to go through ten versions of the same discussion that he knew was waiting at the caucus gathering downstairs.

It was not often that a senator with his sort of tenure left office, even less frequent that they did so under the not-so-subtle advice of their population base. Already in the last two months, he had witnessed a fair number of sideways glances when making his way to the Senate floor for roll call, something he suspected would only intensify in the coming hour.

"It's not so bad," Ridge said, waving a hand in front of him. "I always said this next one would have been my last anyway. This just means I get back out on the rivers while I'm still young enough to enjoy it."

Overhead, the lighted numbers of the elevator informed them they had reached their destination, a single ding of the bell preceding the doors parting wide. As it did so, a flood of sound rushed in around them, the bulk of the majority caucus having already gathered, clusters of people all deep in conversation, each fighting to be heard above the noise.

Holding the door open with a hand, Macon swung his opposite arm forward, motioning Ridge through. "You mean to tell me you're going to miss all this? I can't imagine why."

Exiting the elevator, Ridge took two steps forward, stopping on the edge of the enormous room, surveying the expanse before him.

From where they stood, the space stretched more than eighty yards in either direction, the interior of it lined with round tables under white cloths, ten seats surrounding each. At the front of the room was an impromptu stage with a lectern and a bevy of American flags, a handful of techs putting the final touches on the mechanical necessities for the coming meeting.

Along the back wall was a buffet line, a fair number of people already working their way through, their ages and appearances displaying that some Senators had been quite liberal with bringing along their staff to the gathering.

"Shocking, isn't it?" Ridge replied, his dry tone letting it be known what he thought about everything he saw before him.

Remaining silent, Macon eased up alongside him, he too assessing the room, his features showing he was as unimpressed as his counterpart.

"Most people think what we do is nothing but glamor, getting wined and dined on the taxpayer dollar. What they don't know is how much time we spend on things like this, meaningless meetings that we'd all just as soon avoid if we could."

"Amen to that," Ridge muttered.

Shifting a few inches closer, Macon lowered his voice and said, "And what do we get in return? Bullshit like you got this morning from that constituent of yours. Like you're supposed to know what happened to her son."

Feeling his eyes grow wider, his brows rising, Ridge flicked his gaze to Macon, feeling his body temperature rise a few degrees. "You heard about that, did you?"

His face falling flat, Macon lifted a hand, clapping it around Ridge's arm.

"Of course, Jack. Everybody has."

Chapter Five

The stares as Ridge entered the cafeteria conference room had been bad. They had escalated in frequency and intensity as he worked his way through the buffet line, each passing moment bringing with it an intense awareness of every person around him and the keen interest they seemed to have in the lame duck senator from Wyoming.

All of that paled in comparison to the number of looks he garnered as he finished eating, stood and made his way directly back to the elevators, feeling the collective weight of their eyes on his back.

Leaving his table service right where it was, Ridge had stood in the middle of the elevator with a sneer on his face, almost daring somebody in the room to say something as the doors slowly closed before him, blocking him from view.

The moment he was shut away inside, back to being left free to his own devices, he sagged visibly, releasing the heavy breath he seemed to have been holding since the moment Macon offered his condolences.

Two minutes after entering the elevator, Ridge exited on the third floor, turning a hard right and heading straight back to his office. Unlike his previous trip down the hall, there was no slow amble used to cover the ground, his focus aimed at the floor in front of him, his hands out and pumping along either side.

As he strode forward, he was vaguely aware of a small handful of people filing by, many of them continuing the trend of gawking as they watched him go.

Not that he now, or ever, had really cared what most of the people in the building thought.

"Susie!" Ridge proclaimed as he stepped through the tall wooden door to his suite, the gate always open during business hours, inviting anybody from Wyoming that might be in town to stop by and visit.

Inside the small confines of the front office, his voice sounded much like a cannon blast, reverberating off the walls, causing the young girl seated behind the desk to visibly jump, jostling the tan-colored liquid in her cup.

"Sorry, Ash," Ridge said, stepping past the desk and into the doorway of the office that offset his own, the back half of the suite split into two equal portions.

Unlike his side, which was one large space, the room expansive, housing only a single desk, this one was arranged into an open bullpen, a quartet of desks shoved into each of the corners.

Seated in the back right was Marian Ellerbe, a woman in her late-twenties, the most recent hire of the staff, just two years removed from Duke University. Dressed in a black pantsuit with a white blouse, she was shifted in her chair to stare back at him, a half-eaten deli sandwich on the desk before her.

Ten feet to her left was Kyle Stroh, his white-blonde hair pulled back into a widow's peak, his pale complexion made even more so by the yellow shirt and matching tie he wore, the overall effect making him appear much younger than the thirty-four years Ridge knew him to be.

Together, the two served as legislative aides for the Senator, Ellerbe covering health and human services topics, Stroh sticking with agriculture and education.

Anything else that needed to be covered was overseen by Beckwith, the final desk in the room sitting empty, the third aide for the office having quit abruptly after the election two months prior, wasting no time in moving over to the private sector once it was clear the position was operating under a truncated timetable.

"Yes, Senator?" Beckwith asked, her seat arranged just inside the door, making for optimal entry and egress whenever she was needed.

If she was surprised in the slightest to see him back so soon she did nothing to show it, her features impassive, her voice free of accusation or concern.

"My office, right now," Ridge said, hooking a thumb back over his shoulder before glancing up to his aides and adding, "You guys, too. Bring your food if you want."

Without waiting for any verbal response, Ridge strode across the small landing between the two sides, his footfalls swallowed up by the thick carpeting underfoot. Going straight to his desk, he pulled out his chair and lowered himself into it, arriving just moments before Beckwith, Ellerbe and Stroh coming in on her heels.

Each armed with a notepad and pen, they pulled forward the same chairs that had been used by the constituents that morning, the trio sitting across from him in a line that couldn't help but conjure a bit of déjà vu.

Barely waiting for them to take their seats, Ridge said, "I'm guessing you know why I called you in here."

Across from him, the two aides both glanced down to their blank notebooks, ceding the floor to Beckwith.

"What happened downstairs?" she asked.

"Nothing," Ridge replied, spitting the word out instantly before pausing to reconsider. "Okay, well, nothing down there in particular."

"Meaning?"

"Meaning I rode the elevator down with Senator Macon, who offered me his condolences on what happened this morning," Ridge said, unable to contain his voice as it rose slightly.

In response, he continued to get a view of the top of both Ellerbe and Stroh's heads, their focus intense, the latter even going as far as to jot down a note.

"This morning," Beckwith said, working her way through the statement. "The interview. He saw it."

"Yes," Ridge said, "and apparently everybody else has as well."

Three feet away, Beckwith's lips parted just slightly, creases forming on either side of her mouth as her jaw sagged open. "Oh, my."

"No," Ridge said, waving a hand at her. "Nothing like that. I don't blame you, and we're not about to sit around here feeling sorry for ourselves."

At that, each of the three people before him looked up expectantly, not sure where he was going with things, their faces registering everything from mortification to open curiosity.

"What do we have on the agenda for the rest of the afternoon?" Ridge asked.

Immediately shifting her attention down to the same leather planner resting on her lap, Beckwith hooked a finger around the ribbon and pulled it open, running her gaze down the length of the page.

"You were scheduled to be downstairs until two, after which you have a meeting with Senator Schultz to discuss new zoning laws around Yellowstone and Representative Conrad to talk about the new wind farms in the Wind River Range.

"And this evening is the farewell mixer."

Of everything mentioned, the discussion with his House counterpart was the only thing of even nominal importance, the mixer something that ranked lower than the media event that morning on ways he wanted to spend his final hours in office.

"Never mind any of that," he said.

"I beg your pardon?" Beckwith replied, snapping her attention up from the book spread atop her thighs.

"You heard me," Ridge replied, a hint of an edge in his tone. "We're clearing our schedules. All of us. For the rest of the day, the only thing any of us are focused on is finding the answer to that poor woman's question."

Chapter Six

The image was enlarged from the tiny touch screen on Leopold Donner's phone to the vertical monitor sitting on his desk, though the extra space did nothing to enhance the resolution. If anything, it was only made worse, the picture becoming pixelated and distorted, the original footage grainy, as if taken on an aging device of some sort.

The visual quality of it was of little import to Donner as he worked, though, having seen the entire sequence enough times to know exactly what was contained, the blurry bursts of color more than enough to tell him who was speaking and when.

Using the scroll bar on the bottom of the screen, he pushed the feed along until he saw the burgundy splotch that he knew to be the coat of the woman seated in front of Ridge. With his right hand, he navigated the mouse over the woman's features, cropping out a square more than six inches on either side and exporting it into a secondary program already running on his desktop.

As little as five years prior, the thought of Donner doing such work would have been enough to make the man laugh out loud. Enlisting in the Navy right out of college – a four-year jaunt that was marked more by his time throwing a discus and performing keg stands on the local Greek circuit than anything related to scholarly pursuits – the bulk of his career was spent ankle-deep in the mud.

The first moment he'd been eligible he had enrolled in SEAL training, spending the better part of a decade bouncing across the globe, never ceasing to marvel at the fact that while he was employed by the Navy, most of his time was spent in one desert or another.

Content that that was the life for him, never had the thought of getting out crossed his mind, images of becoming something like Arnold Ames, a man still wearing the uniform well into his fifties, being the ideal he aspired to.

Clear up until the moment he realized just how much money the private sector was willing to dole out to men with his training.

His first dalliance with what many in the service referred to as *the dark side* occurred in Iraq. At the time, he was still in the direct employment of the United States government, forced to be a bystander as men that he had been serving with just six months prior came to town, wearing more comfortable clothes and carrying far superior weaponry.

Not short on braggadocio, they had also been quick to share that just a few months in their current post would garner more than he made in a year.

Without a wife or children, never before had Donner given a great deal of thought to retirement, or saving money, or even anything beyond the world of green camouflage he was living in.

An errant piece of shrapnel from a roadside IED changed all that for him, twisted metal no larger than a silver dollar managing to slice clean through his triceps muscle, cycling him back stateside, requiring surgery and six months of rehabilitation time.

By the time his recovery was complete, he had come to realize his time with the Navy was as well, cashing out five years short of a pension, content that whatever he might miss out on would be more than compensated by the litany of private operators lining up for men with his particular skills.

Turned out, he was right.

Now five years into his life on the civilian side, he had ascended to partner status with his new employer, enjoying near-total autonomy coupled with hefty financial backing.

Along the way, he had also collected no small number of contacts, men such as Ames, people that made the secondary ventures that he knew would serve his actual retirement interests.

"Alright," Donner said, lifting the cropped image of the woman from the screen and transposing it onto the secondary screen. "Let's see what we've got here."

Beginning with a few clicks of his mouse, the moves practiced several times over, Donner ran a basic enhancement. On screen, the program responded to his commands, a horizontal line stretching across the bottom of the image and slowly working its way upward.

With each bit of distance, it filled in the grainy and blurred spots on the image, using a combination of contextual clues and educated guessing to clarify the image.

Less than a minute after pulling it from the video, the resolution had gone from unusable to something fairly clear, the screen depicting a woman that looked to be just north of fifty, her hair trending toward silver, her features pointed and harsh.

"Damn," Donner said, wincing as he looked at the woman, sun lines appearing around his eyes. "Feel sorry for the poor bastard that ever procreated with that."

Saving the new image to his desktop, Donner closed out the photo program, pulling up facial recognition software in its wake.

Entering the new picture into it, he started the program to searching, a status bar appearing at the bottom of the screen.

"Alright," Donner whispered again, waiting as the search got underway. "Let's see who the hell this ugly broad is."

Chapter Seven

The woman's name was Clara Tarby, the search for her being as simple as consulting the guest registry in the front of the office, the information entered in her own stilted handwriting, plain blue letters scribbled across the page.

The first three attempts to contact her had all gone for naught, the calls going directly to voicemail, an automated voice reciting the number they had tried to reach and imploring them to leave a message.

Between each of the calls, there was plenty of speculation throughout the office, the myriad of possibilities for the absence being everything from she was underground in the subway to she had already made her way back to the airport and was currently somewhere over Middle America, headed back home.

The decision to wipe away a half day — the final half day at that — to engage in a hunt for the woman in an attempt to answer her question was not entirely well-received in the office, though nobody went as far as to say anything.

Instead, they had all done as instructed and cleared their schedules, incurring no small amount of pushback from various organizations in the process.

As expected, Ridge's response had been to have them tell everybody to go to Hell.

He had one last day in office, and he would use it however he saw fit.

In the time since their prior meeting, the three staff members had pushed their chairs to the side to accommodate a fourth seat in the arrangement, putting Beckwith and Tarby in the center, the two young aides on either end. As odd a conglomerate as Ridge could ever remember being seated before him, the quartet was spread from one corner of his desk to the other, their faces bearing a variety of expressions.

"Good afternoon," he began, leaning forward and lacing his fingers atop the desk. Giving only a quick glance to either side, he focused on the narrow sliver of space between Beckwith and Tarby, wanting to keep them both squarely in his view.

With her mouth parted slightly, the usual bit of teeth peeking through, Beckwith looked exactly as she always did. Beside her, Tarby was a mirrored contrast in every way, fear clearly etched on her face, a healthy swath of guilt appearing to be present as well.

Still dressed in the same slacks and coat as that morning, a couple of extra red lines crossed the whites of her eyes, as if tears were threatening to streak south at any moment.

"I'm so sorry," Tarby whispered, ignoring his greeting, bypassing offering one of her own. "I know I told your staff I was here this morning to speak about a state park, but-"

Putting on the closest thing he could approximate to a grandfatherly smile, the gesture feeling odd given the myriad of feelings he felt inside, Ridge waved a hand, stopping her mid-sentence.

"Ms. Tarby, I promise, you are not in any trouble. You had every right to come in here and ask what you did."

"And I'm also sorry I missed the first few calls," Tarby continued, "I was touring the Holocaust Museum, and they made me turn off my phone-"

"Ms. Tarby," Ridge inserted a second time.

"And I had no idea anybody would be filming us," Tarby continued, the sheen of moisture that had been threatening finally breaking through and coating her eyes, more red tendrils permeating them.

Again, Ridge raised a hand to stop her. "Please, you don't need to apologize for anything."

Looking down to her lap, staring at the fingers laced tight atop her thighs, Tarby glanced up at him, more tears underscoring each eye.

"I just...I didn't know where else to go, who else to ask," she said, her voice falling away to just barely audible. "These last eight months have been hell, and nobody will tell me anything."

Feeling the smile fall away from his face, his features harden, Ridge stared back at her. Leaning forward another inch, he attempted to impart the seriousness of the situation, the earnestness he felt about it.

"What do you mean *nobody will tell you anything*?"

Opening her mouth to speak, her left hand rising in tandem with it, her open palm twisting toward the ceiling, Tarby said, "I...I wish I had more to tell you."

Over the course of his lifetime, Jackson Ridge had spent just north of forty years involved with the military, first as a soldier, later as a congressman, at one point even as the Chair of the Senate Armed Services Committee. In the sum total of that time, he had heard a great many things before, some of them pushing well beyond the boundaries of logic.

Still, this was a first.

Casting a glance to Ellerbe, he said, "Can we please get Ms. Tarby some tissues?"

Stopping mid-sentence on the note she was taking down, Ellerbe spun out from her chair, padding silently across the carpeted floor. Going straight for the round discussion table in the back half of the space, she grabbed up a box of Puffs in a patterned container and brought it over, setting the entire thing down in front of Tarby.

"Thank you," the woman managed to mumble, reaching forward and taking two from the top of it, immediately thrusting them to the bottom side of her nose.

"Thank you, Marian," Ridge echoed, waiting as his aide returned to her seat and Tarby took a moment to collect herself. "Start at the beginning."

Again, Tarby's head went toward her lap, where it remained for several moments, long enough that her shoulders racked twice with silent sobs. On cue, the tissues came to her face, burying the red-tinged tip of her nose, nobody saying a word as she collected herself.

Sitting and watching her do so, Ridge could not help but think of the situation he was now faced with, the meeting he was having a far cry from how he'd envisioned his final day playing out. On the surface, there was no rightly reason why he should be doing what he was doing.

The woman had certainly pulled a fast one on him and his staff, using a bait-and-switch to gain access and pursue a personal narrative.

To the media, any attempt to help her now would only play like pandering, a scrambling politician looking to cover up one last faux pas on his way out the door.

To his colleagues, it would look like an abuse of power, him spending his final hours to try and gain answers for this woman.

To the voters back home, it may even serve as a final validation of their decision in the fall, both his inability to respond to her initial response and his later attempt at recovery confirming everything they had come to loathe about his performance.

Perhaps it was that very combination of things that had caused the situation to crawl into his core and take hold, refusing to relinquish its grip. There it had settled, and festered, starting the moment she asked the question, growing through his conversation with Macon, reaching a crescendo as he sat in the downstairs cafeteria, painfully aware of the stares cast his way.

Maybe it was the look on the woman's face sitting across from him, the anguish Clara Tarby felt obviously genuine, having stripped away any amount of humanity that she may have once possessed, leaving her exterior hollow, Ridge guessing her interior to be much the same.

Not to be discounted was the fact that at least some small bit of his ego may be getting the better of him, wanting one last victory on his way out, wagging a middle finger at his doubters, letting them know that while they might have ultimately won, he tallied the last score in the contest.

Regardless, each passing second only seemed to confirm what he was doing, naysayers be damned.

"His name was Josh," Tarby whispered, pulling Ridge from his thoughts, jerking him back into the moment. "He was twenty-one years old."

To either side, Ellerbe and Stroh again began jotting notes, the sound of their pens scribbling against paper just barely audible.

"So, Corporal Joshua Tarby?" Ridge asked, piecing together what he knew of the rank structure, superimposing the average time it took to ascend the latter.

"That's right," Tarby replied, nodding slightly.

"Maybe a year or so away from becoming a sergeant," Ridge added, his voice only nominally louder than Tarby's.

"He was hoping to do so in eight months," she responded, adding another nod.

"Impressive. Sounds like he was a real self-starter."

"He was," Tarby said, "always had been."

It was clear there was more she wanted to add, further details that would flesh out the story, though Ridge let it pass, content that everything would come out in due time.

"Where was he assigned?" he asked instead.

"Kabul," Tarby replied, "or, well, just outside of it at a place called-"

"Bagram," Ridge finished. "Yes, I'm familiar with it. There's an airfield there, serves as the drop point for most of the supplies in the region."

Her eyes parting wide, Tarby stared at him for a moment, a bit of surprise registering on her features. "Yes, that's correct."

He wanted nothing more than to remind Tarby that she herself had pointed out that morning how he had voted to send troops into the region. To add that of everything he had done in his time in Congress, that decision was the largest he ever faced, he and Beckwith having pored over every facet of the situation before making a decision.

Knowing he could say nothing of the sort, he again fell silent, waiting for Tarby to continue.

"He had been in country seventeen months," she said, "almost done with his tour, less than a month from returning."

Again her bottom lip quivered, a single tear leaking out from the corner of her eye as she turned her head to look past Ridge, staring through one of the large windows framing his desk on either side.

"His job was to serve as guard detail on those supply runs you mentioned. Three days a week, he would escort the caravan down into Kabul, stand by as they unloaded whatever they had, and then return."

Shifting to look back at Ridge, the emotion of a moment before passing, she continued, "I know it wasn't one of the more glamorous jobs that are out there. Nobody's going to be writing books or making movies about him the way they might a sniper or some hero deep in combat, but the dangers were real, and Josh took his job very seriously."

"I'm sure they were, and I have no doubt he did," Ridge said.

Much like her son, his time in Vietnam was spent performing tasks that would never usually come to mind when someone thought about life in the military.

Didn't make it any less vital to the overall operation, nor, as Clara Tarby had just mentioned, did it mean he was ever immune from peril.

Seeming to gain resolve, Tarby said, "That fact was the reason they decided to shift from day to night runs. Word was they were starting to scale down in the region, meaning that a lot more stuff was beginning to move out than in."

Already knowing where it was going, piecing together what he could remember, adding to it the things Tarby mentioned, Ridge said, "Making them even more of a target."

The skin on either side of Tarby's neck creased into a series of lines as she nodded emphatically, her chin nearly touching her chest before ascending back up.

"Yeah," she said, her faint voice barely matching the defiant look in her eyes, "and on April 14th, the convoy he was riding with was ambushed."

Despite knowing where the story was going, Ridge felt his eyes pinch close, a slight groan sliding from deep in his diaphragm.

"Dammit," he whispered, holding the pose a moment before slowly opening his eyes. "Dammit. I am so sorry, Ms. Tarby."

Moving right by the statement, Tarby said, "Less than a month from getting out."

Again she shifted her gaze to the window behind Ridge and added, "Took them more than twice that long to get him home to me. By that point, I had no choice but to have a closed casket ceremony, which was all I could afford."

Feeling his head twist from side to side, Ridge stared straight at Tarby, her words taking several moments to penetrate before taking hold.

"All you could afford? Pardon my language, by why in the hell did you have to pay for it?"

Chapter Eight

Despite Tarby having left more than twenty minutes earlier - escorted by Ellerbe and Stroh both under instructions from Ridge to grab her things and bring her from the motel she was staying at in Silver Spring to the Hilton three blocks from the Capitol – there was still a clear and palpable current in the air, the office weighed down by the story she had just shared.

The chairs that the three had been parked in were still sitting wide to either side of Beckwith, the woman positioned in her customary stance, the day planner on her lap, her lips parted the usual amount as she sat and waited.

"Well now," Ridge began, the two having reconvened after a short break, the hope being that it would have helped them return to neutral, but the reality being they felt just as they did moments before.

"A grieving mother," Beckwith replied. "I can't even imagine."

"Me neither," Ridge said, shaking his head softly, the fact that neither one of them had children having little bearing on what they'd just seen.

Raw, unbridled, unadulterated, sorrow.

"Anything in that story make sense to you?" Beckwith said, pulling Ridge's gaze from the desktop back up to her, only his eyes shifting her way.

A decent chunk of the time between meetings had been spent chewing on that same question. For the better part of an hour, he and his staff had sat in rapt silence and listened to the story of Joshua Tarby.

His mother had been correct when she posited that guarding a supply line was one of the more unglamorous jobs on the military payroll. There weren't any anecdotes of him being behind enemy lines, not a lot of pictures of the young man returning to base in grease paint after an evening of slipping through the shadows.

Each day he did exactly what he was asked to, his role small and well-defined, making sure that other people in other places were able to keep doing the same with whatever they were tasked with.

The only way an organism as large and multi-faceted as the army could ever hope to continue working as it should.

Because of that, the lion's share of their discussion had focused on what occurred after his time on the supply chain, his final day on earth being where the narrative truly seemed to shift, grabbing everybody's attention and propelling them forward.

Three different times Ridge had gone through the sequence, each pass using a different approach, to the point he realized it probably seemed he was badgering the poor woman, poking at her story as if checking it for veracity.

"Yeah, the first five minutes or so," Ridge said. "Young man, single parent home. Things are tight, enlists right out of high school."

"Good pay, come back and go to college," Beckwith said, having heard the scripted lines from Ridge many times before.

"See the world," Ridge finished, waving a hand before him. "The whole thing, just as we've seen play out a hundred, a thousand, a hundred thousand times before."

"But..." Beckwith prompted, nudging them forward, Ridge recognizing it instantly as her not wanting to go back down the same path again.

"But then...then things started going sideways," Ridge said. "What could a young man have done that night that managed to simultaneously get him killed and dishonorably discharged?"

To that, Beckwith had no response, merely sitting and staring, waiting for him to continue.

"And worse yet, no information at all to be relayed back to the family," he added. "I mean, the poor woman just lost her son. Give her *something*."

This time a single arched eyebrow was Beckwith's only answer, both knowing that was not how the army operated.

Rarely did they even give the soldiers on the ground everything they needed at any particular moment, let alone fleshing out the stories for those back home after the fact.

"Okay," Beckwith said, clear that she was past the encounter with Tarby, was ready to begin working on the task at hand. "How do we go about this? Can we do this?"

Pushing Clara Tarby from his mind, Ridge leaned back in his chair, the springs moaning slightly beneath his weight. "It has to start with his file."

"You don't believe her story?" Beckwith asked.

"It does seem pretty fantastical," Ridge conceded, "but I do believe her, or at least believe that is what she was told, which is why we need to see exactly what happened to this young man."

Lifting her left wrist from the planner on her lap, the cuff of her suit coat pushed back just enough to reveal the face of her watch. "Can we get it in time?"

"In time won't be a problem," Ridge said. "The files are all housed in Kansas City, which is central time, can be emailed or faxed at a moment's notice."

"Meaning the *can we* part could be a bit trickier?" Beckwith asked.

"Could be," Ridge replied, "but I am still a ranking member of the committee, and that does come with some perks, as you might remember."

"I might," Beckwith replied. "And after that?"

"Depends on what the pages reveal," Ridge said.

Falling silent for a moment, he rocked himself back and forth a few inches at a time, trying to envision what the story might be, how things may play out over the remainder of the day.

Just as fast he shook himself free of the notion, knowing it could be either a quick and glorious win or a total train wreck, the two outcomes both presenting with equal likelihood at the moment.

A lifetime of history with the military told him the weight was probably shifted a little higher to the former than the latter, but that did little to change his approach.

"We could end up ruffling a lot of feathers with this," Ridge said, his voice distant, thinking aloud.

"I never thought otherwise, sir."

Chapter Nine

Jackson Ridge was waiting for the call as the phone atop his desk burst to life, pushing a loud, shrill sound through his office. Leaning forward on an elbow, he snatched the polished black plastic up a moment after the ringer began, smashing it against his cheek.

"Senator Jackson Ridge."

There was a clear edge to his voice as he said the three words, not bothering with a greeting of any sort, the man he knew to be on the other end having lost any right to such niceties during their previous conversation.

Gaining access to military records was not an easy process, the sort of thing that was generally restricted to personnel only, usually requiring the authorization of someone pretty high in the pecking order.

As a former chair and current member of the Armed Services Committee – even if only for another twenty-some hours, Ridge was one of the few civilians in the country that could access such things, though the person he was speaking to on the opposite end of the line seemed to think otherwise.

"Good afternoon, Senator," the man sputtered, making it clear that he was a little embarrassed by his previous actions, perhaps even a bit fearful for his position. "I am so, so sorry for our previous conversation. I meant no disrespect."

The first thing the man had said when Ridge had identified himself was to make a backhanded comment about how he was the Pope as much as Ridge was an actual United States Senator.

How that could be interpreted as anything but disrespectful, Ridge had no idea.

"The file," Ridge said, in no mood to rehash their previous talk, even less to placate the man.

If he had more time, or even more energy, he might take the opportunity to put the man in his place, giving him an undressing that wouldn't soon be forgotten.

As it stood, the only thing that mattered was Clara Tarby, figuring out what happened to her son, and being able to give her some small shred of relief.

"I need the file for Corporal Joshua Tarby sent over to me immediately."

"Okay, sir, I can do that, sir," the man replied. "Fax or email?"

"Both," Ridge said, rattling the needed information off in short order, his tone never once rising above frigid. As he spoke, he could hear the man repeating it softly back while jotting things, ending the conversation the moment he was done.

Slamming his phone down, he kept the receiver in its cradle and pressed a single button along the bottom of the front panel, a single tone sounding out. A moment later, a female voice could be heard piping through the speakerphone, filling the interior of the office.

"Hello, Senator, how can I help you?" Ashley asked from the front desk.

"I've got a fax coming in from Kansas City any moment now," Ridge said. "Can you bring it in as soon as it arrives?"

"Certainly, sir," she replied.

"Thanks," Ridge mumbled, cutting off the discussion and leaning back again in his chair. Focusing on the computer monitor on the far right side of his desk, he stared at his incoming email program, waiting for a new line item to appear.

Given his druthers, he would much prefer actually seeing the file printed out and would wait until Ashley brought it in before reading it. Still, he wanted to see how long it would take for it to arrive, if the man would be brazen enough to send it from his own email address.

The answer to the first part of that turned out to be two minutes, a ding sounding out from the screen as a boldface entry appeared at the top of the screen. Sliding open the top drawer beside him, Ridge grabbed a pair of reading glasses, unfolding the arms and resting them on the tip of his nose.

The second part of his question turned out to be just as he had imagined, the message arriving from a generic military email, the name assigned to some department within the National Archives.

Feeling one corner of his mouth curl up slightly in a smile, Ridge muttered, "Chickenshit," his attention still on the screen as a quick double-tap could be heard against his door.

"Come on in, Ash," he called, raising his voice to be heard. Keeping his gaze on the screen a moment longer, he waited until she was just in front of his desk before turning her way, not bothering to remove the glasses from his nose.

"Here you are, sir," she said, "seventeen pages in total."

"Thank you," he replied, watching her bow slightly at the waist before retreating from the room, closing the door in her wake.

Leaning forward in his seat, he grabbed up the stack of pages and pulled them over before them, running his focus down the length of the first page. Found there was nothing more than the usual basic information, including Tarby's name and rank, his date of enlistment, his hometown, and the unit he was assigned to.

Shuffling ahead to the second page, he saw that the young man had done his training at Fort Benning in Georgia, a mainstay that had been pumping out soldiers by the thousands for decades. During his time there, Tarby had received solid if unspectacular marks, his instructors all praising his discipline and willingness to learn.

Moving quickly on to the third, he felt his insides begin to clench, the air pulling from his lungs as he processed the scant information before him. Shuffling the page off to the side, he went through the fourth page just as fast, followed in order by the fifth and sixth.

By the time he made it to the seventh, there was no point in reading further, his core feeling as if an iron spike had been driven into the center of it, his entire digestive tract wrapped around it, trying in vain to process the lunch he'd thrown down a few hours before.

Snapping the glasses down off his nose, he left them upside down on the pages before him, leaning back in his seat and closing his eyes, using a hand to rub hard at his forehead.

"Now what the hell am I supposed to do with this?"

Chapter Ten

The afternoon sun was clear and bright overhead, though there was no warmth to it as Arnold Ames stepped outside the enormous vertical walls of the Pentagon. Stopping just beyond the front doors, he ignored the steady flow of foot traffic that streamed by him on both sides, his eyes hard as he stared into the distance.

On the roadway nearby, afternoon traffic had already begun, the term being a very literal moniker, the cars starting to line up around lunchtime each day, commuters having adjusted their schedule so that it started well before the sun, ended well after dark, all with hopes of avoiding the dreaded crawl of sitting in their car.

What on paper might have made sense, may have even worked out for a while, had long ago lost any semblance of reasonability, the city so overpopulated, the number of government jobs downtown so robust, that there was no way to ever avoid the slog.

Hearing their errant honks and the occasional squeal of brakes, Ames turned west, putting his face into the brisk breeze, moving parallel to the Potomac River. Flowing in the opposite direction, the surface of it was a hazy silver color, darkened by the rise of buildings behind it, only the occasional flash of light reflected from the pale sky above.

With his shoulders square, his cap pulled low over his cropped hair, the general walked for more than ten minutes at a steady pace, making it far enough that the Pentagon receded from view behind him.

Along his left, the iron gate surrounding Arlington National Cemetery ran along the sidewalk he was on, stretched out for well over a mile before him, the far end of it demarcated by a steady throng of tour buses all pushing to get inside.

Why anybody would want to travel across the country, or further, to take pictures and gawk at the resting place of heroes and patriots, Ames had no idea, the notion still inciting ire within him, something he would no doubt carry for the remainder of his days.

Just past the corner of the cemetery, the general fished his cellphone from his pocket and gripped it in his right hand, inserting the small Bluetooth device into his opposite ear. Opening his bank of text messages, he moved down to the most recent entry and highlighted the name attached to it before pressing send.

The moment it began to ring, he slid the phone back into his pocket, the tiny ear bud the only external sign he was making a call, his left cheek just a couple feet from the fence beside him.

Three times the line rang before being snatched up, the voice on the other end panting slightly, as if out of breath.

"Good afternoon, General," the man said. "Sorry about that, I was on my way back from the head when I heard the phone ringing."

As he made the apology, the sound of a door rattling against its casing could be heard, the man shutting himself into his office. Even though there would be precious little actual information shared, both knew there was the extreme need for privacy.

"What is this about?" Ames asked, ignoring the opening and the attached apology.

The day had gotten off to a rocky start for Ames, beginning with the initial request to meet from Donner, only growing worse over the course of their conversation. By the time he had made it back to his desk, a tempest of thoughts and concerns were at work behind his steel gray eyes, the Lagavulin and accompanying cut of beef being the only two things that had gone remotely right since he woke.

Receiving the text message he had just referenced an hour after returning only made things worse, deep frown lines etched into either side of his face, neither appearing like they may leave anytime soon.

"This is about the list," the man said, keeping his answer intentionally vague, just as he had been instructed to do.

"The list," Ames repeated.

"Yes, sir," the man replied. "We've been pinged."

Forcing himself to keep his pace even, his eye level high, not giving the slightest external sign that anything was amiss, Ames said, "Pinged?"

"Yes, sir," the man said again. "There's been a file request."

Ames's initial reaction was to ask who it was for, though he refrained from doing so.

That too was part of the long established protocol.

"Cause for concern?" he asked instead. Already he knew the answer to the question, just as he knew the reason why Donner had asked to meet that morning.

The particulars of either situation weren't overly important, but the fact that these men were reaching out to him meant something was wrong.

That simple fact was about the only thing that these men seemed to share with the ones he oversaw from his desk each day at the Pentagon.

"I wouldn't be calling otherwise."

Drawing his lips into a tight line, Ames pushed a long breath out through his nose. Beside him, cars continued to move in an unending snake, all running forty or more miles an hour, none allowing more than a couple of feet between their bumper and the rear of the one in front of them.

Reaching the fence post that demarcated an exact mile and a half from his desk, the general stopped abruptly, rotating on the ball of his foot and heading back in the opposite direction.

"Call it in. You know the rest."

Sliding his left hand up to his ear, he swapped the Bluetooth out and pressed the button on the side to end the call, sliding it back into his pocket. Keeping both hands buried inside the warm trousers, he retraced the steps he had made just a short time before, nothing more to the curious observer than a man that had needed a few minutes away from his desk.

Even to the trained eye, there was nothing to give away what had just taken place.

Just as there would be precious little to hint at what surely lay ahead.

Chapter Eleven

Standing over his desk, both palms pressed flat against the polished cherry top, his weight shifted onto this right foot, his left heel elevated just slightly, Jackson Ridge leaned forward, feeling the stretch in his shoulders, his glasses balanced precariously on the tip of his nose.

"You know what the easiest way to draw attention to yourself is?"

For a moment there was no response, nobody even in his office to reply, before Susan Beckwith entered, a slip of paper between the index and middle finger of her left hand.

"Hmm?" she asked, not bothering to offer anything more, trusting that the question was rhetorical.

"Trying too damned hard to hide," Ridge replied, shaking his head slightly as he stared down at the papers.

Across from him, Beckwith walked forward until she was even between the chairs she and Tarby had used a short time earlier, the quartet still in place before the desk.

"And who is trying too hard?"

Waiting a moment, continuing to stare down at the pages strewn across his desk, Ridge heard the question. He felt it resonate within, ping-ponging across his mind, though no answer came back to him.

Pushing himself back to upright, he extended a hand at the mess of papers, sliding the glasses from his nose with his opposite paw.

"I mean, look at this. How the hell is anybody supposed to make heads or tails of this mess?"

Glancing down, only her eyes moving, Beckwith flicked her gaze over the expanse of the desk before looking back to him.

"I'm guessing that's the idea?"

Fixing his stare on her, Ridge said, "Yes, but *why*? This wasn't some highly classified operation, this kid wasn't on a clandestine mission somewhere he wasn't supposed to be.

"This guy was a truck guard, as nameless and faceless as a thousand just like him, yet somehow *this* is what his file looks like?"

On the last part of the sentence, he again jabbed a finger at the pages before him, disgust plain in his tone, on his face.

With the exception of the first four pages – the most basic of information from Tarby's enlistment and early training period – most everything else had been redacted. Page after page of nothing by thick black bars, most of them stretched the width of the page, others stopping long enough to just allow a few stray words in odd places.

Cumulatively, they effectively managed to wipe out anything of use, almost all of Josh Tarby's time in service, certainly every minute spent in Afghanistan, effectively gone.

"No," Ridge said, twisting his head and glancing up to Beckwith, the woman remaining as impassive as she had in their briefing first thing that morning. "Something's not right here."

Considering the statement, Beckwith allowed the top of her head to dip just slightly to the side.

"The man was dishonorably discharged. Perhaps something happened that needed to be struck from the record."

"But wouldn't that be all the more reason to leave it there?" Ridge fired back. "There needs to be some explanation as to why the military suddenly kicked what appears to be a pretty good kid out on his ass."

Taking a half step forward, Beckwith extended the piece of paper she held across the desk, the small white square still tucked between the first two fingers on her left hand.

"And just weeks after his death," she added.

"Right," Ridge snapped, raising a hand at her, his voice growing more animated. "What the hell?"

Saying nothing, Beckwith wagged the paper in his direction, waiting as he reached out and accepted it before slowly starting to withdraw from the room.

"Hopefully, he can help."

Looking down at the paper, Ridge unfolded it to see a name and a phone both scrawled across it in plain blue ink.

"Thanks, Susie," he mumbled, his Chief of Staff raising a hand and fluttering her fingers at him as she exited, saying nothing.

Placing the piece of paper down on the desk, Ridge stared at it a moment before reaching out and grasping his phone. Raising it just a few inches, he immediately reconsidered, lowering it back into place.

Bending at the waist, he instead went into the top drawer of his desk, into the same space his glasses had been, the small wooden box his only repository for personal items in the office. Nudging aside his wallet and house keys, he grabbed up the ancient flip phone that had been with him for a decade and snapped it open, the hinges creaking slightly from the effort.

Peering down his nose at the paper atop his desk, he punched the digits into the phone and pressed it to his face. Stepping out from behind the desk, he moved over and stood before the window along his left flank, feeling the cool outside air permeate the glass, the sun already beginning a slow descent in the western sky.

"Hey, it's me. You have time to meet right now?"

Chapter Twelve

There was never a question of where the meeting would take place, the site being one that had been used countless times over the years, this being the first in the better part of a decade.

Much smaller in stature than the other monuments dotting the National Mall and the area surrounding it, the World War I Memorial was first erected in 1981. Little more than a marble gazebo, columns supported a domed roof above an open air floor, the total structure no more than fifteen feet across. Tucked away in the corner of Pershing Park, it afforded a decent view of the nearby pond and gardens, well off the beaten mall footpath, frequented only by picnickers and others looking for a few moments of solitude within the city.

It was in the latter category that Jackson Ridge found himself as he cut a diagonal path across the grass between the sidewalk surrounding the Reflecting Pond and the memorial. Bent forward at the waist, the stiff breeze pushed the short hair atop his head back and forth, riding along the inside of his overcoat.

Underfoot, the ground was frozen nearly solid, the grass having just a slight give as he maneuvered his way through errant pockets of snow.

When he had first arrived in the city, not far removed from the ranching life of Wyoming, the East coast version of cold had barely registered with him. While there was a certain undeniable edge to the extreme moisture that was always in the air, the city had nothing on the open expanses of his home state, where temperatures dropped precipitously below zero, winds tearing through and pushing things down even lower.

In those first days, it was the opposite end of the calendar that bothered him far more, the mid-summer heat and humidity leaving his clothes damp with sweat, a condition that seemed to arrive in early June and not depart until well after football season had started for the year.

The thought brought a hint of a smile to his face as he moved forward, pushing one foot out in front of the other, his gait suggesting he was stepping through an invisible field of knee deep snow.

Now, both of the extremes seemed to bring out the worst in him, the summer giving the impression he was perpetually melting, the winter causing him to ache to the core.

East coast living had made him soft.

His parents would be ashamed.

"Excuse me, sir, might you have the time?"

The voice snapped Ridge from his thoughts, his head remaining aimed forward as his eyes swept the area around him, seizing on the man he had called just an hour before. Seated on a park bench less than fifty yards from the memorial, the man had a small paper bag in his lap, puffs of popcorn extended from the top.

Dressed in dark jeans and a black leather coat, a black-and-white plaid scarf was wrapped around his throat, a pageboy cap tilted on his head. A ring of gray hair was visible beneath the bottom of it, what little skin that was exposed to the elements the color of milk chocolate.

In front of him, a bevy of white and gray pigeons hopped about, imploring him to continue tossing more of the feast their way.

"Time?" Ridge said, glancing around to ensure they were alone before settling onto the opposite end of the bench. "Time seems to be the only damn thing I have a lot of these days."

A small chuckle rolled from the man, the gesture lifting his shoulders just slightly. "You and me both, brother."

Breaking their usual posture for just a quick moment, Ridge pulled his right hand from his coat and reached across his body, feeling the chilly air grip his fingers.

"It's good to see you, Sea Bass. Thanks for coming."

Pausing his orchestrated action of feeding the birds for just a moment, Sebastian Murray accepted the shake, pumping it twice before going back to his previous endeavor.

"Good to see you as well, Jack."

The two men had first met forty years and what seemed a million miles ago, both literally and figuratively. Two years older than Ridge, Murray was a sergeant in a neighboring platoon, the two having crossed paths briefly a time or two, neither thinking much of it at the time.

Not until they were back stateside more than a decade later – Ridge in the House of Representatives, Murray with the CIA – did the two actually become more than acquaintances, a relationship that began with wary reluctance and evolved over time into what it was now.

The type of thing where one or the other could be counted on in a time of need, if not for results, then at least for an ear and a bit of unbiased analysis.

"How in the world did you even get my number?" Murray asked. "I haven't had the new one but a few weeks."

"Susie," Ridge said simply, having tried the old contact he had on file before giving it over to his Chief of Staff. "That woman is a bloodhound."

"That she is," Murray agreed, Ridge able to almost hear the smile in his voice, not needing to glance over. "Which is exactly what an old coot like you needs watching over him."

This time it was Ridge's turn to chuckle, the ends of his mustache riding up slightly.

"How's retired life treating you?"

His hand pausing just slightly, Murray thought on the question a moment before beginning anew, tossing more popcorn out before him.

"You'll find out, soon enough."

"That I will," Ridge conceded, "but before I go, I have one last thing I need to do."

This time there was no pause from Murray, the answer seeming to be what he already expected.

"Yeah, after that mess this morning, I imagine you do."

Again feeling the same stab in his stomach that had been present most of the afternoon, Ridge said, "Saw that, did you?"

"Mhm," Murray replied. "Even if I didn't make a habit of looking in on my friends, that one would be hard to miss."

Having long suspected the first part of the statement, never before had Ridge heard it stated explicitly.

The friend part, anyway. He'd always known Murray made a habit of poking through the dirty laundry of him and countless others.

Tossing out the last of the popcorn, Murray carefully folded the bag and tucked it under his thigh, the flock of birds continuing to bounce around before them, all stooped at the hip, pecking at the ground. Slapping his hands together to knock away any salt and butter that remained, he said, "So, what can I possibly do that would warrant getting a call on your very last day in office?"

With his gaze fixed on the birds, watching them hop to and fro, the symbolism was not lost on Ridge, feeling as if most of the time he had spent in D.C. was much the same, hopping after whatever morsels were tossed his way.

"Oh, you already know the answer to that," Ridge said. "I told that woman I'd find out what happened to her son, and I aim to do it."

"Even if it's the last thing you do in office?"

"Even though it's guaranteed to be the last thing I do in office," Ridge replied.

Beside him, he could sense Murray cast a glance his way, though no comment was made. Instead, the man asked, "And the reason you're doing this?"

Recalling the conversation he'd had with Clara Tarby, remembering the stack of redacted pages on his desk, Ridge said, "Because something isn't making sense, in a big way."

"Not because you want to make amends for a poor showing this morning?" Murray pressed.

Feeling a scowl creep onto his face, Ridge said, "You ever known me to give a damn about that?"

"Wouldn't have been very good at your job if you did," Murray replied.

"Besides," Ridge added, "bastards already voted me out, I'd say I know pretty well where I stand with them, wouldn't you?"

A grunt was the only response from Murray, the two men falling into silence for the better part of two minutes, the occasional coo of a pigeon and the errant sound of a car door slamming the only sounds between them.

"Did you start with the file?" Murray eventually asked.

"What there was of it."

"Ahh," Murray said, picking up on the insinuation as he slid the popcorn sack from beneath his leg and stowed it into the pocket of his coat. Keeping his hands buried inside the leather shell, he stood, a pair of pops ringing out from his hips and lower back.

"Good seeing you, Jack. I'll be in touch."

Chapter Thirteen

Marian Ellerbe was the first one through the door, leading the impromptu trio into the suite. Pushing the heavy wooden door open with both hands, she stood to the side and held it wide, the square heels of her shoes pressing down into the thick carpet on the floor.

"And here we are, Ms. Tarby."

Second inside was Clara Tarby, her mouth and eyes all stretched into congruent circles as she passed into the palatial spread, her face arched upward as she gaped at what she saw.

"Oh, my," she whispered, the sound just barely audible, bringing a thin smile to Ellerbe's face. Remaining in place, she waited as Kyle Stroh crossed over as well, gripping one small bag in his right hand, a second matching bag tucked under his arm.

Reaching out, he accepted the door from Ellerbe, slowly easing it back into position, the gate closing with a click that could be heard throughout the room.

"Where would you like your bags, Ms. Tarby?"

Whirling toward the sound of his voice, her eyes still wide, Tarby extended both hands his way, fingers splayed out wide.

"Anywhere is fine. Please, just drop them beside the door and I can get them."

"No, ma'am," Stroh replied, a smile on his face. "We aim to please in Senator Ridge's office. Where would you like them?"

Keeping her hands outstretched for a moment, Tarby gave him a look that seemed to border on pleading before finally capitulating.

"On the bed would be great, if you don't mind."

"Bed it is," Stroh replied, nodding once and setting off for the far side of the spread, his footfalls silent atop the carpeting.

The process of taking Tarby to her motel in Silver Spring and bringing her downtown had taken the better part of two hours. Given the close urban location of both destinations, there was no highway reprieve to aid them going either way, no break from the urban grind that had kept them from ever moving more than a few dozen yards at a time.

In that time, Ellerbe and Stroh had taken turns attempting to engage the woman in small talk, most of it stymied with varying degrees of forcefulness, almost always to the tune of the entire thing being unnecessary.

From where she stood, Ellerbe couldn't say that she rightly disagreed, though the decision made was something far above her head, daring not to ever question it.

Turning away from the door, she extended both hands toward the picture window framing the seating area of the suite. Below, the Potomac River moved slowly by, scads of tourists lining the shores, many in heavy coats with cameras hanging from their neck.

Behind them, the white marble of the Capitol rose against a steel-colored sky, the Washington Monument just peeking out from behind it in the distance.

"How about this view, Ms. Tarby?" Ellerbe said, putting her best smile on display, hoping that the new topic would give her something to fill their last moments together.

Keeping her hands folded before her, Tarby remained in place, turning toward the window.

"I really can't afford this place, you know."

Feeling the smile disappear as quickly as it had arrived, Ellerbe said, "Nobody can, Ms. Tarby. These suites are set aside for special guests here on the Hill."

"And even if they weren't," Stroh added, exiting the bedroom to join them, "Senator Ridge wouldn't dream of letting you fit the bill, even if he had to pay for it himself."

Giving them each a quick glance, a bit of wariness obvious along the edges, Tarby took a few steps closer to the window, sidling up along the far side of it, easing one hip against the wooden casing.

"First time to D.C.?" Stroh asked.

"Mhm," Tarby replied, nodding slightly. "Hopefully, first and last."

Again the plastic smile appeared on Ellerbe's face, she too taking a step forward, cutting down the distance between them. "Is it really that bad?"

With her gaze still aimed out the window, Tarby asked, "Where are you from?"

"Jacksonville," Ellerbe replied.

"And you?" Tarby asked, flicking a quick glance to Stroh.

"Nashville."

"Hmm," Tarby replied, falling silent for a moment before starting anew. "Both of those are cities that people recognize immediately, probably full of tall buildings and big crowds and loud noise.

"Me, I come from a place called Ten Sleep."

Shifting to look at each of them, she said, "Actually, six miles outside of Ten Sleep. Can you imagine how many cars I see in any given month?"

"I can't," Stroh said.

"Not many?" Ellerbe added.

"Fewer than I can see from this window right now," Tarby said, glancing to her shoes before again forcing herself to examine the view before them.

In the wake of her confession, most of the air was sucked out of the room, silence flooding in behind it, Ellerbe casting a look to Stroh, his face showing he had as little idea how to proceed as she did.

Between the two of them, they had spent more than half a decade under the employ of Senator Ridge. While it was not entirely uncommon for them to be given random tasks, or make seemingly illogical errand runs, this was an absolute first.

"Well, just one more night," Ellerbe said, attempting to salvage the situation, hoping to exit as quickly as possible. "This place has a fabulous room service menu, I'm told. Stay here, rest up, and you'll be headed back to Ten Sleep soon enough."

Where Ten Sleep was – or even if it really existed – Ellerbe had not a clue.

At the moment, it was far from the most important thing on her mind.

Again, there was no response from Tarby for a moment, her eyes glassing over as she stared out the window. In that position, she remained for several seconds before slowly turning back to them.

"I'm so sorry you've been forced to do this. I never asked for any of this."

Feeling her mouth drop open, unsure of how to respond, Ellerbe merely matched the woman's stare, hoping Stroh might have the proper response for the situation.

He did not.

"Senator Ridge...I know it wasn't a fair thing to put on him, but nobody else seems to know anything. I just..."

Yet again she paused, cracks in her voice betraying her, the raw emotion she had shared in the office earlier still on plain display.

"All I want is to find out what happened to my son," she whispered, the moisture belying her eyes growing more pronounced, a warble forming in the middle, threatening to streak south. "I just want to be able to sleep at night."

Feeling mist rise to her own eyes, Ellerbe said nothing, pulling in long drags of air through her nose.

"Does that make sense?" Tarby whispered. "Does any of this even make sense?"

Her legs wobbly beneath her, Ellerbe slowly moved forward, extending a hand before her. Reaching out, she found both of Tarby's still clutched tight, her fingers cold to the touch.

"It doesn't have to, Ms. Tarby."

Chapter Fourteen

The walk back from the World War I monument took just over twenty minutes, a time aided considerably by the wind pushing at Jackson Ridge's back.

Bent forward at the waist, he plunged his hands into his pockets and lowered the top of his head, the collar of his coat flipped up. Staying a few feet off the concrete sidewalk, he pushed past the Reflecting Pond and by the World War II spread, everything from the set of his jaw to the pace of his steps letting it be known that it was not in anybody's best interests to stop him for a chat.

Based on the comments of both Macon and Murray, the video of him that morning had gone viral, meaning he was in no particular mood to stop and discuss the matter with any curious bystanders.

Compounding that mood were the events of the afternoon, his search for the answer to Clara Tarby's question no further along than it had been when she first asked it.

Part of the reason for his wanting to pursue the topic was to help her and to do right by a fellow soldier, though there was certainly far more to it than that.

No person that had ever submitted their name to run for office did so without at least some small sliver of ego attached, and he was no different.

Getting voted out in November had been a massive blow to his. Finding out there was a video circulating out there, seeking to make him a laughingstock on his final day in office, wasn't much better.

Stepping inside the door at the foot of the Dirksen Senate building, Ridge nodded to the guards working the metal detectors and unloaded his pockets into the bins. After being out in the cold, he could feel the flaps of his ears burning as blood rushed back in, bits of prickly heat running the length of them as he passed through the scanners and collected his belongings.

On the heels of his walk, he opted to bypass the stairs, going to the far bank of elevators and ascending to the third floor. Less than a minute later he emerged to find Beckwith waiting for him, the planner and a sheaf of papers pressed tight against her chest.

How she had managed to know he was on his way up, he had no idea, it being somewhere around the hundredth time she had managed such a feat over the years.

"Have a nice walk?" she asked, the question seeming innocuous enough, clearly meant to relay a message.

There was somebody nearby. Speaking freely at the moment would not be a good idea.

"Very," Ridge replied.

"And the knee?" Beckwith asked, taking another half-step closer.

Feeling his eyes narrow, knowing that the person she was warning him about could be any one of a thousand people, he said, "Started tightening up a bit there at the end. You know how it gets in the cold."

"I do," Beckwith said. "I don't envy your return back to Wyoming."

126

Unsure how to respond, having taken the charade as far as he could, Ridge pulled his brow together, a deep crease appearing between them.

"What's up?" he mouthed, no sound passing his lips.

"Hodges," Beckwith mimed.

Confusion gave way to agitation, a sour taste rising to Ridge's mouth. Every part of him wanted to storm right past Beckwith, striding directly into his office and throwing his successor and anybody else that might be along for the ride out on their asses.

The voters may have seen fit not to give him another term, but that still meant he had a task to perform and until noon on January 3rd to do it.

"No," he said, this time unable to keep himself silent, the word coming out an angry whisper. "Absolutely not."

Offering him a look that resembled something his mother might have at one point given him when she thought he was being absurd, Beckwith pushed out a long sigh.

"Sir," she muttered, "it *is* customary-"

"I don't care about customary," Ridge spat back. "We've actively avoided it for thirty-six years now, I see no point in starting today."

Deep in the recesses of his pocket, his phone began to vibrate, the pulsating object buzzing against his fingertips.

"So you're just going to march in there and tell them no?" Beckwith asked.

"No," Ridge said, pulling the phone from his pocket and flipping it open, a string of digits with a local area code staring back at him. "You are, while I take this call."

The left eyebrow of Beckwith rose to a pointed arch as she stared at him, the corners of her mouth turned downward, letting him know that she didn't appreciate being cast as the bad guy yet again.

Raising his voice again, this time loud enough to be heard, Ridge added, "Tell him he assumes office tomorrow at noon. Come back then."

Chapter Fifteen

The rooms had been installed sometime decades before, small alcoves carved into the sides of the expansive hallways of the Dirksen building. Originally meant to serve as telephone weigh stations, the rotary machines had long ago been removed, replaced by solid steel plates bolted flush against the marble walls.

For years the small spaces had gone virtually unused, far too expensive to bother filling in, left standing idly along the side. With the advent of cell phones, they had taken on a second life, providing a place for staffers to step away for conversations they didn't want to be overheard, the closed doors providing excellent sound proofing, the clear glass on them making it possible to keep an eye out for anybody that might be coming.

It had been years since Jackson Ridge had had any reason to step into one of the bays, his office being more than sufficient, his status making it possible for him to simply ask whoever might be standing by to give him a few minutes.

Not wanting to face the annoyance of Hodges or his staff, Ridge slid into the closest closet and pulled the door shut behind him, slamming it home in hopes that the sound would carry into the lobby of his office, a clear point being made.

"Sea Bass," Ridge said, thumbing the phone to life and pressing it to his face. "I wasn't expecting you to get back to me so quickly."

"Can you talk?" Murray replied, his smooth voice low, making it clear there was a trace of something present, even if Ridge didn't quite know what it was.

"Just you and me," Ridge replied, his previous tone matched in kind. "What did you find?"

"Didn't find a damn thing," Murray said, "which is why I'm calling back so quickly."

"Sonuva..." Ridge muttered, letting his voice trail away.

"Yup," Murray said. "You said you got a peek at his file earlier. Let me guess, nothing but black bars?"

"Like a horizontal prison," Ridge answered. "One page after another."

"That's what I got too," Murray replied, "which is saying something."

Shifting slightly, Ridge bent at the waist, peeking out to make sure there was nobody nearby. At the far end of the hallway, he could see a tuft of thick brown hair and a blue suit appear, presumably his successor Willis Hodges, the sight of him only adding to the frown on Ridge's features.

"How so?"

"Well," Murray said, "most of the time, files are redacted by just covering portions of texts and making a photocopy. That way, whatever they want hidden does so without damaging the original wording."

"Just in case they ever need it," Ridge reasoned.

"Right," Murray replied. "I mean, just because they don't want a particular story getting out to the masses doesn't mean they shouldn't have it documented somewhere."

Never before had Ridge given a huge amount of thought to the topic, though what Murray was saying made sense. There were certainly a great number of incidents that had occurred during his time in the military - things that he and many others would like to pretend never happened – that he would prefer never reached the media.

That didn't mean they needed to be wiped from history, for a variety of reasons.

"But Tarby's?" Ridge asked, already feeling a draw deep within telling him where the conversation was going.

"Let me put it this way," Murray replied. "I don't know what the hell that kid did exactly, and the way that file looks right now, nobody else ever will either."

Leaning a shoulder against the door, Ridge again glanced down the hall, watching as Hodges and a pair of staffers stepped out and began plodding in the opposite direction.

Twice the man turned back and glared at his future office as he went, Ridge too far away to make out his facial features, but clearly seeing the body language that was on display.

"Piss on him," he whispered, bitterness contorting his features.

"What was that?" Murray asked, his voice pulling Ridge back to the conversation, his attention away from the hallway outside.

"Nothing," Ridge replied, "just some bastard here at the office trying to overstep his boundaries again."

"Ah," Murray replied, offering nothing more, leaving it at that.

"Okay," Ridge said, shoving the word out with a sigh. "It was worth a shot, thanks for taking a look, Sea Bass. I appreciate it."

"Well, now, hold on," Murray said, raising his voice just slightly. "I said I didn't find a damn thing in the file, not that I didn't have a damn thing to offer you."

Pausing for a moment, Ridge considered the words, not sure quite what was being alluded to.

"Okay," Ridge said. "Meaning?"

"Meaning one of the few pieces of information I was able to strip away from those pages were the letters CID."

After his years with the Armed Services Committee, Ridge was more than familiar with the acronym, the group serving as the investigators tasked with all felonies occurring within the jurisdiction of the military system.

"So there was an investigation," he whispered, linking the information up to what he already knew in his mind.

"Yup, and it must have been something big," Murray said, "because we're not talking basic on-base military police here. Somebody flew these guys in to poke around for a while."

Again falling silent, Ridge felt his eyes narrow slightly as he ruminated on the information.

"Flew them in from where?" he asked.

On the other end, he could hear a small chuckle, enabling him to envision the smile spread across Murray's face. "Now you're starting to see, old man."

It was the second crack that had been made about his age that afternoon, but it hardly registered with Ridge, his focus still on the unanswered question he had posed a moment before.

"Flew them in from where?" he asked.

When Murray spoke again, the previous mirth was gone from his voice, the grave tone back into place.

"CID is headquartered down the road at the Marine Corp Base, sharing space with the boys at Quantico."

These too were names Ridge was familiar with, the Marines and the FBI sharing a joint facility a couple of hours outside the Capitol.

Pushing back the sleeve of the jacket he was still wearing, Ridge checked his watch, seeing it was already well into mid-afternoon.

"Dammit," he muttered. "There's no way anybody down there will start willingly answering questions over the phone."

"Right you are," Murray replied.

"And with outbound traffic being what it is, it would take forever to get there right now."

"Right again," Murray answered, "but luckily for you, there isn't a need for you to go jumping into the Batmobile and rush off to save the day just yet."

Allowing the sleeve of his coat to slide back into place, Ridge again felt his brows come together, confusion etched in the lines outlining his face.

"Meaning what, exactly?"

Chapter Sixteen

The crowd at the Iwo Jima monument was just beginning to thin, the hordes of Japanese tourists that had spent the last forty-five minutes milling around the base of it starting to disperse. Slowly, in clumps of two and three, they made their way back to the quintet of buses idling nearby, ready to take them to their next designated stop on their tour of America's capital.

Seated on the outer edge of the concrete encircling the structure, General Arnold Ames leaned back against the metal support behind him, doing his best to appear impassive, to look just like any other person out on the blustery January afternoon.

Dressed down from his uniform before leaving the office for the day, he sat in jeans and a plaid button-down, a canvas coat atop the ensemble, his

136

hands shoved into the front pockets. In that position he sat and waited, watching as people took unending photos of the iconic image before him, the afternoon sun shining down at an angle, providing the optimal light for the endeavor.

Not that Ames was one to be bothered with such notions, photography just another hobby he had little time or patience for.

Instead, his thoughts were on the call from a short time earlier, on the words shared from his contact in Kansas City. Matching it up against what Donner had said earlier in the day, dozens of thoughts and permutations ran through his mind, none of them seeming particularly appealing.

"We've really got to stop meeting like this," a voice said, arriving a few moments before its owner, "people are going to start talking."

Feeling a scowl cross his features, Ames sat without giving any other visible reaction, not even bothering to glance to the side as Leopold Donner dropped himself on the opposite end of the bench. Despite the seat being constructed of rubber-coated steel, he could still feel a small tremble pass through it, his counterpart's bulk sending a tremor throughout.

"Donner," Ames said, his voice terse, letting it be known that this was hardly a time for joking.

"General," Donner replied, "to what do I owe the pleasure of a second face-to-face today?"

There was no way Ames would ever refer to a meeting with Donner as a pleasure, knowing with reasonable certainty that his cohort felt exactly the same way. Theirs was a relationship of circumstance, something that had been borne out of opportunity, had remained out of necessity.

In no other context would they even be having a conversation, much less be anything approaching friends.

"What were you able to find out?" Ames asked.

To the right, he could feel Donner shift to glance his way, a half-smile on his face, before turning to face forward again.

"Wow, at least you bought me lunch the first time."

Feeling his features tighten, his core doing the same, Ames shoved out a slow breath through his nostrils, careful to make sure it was loud enough to be heard, before speaking.

"I really don't think-"

"Yeah, yeah," Donner said, "I know. Just buttering you up a little bit."

Having seen this play out before, knowing that it never went anywhere good, Ames said, "Just get on with it. No amount of bush beating ever helps anything."

Beside him there was no response for a moment, the two of them watching as the crowd continued to thin, stragglers taking a final few selfies before drifting off toward their waiting carriages, the engines already running, the sound a steady purr providing background noise over the grounds.

Meeting at most of the monuments downtown was so common it had almost become a cliché, that being the very reason Ames made such a point to avoid it.

At any given moment there could be spotted a host of people in business attire huddled up, all pretending to be doing nothing more than feeding the birds or reading a newspaper, thinking they were invisible to the world around them.

To Ames, they might as well have posted a billboard with flashing lights above them, that being the only way they could possibly draw any more attention to themselves.

Situated on the opposite side of the river from the hub of the city, the Iwo Jima was one that he didn't mind using, the place far enough off the beaten path to avoid most of the D.C. crowd, but sufficiently established to ensure there was always more than a few tourists on hand.

"The woman wasn't an easy ID to make," Donner said. "Nothing in facial recognition, meaning no prior criminal offenses, not even a legal driver's license."

Ames knew exactly what the lack of facial recognition meant, his agitation only growing, though he remained silent, wanting nothing more than for Donner to get to the point.

"Ended up having to go through a contact in the media at a station that had reported on the little gathering with Ridge this morning," Donner said. "Promised her a few things I wasn't particularly proud of, but in the end, it paid off."

The last line was tinged with mirth, the sort of playful posturing that was better served in a locker room than in their current position.

"And they said?" Ames asked, again spurring things along.

In his periphery, he could feel Donner turn and stare his direction, blood rushing to Ames's cheeks, more from the man's complete lack of decorum than for the glare he was receiving.

"Clara Tarby," Donner said, "none other than the mother of one-"

"Joshua Tarby," Ames finished.

"Joshua Tarby," Donner echoed, "which, as you know-"

"Yes, I know," Ames snapped, cutting him off for a second time.

"Which means you also know, that ain't good."

For no less than the fifth time that day, Ames felt his acrimony for the man beside him grow, wondering what had possessed him to ever get in league with such an individual.

"But what I don't know," Donner said, "is why you called and asked to meet with me first. I only just found out a few minutes ago."

Watching as the side doors to the buses closed up one after another, the enormous machines shifting into gear and beginning to rumble away,

Ames said, "It's actually much worse than just her being Tarby's mother."

Falling silent for a moment, he waited as the buses passed, their noise too great to be heard over, before casting a quick glance to Donner and saying, "I got a call from our guy in KC. Apparently, Ridge put in a file request earlier this afternoon."

"For Tarby?" Donner asked, as if there was another possibility, any other reason Ames might be sharing the information.

"For Tarby," he confirmed, leaving his response at that.

"Oh, shit," Donner said.

Not wanting to agree with the assessment, or to comment on the lack of help that it was, Ames simply sat and stared, waiting for Donner to put things together beside him.

"Okay," the younger man said, "that thing has been doctored to Hell and back, so we don't have anything to worry about there."

"Unless somebody starts to wonder *why* it's been doctored," Ames retorted.

"Unless that," Donner conceded, the two rattling off things in a rapid fashion, the two more thinking out loud than having an actual conversation.

At the conclusion, they fell silent for several moments, each staring as the sun dipped a little lower in the sky, hiding behind the outstretched legs of the last man in position, the frozen figures all fighting to plant the flag on some far-off shore.

"So how do we handle this?" Donner asked.

Without a doubt, it was the most cogent thing the man had said since arriving, the very same question Ames had been rolling around all afternoon.

Right now, it was still possible that this was nothing more than a fishing expedition, Ridge placing a few phone calls to try and atone for an embarrassing meeting that morning. If such was the case, they had nothing to worry about, the redacted file being everything they needed to stymie his efforts.

Should he feel the need to dig further, things could start getting complicated, especially if he began to assert any amount of pressure on the sort of contacts he had surely developed over the years.

"I don't think we need to move in yet, but the time has come for us to at least be aware of what he is up to," Ames said.

A small grunt in the affirmative was Donner's first response, followed by, "Team approach or solo effort?"

"As little as possible to get the job done," Ames replied. "But make damned sure it gets done."

Chapter Seventeen

Jackson Ridge was barely more than back in his office, still hanging his formal overcoat on the polished wooden rack in the corner, when Susan Beckwith strode in. With her footfalls silent, she made it within just a few feet before stopping and clearing her throat, the sound causing Ridge to flinch, his adrenaline spiking as he turned to face her, hands clutching the coat on either side of the peg he was aiming for.

Seeing it was her, the feeling receded, his heart rate slowing, his ears glowing a bit with embarrassment.

"Damn, Susie..." he muttered. "Next time make some noise or something. You're liable to give an old man a heart attack."

Opening her mouth, as if about to point out that she had made a noise before speaking, she closed it just as fast, the corners of her mouth turning down only slightly.

"Of course, sir," she replied. "I just came in to say that a Lucious McVey is here to see you."

Shifting his focus to the rack just long enough to finish hanging up his coat, Ridge said, "Tell him I'm sorry, but I'm not available this afternoon."

Leaning forward, he lowered his voice and added, "You know what I'm working on right now, the time frame we're up against."

"I do," Beckwith replied, making no effort to match the tone or the stance, "and I believe he is here to help with that."

Leaving her explanation at that, she turned on a heel and strode for the door, stopping just short of it and standing to the side.

"There we are, Mr. McVey. Please, come inside and have a seat."

"Thank you," a light, high-pitched voice responded. An instant later a man strode through the door that didn't seem to match it in the slightest, his light brown head shaved clean of hair, creases on either side of his mouth seeming to frame his face in a constant grimace.

Standing more than a head taller than Beckwith, he wore chocolate-colored slacks and a black knit sweater beneath a baggy coat, a scarf hanging from his neck.

"Can I get you anything?" Beckwith asked. "Coffee? Tea? Water?"

"No, thank you," the man replied, striding across the floor and moving directly for Ridge, still standing by the coat rack.

With each step he seemed to grow even taller, the senator's eyes growing large as he took the man in, rifling through his internal Rolodex and coming back quite certain he had never encountered him before.

"Hello," he said, extending a hand before him, not trying to mask any confusion in his voice. "Jackson Ridge."

"Senator," the man replied, accepting the shake in his massive paw and pumping it twice. "Lucious McVey."

Still feeling uncertainty etched across his face, Ridge said, "Good to meet you. Please, have a seat."

Releasing the shake, the two men retreated to their respective sides of the desk, McVey unfurling the scarf from around his neck and dropping it into his lap, leaving his coat on as he settled down into his chair.

After spending most of the day holding the likes of Beckwith and Clara Tarby, the seat seemed many sizes too small, the sight almost comical as McVey folded himself down into it.

"There's no way you have any idea who I am, so let me get right down to it," McVey said, taking the lead. "The reason you don't know my name or my face is because for the last twenty-two years I have worked for Army Counterintelligence."

Like a great many of the things Ridge had heard bandied about over the course of the afternoon, the term was something he had at least some passing familiarity with, his knowledge being more on the surface than to any deep level of understanding.

"I see," he managed.

"And our mutual friend Sebastian called and asked if I wouldn't mind stopping by for a few minutes to help clear up a few things for you."

The mention of Murray brought things a bit more into focus, explaining the man now seated in his office, the reason for his unexpected visit.

When he had gotten off the phone a few minutes earlier, he wasn't entirely sure what Murray was alluding to when he said help might be on the way, though this certainly wasn't quite what he had planned on.

"I see," he said again. "And you just happened to be in the area?"

Across from him, McVey leveled a stare, holding the pose for a moment, letting it be known that despite the office they were sitting in, he was very much in charge of the conversation they were having.

"Yeah, let's go with that," he finally said, a point of finality clear.

"Sounds good," Ridge replied. The thoughts of thanking the man for stopping by, of a dozen follow-up questions, all filed through his mind in short order, each dismissed just as fast as they arrived.

Instead, he leaned back in his chair and folded his hands across his belt, waiting for McVey to continue.

"Now, Sebastian gave me a quick overview of what you're looking at here," McVey said, "and let me be right up front and say, I don't know a damn thing about any of that. I have no idea what happened to that boy, and I've got no pull with tracking down or recreating redacted files."

Again, Ridge forced himself not to display an outward reaction, not to tip off the fact that internally he was already feeling a bit of disappointment, his stomach dropping slightly.

"What I do have is some institutional knowledge that might be able to help you out along your way," McVey said.

"Okay," Ridge replied.

"And when we're done and I leave here, this conversation never took place."

"Okay," Ridge repeated.

"And if you ever see me again – in a restaurant, at a ballgame, walking along the street – you don't know me."

The gambit seemed a bit much, the sort of thing that only drove home many of the stereotypes that existed about counterintelligence, though Ridge again made no sign of his thoughts.

In a week's time, he would be back in Wyoming, living on the family ranch, unlikely to ever attend a ballgame or walk down many public streets again. The sole restaurant in his town he had a hard time ever picturing McVey in, for a variety of reasons.

"Understood," Ridge replied.

Waiting a moment to make sure each of the previous points was made, McVey nodded once, lowering the top of his shaved pate in confirmation.

"Okay, then," he said. "So here's how it goes. As I'm sure you are aware, in the Army, the law enforcement division is broken into a series of different departments.

"You've got your basic Military Police – the MPs – which handle everyday things. Bar fights, domestic disturbances, basically everything short of a felony.

"These guys are housed in every base in the world, each with their own division, their own chain of command. Their jurisdiction is largely contained within the base and the surrounding area, though they can go outside of it after a soldier stationed there, or if they are called in from another base."

Most of the information Ridge was already familiar with, the data sounding similar to what he had encountered decades before in Vietnam. Some of the jurisdictional stuff he wasn't quite as familiar with, though he let any further questions slide by, content that McVey would tell him anything extra he needed to know.

"When the offense gets a little larger, rising to the level of a felony," McVey said, "that's when you start talking about CID, the Criminal Investigation Command."

Stopping for a moment, he waved a large hand before him, a flurry of long fingers passing by.

"I know the letters don't fit, but this is the army. Don't try to understand it."

Unable to stop himself, Ridge felt his mouth curl up into a small smile, a smirk rocking back his head a half inch.

"The CID uses special agents that come in to look at things," McVey said, rattling off the information as if he was there just to impart knowledge and leave before anybody even noticed he had been in the building.

"They can be employed by the military or civilians, and they can look into anybody – soldier or outsider – so long as the crime pertains in some way to dealings with the army. You follow me?"

Surprised at being drawn back into the discussion, it took a moment for Ridge to respond, his mind registering one was needed just a split second before nodding.

"I do."

"Good," McVey said. "And then the third wing, the place they turn when things really get hairy, is my department - counterintelligence.

"The elite of the army, we look at offenses like treason, sedition, espionage, things with some high-level ramifications."

Envisioning the structure in his mind, Ridge pictured it like something akin to a pyramid, MPs at the bottom, men like McVey at the top.

"So I'm guessing the higher in the pecking order you go, the lighter the case load?"

"Lighter in terms of numbers only," McVey corrected. "I once worked a case for four years that probably saved a couple million people.

"That was only one case, but..."

This time he raised both hands, splaying his fingers out and spreading them wide, letting the gesture make his point for him.

"Understood," Ridge said. "And, thank you."

"You're welcome," McVey said, no irritation or pride present on his face or in his voice, the response a simple reply to the thanks given.

Waiting to see if there was anything more to be shared, Ridge paused a moment, until it was clear McVey was done speaking. Raising his elbows up onto the arms of his chair, he tapped the pads of his thumbs together, computing the last couple of hours, trying to make things fit together.

"When I spoke to Sea Bass," he said, reasoning through things out loud, "he mentioned CID being stated in the file."

"Right," McVey said, "and he wouldn't have asked me to stop by unless he thought counterintelligence had also been called in by CID to lend a hand."

Nodding, Ridge fixed his gaze on the desk before him, drawing his mouth into a tight line, continuing to parse through what he knew.

"So whatever it was that Josh Tarby was involved in, or at least whatever got him killed, must have been some pretty weighty matters."

154

A few feet away, McVey shrugged his eyebrows, the top of his head listing slightly to the side.

"Like I told you before, that I don't know."

Seizing on the insinuation, Ridge flicked his gaze to McVey, staring intently, waiting for the man to finish the thought.

"But what I do know is, it would take something pretty heavy to get someone dishonorably discharged after they died on duty, and a hell of a lot of pull to make it all completely disappear from their file."

Chapter Eighteen

Despite the bravado he had displayed in front of Ames, Leopold Donner could feel the tension of the situation they were now faced with. Jackson Ridge was a man on borrowed time with egg on his face, a combination that could easily push someone into the realm of doing something desperate.

In his experience, little good ever came from someone that found themselves in such a situation, the old adage *a drowning man will always pull someone down with them* being something Donner had learned at an early age, had always fully believed in.

Most of the time, the predicaments people found themselves in didn't really amount to much worth fretting over, their own heightened sense of self-worth and a societal inability to handle stress both contributing to making inconsequential matters seem much more severe.

This case was different, though, something Donner had known from the moment it first showed up on the newscast, the very reason he had called Ames out of the blue and asked to meet.

Sitting on the outer ring of the grounds of the Iwo Jima monument, Donner had waited until the general rose and walked away, following his stiff-legged gait as he limped across the open expanse, eventually disappearing from view.

Once he was gone, Donner waited another full ten minutes, ignoring the cold as it nipped at his features, fighting the urge to so much as draw his phone out and glance at the screen, before rising and cutting a path in the opposite direction. Climbing into the front cab of his mid-sized SUV, he slid a compact laptop from beneath the driver's seat and powered it to life, his every movement hidden behind glass tinted to within a degree of the legal limit.

Outside, the sun sat just above the horizon, the calendar only a few days past the winter solstice, the shortest days of the year still upon them.

Around him, the last few stragglers of the day hurried for final photo opportunities, many pushing out plumes of white with each breath, their cheeks rosy as they walked in exaggerated strides.

Ignoring them, turning his focus down to the device on his thighs, Donner started by opening a basic web page, going to the Senator's website and scrolling quickly through the available tabs. Having already brushed up on Ridge, his background, and his policy measures earlier that day, he instead clicked through until he found a listing for staff.

Operating under the fastest available web provider in the D.C. area, the laptop returned the site he was looking for in just a matter of seconds, the front page – replete with smiling photo of Ridge – disappearing from view, replaced by a vertical listing of a half dozen names.

Beginning at the top was Susan Beckwith. Listed as Chief of Staff, her contact information was lined out as hyperlinks beneath it. Below her, in order, there were three entries for legislative aides, each of them parsed off according to subject matter, data on how to reach them appearing as well.

Fifth in order was Ashley Guthrie, her official title listed as administrative liaison, which a lifetime of dealing with the bureaucracy of the military and their obsession with titles told Donner that the girl was a receptionist, most likely manning the front desk, answering the phone and smiling for the occasional guest.

Last on the page was for someone named Micah McArthur, Office Coordinator for Ridge in Wyoming, the mailing address listed as Cheyenne.

Lifting his right hand, Donner formed his fingers into a bracket, clustering the group of legislative aides together, flicking his gaze between the entries for Beckwith at the top and Guthrie at the bottom.

For a moment he remained in that position, long enough to let his gaze blur, thinking on the best way to approach things.

Ames had said to be as small and inconspicuous as possible, though he had also stressed the need to be thorough. Given what had happened so far, there was no reason to believe that anybody but Ridge had acted on things, at most perhaps sharing some information with Beckwith.

Still, with less than twenty hours remaining on the man's term, he might also be straying into a gray area, looking for help in places he may not otherwise, forcing Donner to do the same.

For one last instant Donner kept his hand in place, staring at the screen, before pulling it back and snatching up his phone from the middle console. Using his thumb, he entered his passkey and moved down through the address book, finding the entry he wanted listed simply under the letter P, and hitting send.

Three rings were all it took for the line to connect, a small burst of sound the first thing audible, followed quickly by total silence.

"Packard," a female voice said, short and terse. Despite the fact that Donner knew her well, spoke to her at least twice a week, had worked with her for a number of years, there was no greeting of any sort, nothing to pretend that his reasons for calling were anything but serious.

Which was exactly why he had opted to go to her in the first place.

"Donner," he said, pausing for a moment to let her clear the room if she needed to.

"Go ahead," Packard replied.

"We've got a job," Donner said.

"The Ridge thing this morning?" Packard answered, having already seen the footage, sounding like she had been waiting all afternoon for the call.

"Very same," Donner said. "General wants things to be as small as possible, so for the time being it'll be a two-person op. You cool?"

"Frosty," Packard replied.

"I'm splitting the targets in half," Donner replied, keeping things as generic as possible over the phone. "Half for each of us."

"Roger that."

"Everything you need will be emailed within two. Follow encryption protocol six to view it."

"Roger that," Packard repeated.

At that, Donner ended the call, flipping the phone onto the passenger seat before going back to the device on his lap.

He had an email packet to send.

Chapter Nineteen

In the wake of Lucious McVey leaving, Jackson Ridge sat at his desk and pondered the information he'd just been given. Reaching to his collar, he loosened the tie he was wearing, undoing the top button and pulling the material a half-inch away from his neck. Running a finger along the inside of it in either direction, making sure things settled just so, he could feel late day stubble already beginning to form, loose skin shifting as well.

Once he was a slight bit more comfortable, he returned his hands back to his lap, lacing his fingers over his stomach, his gaze fixed on the desktop before him.

His first hope was that Murray might have been able to pull some information from the original file, though that had turned into a dead end.

Instead, he had gotten a visitor that knew even less about the situation at hand, making it quite clear that he had no interest in being dragged into the fray.

What the man did have, though, was a mountain of tangential information, the subject matter something Ridge had familiarity with to varying degrees, though nothing to the level of depth that had just been dropped on him.

With the introduction to so much new data, what had started as simply trying to make good on an awkward conversation with a constituent had now morphed many times over, shifting from a vanity play to an appeal to basic humanity to whatever it now was, which felt a lot more like a detective novel than something he had envisioned a few hours earlier.

Such a realization also managed to compound the repercussions of the meeting with McVey, causing Ridge to wonder what all the new information could possibly mean, and more importantly, what he was going to do with it.

Sitting behind his desk, the last gasps of the afternoon sun pouring in through the glass behind him, offering bright light completely void of warmth, he allowed the milieu of thoughts and facts to percolate through his mind.

On one hand, he had already done what he said he would. He had made some phone calls on behalf of the Tarby family, had even cashed in a favor, which had in turn cashed in a favor. He had braved the cold, and even put the woman up at the Hilton on his own dime.

Any bit of bad press he might have received that morning was now more than corrected, by the woman and by public opinion. He could walk away now, and never once be the worse off for it.

He might have to turn his head and squint a bit, but an argument could be made that he had his win.

That was no small part of what this was all about anyway, if he really wanted to get down to it.

For as much as he wanted to believe that, though, to put it behind him, to call his staff back and have one last nice dinner on the taxpayer dime, he knew whatever he was now wading through went much further than that.

The tone of Murray's voice had made it clear that something was awry, the general comments from McVey only adding to that impression.

Beyond that, there was something even more basic that Ridge knew would never leave him if he were to quit now, a fact that would perpetually bother him, perhaps more than anything else that he had done in his time in Congress, and that was the face of Clara Tarby seated across from him.

The emotional turmoil she was in, the psychological carnage she had endured, was as real as anything he had ever witnessed.

With it came back memories, recalled days gone past, bringing with them things that would never leave him as long as he lived.

There was no way he couldn't see this through, come what may, and he knew it.

Rising from his chair, Ridge crossed back over to the coat rack, grabbing at the lapels of his overcoat and pulling each side out wide. Rifling down through the pockets, he found the personal cell phone that he had used to talk to Murray just moments before, the device still stowed away, McVey's unexpected arrival keeping him from taking out it earlier.

Padding back across the room, he moved parallel to his desk and stood in front of the window facing toward Union Station, a steady line of Hill workers already heading toward the train, their clothes all uniformly dark and drab in color, battered bags hanging from their hands or shoulders.

Flipping the phone open, he scrolled through the meager list of contacts he had, finding the one he was looking for. Not even sure if the digits there were still good, he felt his pulse rise slightly as he clicked on the number to call, his shoulders rising and falling with a deep breath before he pressed the phone to his ear.

The tone on the other end sounded abnormally shrill, no question a result of his own trepidation more than any change in the device's settings, as it rattled off a half-dozen times, concluding with a mechanical voice telling him to leave a message.

Nothing more, not even a mention of the owner's name came with it, Ridge's shoulders sagging another inch as he cut it off without leaving a message and turned back toward his desk.

Just three steps into his journey the device in his hand began to vibrate, a single name popping up onto the screen, the very same one he had tried to contact a moment before.

Stopping where he stood, Ridge accepted the call and returned the phone to his cheek, saying nothing, waiting for the other side to initiate.

It took the better part of a minute, but eventually, they did.

"I was hoping I would never see this name pop up on my phone again."

The voice was male, older, gruff, heavily laced with a vitriol Ridge couldn't help but match in kind.

"August 11-" Ridge began.

"Yeah, yeah," the man said, cutting him off. "I know the date and I know what happened."

Still standing at an odd angle in his office, Ridge said, "And now I'm calling it in."

On the other end, there was no response for a moment, nothing but dead air before a long sigh could be heard.

"Yeah, I figured this call would be coming at some point."

"And now it has," Ridge replied.

"No good deed, and all that shit, right?" the man shot back.

Raising his gaze from the carpet he'd been staring at, Ridge felt the skin around his eyes tighten as he focused out through the rear window of his office, dead tree limbs swaying with the winter wind.

"I would hardly call what happened out there that day a good deed."

"Seemed to have worked out okay for the both of us, didn't it?" the man snapped back, defiance obvious in his tone.

Opening his mouth to respond, Ridge pulled up just short, not wanting or needing to rehash something that had happened ages ago, knowing full well neither man would ever be able to see things the same.

"Well, either way, I'm calling now to cash in," Ridge said.

Again the man could be heard sighing. "And then we're square?"

"The slate is clean," Ridge promised without hesitation.

Based on what Murray and McVey had given him, he only had one clear logical next step, this being the best and very nearly only way he knew to take it.

Holding his breath he waited, counting off seconds in his head.

"This had better be important," the man said eventually. "Mulligans. One hour."

Chapter Twenty

The front lobby of the Washington, D.C. Hilton was abuzz with activity. With the new Congress opening the next day, press and local politicians from all over the country were in town, many the personal guests of legislators wanting to get their pictures in the papers back home, intent on telling all their voters how grateful they were to be there and how much they aimed to accomplish.

Manic energy seemed to roll from each person as they moved in a quick and stilted manner, all fearful of missing out on something as they streaked through the space, their heads swiveling from side to side, looking out for whoever may be nearby.

At the polar opposite end of that spectrum, Marian Ellerbe and Kyle Stroh shuffled across the polished marble floor, neither so much as lifting their feet from the ground as they processed what they'd just been through.

The task, on the surface, was a simple one, on the easier end of things they'd been asked to do in the preceding months since the election. Gone were their original charges for the day, sprinting to clean up any lingering issues, instead replaced with driving a single woman to her hotel, grabbing her things, and returning her to a nicer post downtown.

Given what they both knew about D.C. and the traffic patterns, it was clear from the outset that the task would take the better part of the time they had remaining on the clock.

What they hadn't anticipated was it draining away most of their energy also.

Not so much as a word had passed between them since leaving her room, the elevator down mercifully aided by a pair of out-of-towners, their accents and fleshy faces giving the impression of Wisconsin or Minnesota, though neither one had felt up to the task of engaging them far enough to find out.

"Well now, that was…" Ellerbe opened, her voice low, pulling Stroh's glance in her direction.

"Yeah," he agreed, one corner of his mouth flickering slightly before lowering itself back into place.

Again both fell silent as they pushed through the lobby, the two of them serving as the eye of a storm of chaos, people filing by on either side, moving fast.

"You ever?" Ellerbe asked, not bothering to finish the statement.

"Not even close," Stroh replied. "You?"

"Huh-uh," Ellerbe said. "Hope to never have to again, either."

"Right? Normally after something tense I'd suggest we stop by the bar before heading back, grab something to smooth out the rough spots, but..."

"No kidding," Ellerbe said, picking up on his insinuation, offering a small shake of her head to let him know she was of the same opinion.

Ahead of them, the front door loomed, each steering away from the oversized revolving option and instead going for the regular affair positioned off to the side. Arriving first, Stroh reached out and pulled it open, allowing Ellerbe to pass through before following her out onto the street.

Around them, the world had transitioned from midday to early evening, the hour not yet even five, though that could hardly be ascertained. Overhead, much of the daylight was already extinguished, the skyscrapers to either side blotting out most of the residual glow that remained.

In front of them, traffic had swelled considerably, city buses and taxi cabs jockeying for position, cars lined back through every intersection, oblivious to what the posted lights indicated above.

On the sidewalks, most of the working world had opted to get a few minutes jump on the end of the day, post-holiday malaise on clear display, deep frowns crossing most faces as people strode for home.

"Does this mean we should head back to the office?" Ellerbe asked, her eyes adjusting to the low light, the rest of her still fighting to shake off what had transpired upstairs.

"I guess," Stroh replied, looking out at the street before him, his gaze sweeping in a full one hundred and eighty degree arc. "Though, given how crazy the traffic is right now, I don't think anybody would say anything if we took a few minutes extra getting back."

Beside him, Ellerbe heard the words, blinking twice before they penetrated, casting a glance his direction. "Yeah?"

Matching the look, Stroh said, "I mean, if we can't grab a drink, there are other ways to snap out of a funk."

A hint of a smile pulled at Ellerbe's mouth as she looked at him another moment before shifting to see the unending snake of brake lights stretched out before them.

"I'm thinking brownies. You?"

"I was more along the lines of ice cream, but given the cold, I think you might be right."

Chapter Twenty-One

The suit was a Michael Kors, a three-button affair that Leopold Donner had gotten off the rack from a Kohl's sale two years prior. Coal black in color, it was still in the plastic from a trip to the dry cleaners thirteen months prior, that being the only other time he had ever worn it.

Which, for his money, was two more times than he would have liked.

Changing in the back seat of his SUV, Donner had worked the garment into position as much as he could, trying his best to smooth out the horizontal crease along the pant leg from the hanger they'd been on. After a few moments, he gave up on the notion, casting aside any attempt at wrangling the tie into place as well.

Instead, he opted for the open-throat look, marching into the first floor of the Senate Dirksen building just minutes before five, a black leather satchel containing absolutely nothing under his arm.

Not that it really mattered. There was no way his ruse would work, the end goal being solely to get visual confirmation of the three people he was in charge of covering.

From there, he would play things however the situation warranted, the building too large, the exits too numerous, for him to simply leave things to chance.

Passing through the metal detector, Donner remembered the office number from Ridge's website. Eschewing the elevator, he jogged up the stairs to the second floor, exiting into the hallway and moving quickly for the far end, scanning each person he passed.

There was no way to know what Susan Beckwith or Ashley Guthrie looked like, though the few women he passed were already in their coats and headed home for the day.

If any of them were who he was looking for, he could already cross them off the list, they being of no further threat to his concerns the moment they signed off for the day.

Hoping that were the case, Donner kept his stride elongated and went for the far corner, counting office numbers down in his head as he went. Sliding his phone from his pocket, he clicked a button on the side to illuminate the backlight, seeing that it was a just two minutes before five, his pace increasing slightly again.

Perfect, just as he had planned it.

An uneven triangle of light was spread on the floor from the corner office as Donner covered the last few feet, the interior of the space much brighter than the hallway he was standing in, a harsh contrast to the dark marble flooring of the outside.

Almost jogging the last few steps, Donner slowed just slightly before sliding into the office, panting slightly, forcing himself to appear as if he were out of breath. Stopping right on the threshold of the door, he extended one hand out to his right, propping himself up, an embarrassed smile on his face.

The charade was one he had used a time or two before with varying degrees of success. Though he had never been inside Ridge's office - or any congressional office – he had felt reasonably certain that the approach would work, most any basic setup providing what he needed.

This one was no different.

The front room to the spread was maybe fifteen feet on either end, an American flag and a Wyoming flag framing the entry. Along one wall was a small leather sofa, the other a pair of matching armchairs. In front of each sat narrow coffee tables, books of photography from the American West strewn atop them, landscape portraits on either wall.

In front of him was a wide desk made from a dark wood, a blonde twenty-something sitting behind it, a nameplate identifying her as Ashley Guthrie by her side.

One down.

"Good afternoon," Guthrie said, smiling at him, her teeth enhanced tremendously by what he guessed to be a small fortune in dental and orthodontic work.

"Good afternoon," Donner replied, releasing his grip on the door and stepping forward. Wiping a hand across his brow, he rubbed his palm across the thigh of his pants, cleaning it of sweat that didn't exist, the same sheepish grin still in place.

"I'm so sorry to stop by so late," he said. "My name is Tim Davenport from *The Oregonian* in Portland, and I was hoping that I might be able to snag a few minutes with the Senator."

The smile never wavered from the girl's face as a small wrinkle appeared between her brows, her upper body shifting to consult the computer monitor before her.

"Do you have an appointment with Senator Ridge?" she asked.

"No," he said, moving until he was flush against the desk and resting his hands atop it. "I'm working on a piece about our outgoing Senator and thought I might be able to get a quote from some of his colleagues before I wrap it up."

As he rattled off the prepared response, he glanced over the girl's head to the office behind her, seeing a small landing area with doors spread wide to either side.

On the right appeared to be where the staff was housed, a frumpy middle-aged woman staring straight ahead at what he guessed to be a computer, pretending not to be listening to every word transpiring out front.

Without having a picture to work from, he would guess the woman to be Susan Beckwith, though there would be no way of knowing for sure.

Even at that, he felt reasonably certain, his little visit so far having provided two of three targets he needed.

That left only the man himself, the person Donner was most concerned with pinning down immediately.

The door on the left was pulled shut, no insignia or nameplate of any kind on it, Donner guessing that to be Ridge's office. Whether or not he was behind it was open to speculation, Donner rifling through possibilities in his mind, trying to determine the best way to handle things moving forward.

"I'm very sorry, Mr.-"

"Davenport," Donner said, snapping his attention away from the door and back to the young lady before him.

"Davenport," she said, her face folding into a smile again, "but as you might have heard, this is actually the Senator's final day, so his time is booked pretty solid."

Feigning disappointment, Donner glanced down to the desk a moment before looking back up to her. "Oh, well, that happens. I do appreciate you trying, though."

"Certainly," the girl said. "And if you want, you might try ducking in on Senator McCaskill from Tennessee next door. She's been here even longer than we have."

Leaning back a step, Donner let one hand slide away from the desk, his other dragging atop it. Extended one finger down, he tapped twice at the wood, a hollow sound just barely audible.

Given what he had to work with, the attempt was worth the time needed, securing two of the three people he was tasked with, getting an even fifty-fifty on the third. Better than he actually had any hope for, the suit was beginning to become hot, his own patience with the character of Davenport and his reason for being there wearing thin.

It was time to finish up and move on.

"McCaskill," he repeated. "Great, thanks, I'll do that."

Turning away from the desk, he made it three steps across the floor, Guthrie starting to reply, her voice drowned out by the sound of a door jerking open.

Twisting at the waist, Donner looked back to see none other than Jackson Ridge emerge from behind it, the older man shrugging a coat on over his suit, a phone in his hand.

"Ash, I need to step out for a few minutes. Be back in an hour."

Chapter Twenty-Two

Residing only eight blocks from the capitol, Mulligan's was hardly what could be considered a Hill favorite. While most staffers headed west at the end of each day - the evening task of being seen in the right places talking to the right people just as important as what happened during work hours – it was situated to the Northeast, tucked away past the eastern market, on the edge of what could be considered a residential area.

Or at least could have been twenty years ago, before urban blight took down most of the dwellings positioned to either side, leaving the establishment as the last enterprising business on the block.

Certainly not the type of place that a sitting United States Senator would be ever walk to, at least not alone.

Which was exactly the point.

With the clock just a shade past five, the evening gridlock leaving the streets at a complete standstill, Jackson Ridge opted against calling for a cab, even more so for requesting a ride, not wanting the slightest record of where he was heading or of having to sit an extra twenty minutes waiting to get there.

Crossing over into the Senate Hart Building from his office in Dirksen, he shot out the North exit, flipping his collar up and walking fast, his shoulders hunched high, letting his body language show anybody that might recognize him that it was not the best time to try and stop him for a chat.

Not bothering to wait for the crosswalk, he shot straight across through the traffic standing idle on the North side of the building, disappearing down a narrow side street. Within seconds he was hidden from view by apartment buildings rising to either side, the waning gasps of daylight doing nothing to penetrate the shadows, providing him added cover.

In as little as four or five hours there would be no way he would even consider making the trek, the telltale signs of hardship and poverty already lining the path, though, for the time being, he felt reasonably certain nothing too worrisome was out, his mood such that he practically dared somebody to try something anyway.

Walking with elongated strides, Ridge covered six blocks going due north before turning east and winding his way through the last few blocks to his destination. Every few minutes he flicked a glance over his shoulder, even a time or two using reflective surfaces to see if anybody was following, the sum total being nothing more than a wry smile.

A couple of hours of making calls and talking to old friends and already paranoia was setting in.

Nine minutes after exiting the Hart building, Mulligan's came into view, a squat corner affair made from dark brick heavily splotched with spray paint, graffiti of oversized letters spelling out messages Ridge couldn't hope to decipher. Along the front window was a single sign indicating the name of the place in green letters, a shamrock serving to dot the I in the name.

No other insignia of any kind was visible to indicate what was housed inside, black iron bars over the windows and front screen door exuding a vibe that would keep most from venturing any closer to find out.

Much like the World War I monument earlier in the day, Ridge knew the place to be a favorite of the man he was coming to meet, though the two of them had only set down together once before.

That particular gathering had been years before, had resulted in the favor that was now being called in, the type of thing that most Americans would wince at if they knew happened on their watch, would openly weep if they realized just how often.

Stepping in through the front door, a wave of warm air washed over Ridge, bringing with it the scents of sour beer and stale sweat, the combined mixture tickling his nostrils. Standing just inside the door, he could feel the damp air begin to lay heavy on his skin almost instantly, a light film coming to his forehead and the backs of his hands.

On first impression, the place looked exactly as it had the last time he was present, the building consisting of one large room with restrooms along the back wall, doors to a kitchen and pantry in the corner.

To his right was a waist-high bar cut from dark wood, nicks and gouges visible along the top, a ring of black leather bar stools around the outside. Behind it stood a man that looked to be even older than Ridge, a tuft of white hair standing high on his head, a towel thrown over his shoulder.

The remainder of the space was split between tables and booths, the place not the sort to bother with pool tables or a dance floor. In their stead was a host of golf memorabilia, framed pictures on the walls, display cases featuring aging equipment set up at random intervals.

With his back to the exit, Ridge scanned the place in one quick pass, ignoring a pair of stares from the bar before settling his gaze on a dark lamp along the far wall.

"Get you something?" the barkeep asked, raising his voice and his chin in unison to fire the question.

"Whatever you have on tap," Ridge replied, barely even glancing over as he felt his core draw tight and began making his way over.

Just as the man had said he hoped to never receive the call earlier in the day, Ridge had wanted even less to make it. His trepidation had nothing to do with the fact that he was letting go of a valuable marker that he had earned long before, but more the fact that he would have to do what he was doing now, which was sit down with the man that had given it to him.

Looping out wide to the right, making sure he could be seen in the man's periphery, Ridge came up perpendicular to the table, the man leaning forward onto his elbows, a beer already down to the dregs sitting before him.

"Whitner."

Without turning to acknowledge him in any way, the man replied, "Ridge," a single word serving both as an invitation to sit and a clear message that he would rather be anywhere else in the world.

A sentiment Ridge more than shared as he slid down into the opposite side of the booth.

"Thanks for meeting with me," Ridge said, not bothering to remove his coat as he settled into position atop the smooth black leather, the seat squeaking slightly beneath his weight.

In response came only a smirk, as clear *as if I had a choice* message as could be delivered without actually saying as much.

Ridge knew the man as Terry Whitner, though if that was in fact his real name, there was no way of knowing, the man residing somewhere between the realms of spook story and fable around the Hill.

Rumors persisted that he had at one time been a Special Forces operator; others insisted he had been trained by the CIA. All anybody seemed to know for certain was that for the last twenty-five years, he always seemed to be around, having a finger on the pulse of things that were necessary, injecting himself on occasion when absolutely vital.

It was in that capacity that Ridge had first encountered the man, back when he was chair of the Armed Services Committee and a very delicate matter appeared before him.

If not for the fact that Ridge was aware of his track record, he would have no idea of the man's age, his looks completely indeterminate, appearing as if not a day had passed since their last encounter.

Thick black hair crowded in on a narrow forehead and spilled over the tops of his ears without a gray to be seen. His face was cut from plains and angles, clear ridges etched into his cheekbones, offset by a scar slicing through his right eyebrow.

Picking up the red flare of the bartender's sweater headed their way, Ridge paused long enough for the man to deposit a paper napkin and his beer, nodding in thanks as he retreated, before beginning anew.

"The reason I called-" Ridge began, ignoring the glass before him, hoping that the interaction would be over before he even so much as touched it.

"I know why you called," Whitner said.

Nodding slightly, Ridge said, "So you'd already caught wind of it."

Staring at him a moment, the first response was an eyebrow rising just slightly, followed in turn by a quick smirk.

"No. Something like this would hardly make it onto my radar."

Not knowing how to respond, feeling his jaw sag just slightly, Ridge again only nodded.

Already it was clear who was in charge of this meeting, there being no need to pretend otherwise, to even attempt to steer things where he wanted.

Calling in a favor owed or not, Terry Whitner was not the type of person to be told what to do.

"I won't say you were right to give me a call," Whitner said, "but I will say there's no way you would have sorted through this mess on your own."

Again Ridge gave no response.

"Because hell, right now I don't even know the whole story."

Internally, Ridge could feel every muscle fiber he had drawing in tight, seizing around his core, threatening to choke the air from his lungs.

What had started as a promise to a constituent, a hope for closing out his tenure on a high note, was already turning into something much larger, having stumbled into the throes of a situation he wasn't sure he wanted any part of.

Just as Whitner had said earlier, no good deed and all that.

"Nor do I have the time to be looking into it," Whitner said, "let alone sitting here in this bar talking to you."

Shifting onto a haunch, he extracted a metal money clip and peeled a fifty dollar bill from the outside, dropping it into the space between them.

"So here's what I'm going to do," he said, returning the clip to his pocket. Taking up his glass, he downed the last bits of his beer, a trail of frothy bubbles lining the side of it.

"I'm going to give you the next piece of the puzzle," Whitner said, "which will let you keep digging on your own."

The news was hardly what Ridge had expected when calling in the favor, especially from someone with the reputation of Whitner, though again he knew not to overstep, keeping any disappointment in check.

"And as a special gift, I'm going to let you keep your marker, since I'm not exactly holding up my end of things here."

While it had been presented as a quasi-deal between the two of them, it was clear that the terms were final, absolutely non-negotiable.

Not sure how to answer, or even if he should, Ridge gave only a small nod, his focus entirely on Whitner.

Across from him, the gaze was met, the other man clearly sizing him up, before saying, "The man who investigated the incident for CID is named Harold Golding, a lifer that's actually not bad at what he does."

There he paused for a moment, considering the statement, before shaking his head and sliding to the edge of the booth.

"Which makes the fact that they shipped his ass off to Alaska the minute he was done all the more curious."

Chapter Twenty-Three

The job was simple, definitely one of the easier tasks that Joselyn Packard had ever been given.

The list Leopold Donner handed over was three names in total, all legislative aides for Senator Jackson Ridge, each somewhere between their late-20s and mid-30s. After hanging up the phone from the initial call, she opened the encrypted file that was sent over and went directly to work on the trio, starting with a girl named Marian Ellerbe, fast discovering she had made her way to the capitol via Jacksonville and Duke University, with pending applications out to a number of law schools up the East coast.

With stellar LSAT scores and undergraduate grades, no doubt coupled with a strong recommendation from the senator, she was likely a shoo-in for most any school she wanted.

While not out of the question, the odds of her doing anything that might upset her future, especially while clutching at a last day gasp for legitimacy by a retiring politician, seemed unlikely.

Next up in order was Kyle Stroh, a thirty-five-year-old from Nashville that had stayed home and attended Vanderbilt, earned both a B.A. and a Master's in public administration before coming to the Hill. Beginning with the Representative from his home state before shifting to Ridge, this was his second gig that was being cut short by the voters, his CV bearing all the earmarks of a lifer that would likely be latching on with another office in the near future.

Packard had seen the type many times before, even made the mistake of getting involved with one for a while.

It hadn't ended well for either.

The final entry was a girl just north of thirty that had cut bait right after the election, jumping to a support spot on the Judiciary Committee once the results were tallied and she would fast be unemployed.

While Packard couldn't help but give a tip of her hat to the girl and her enterprising mentality, she also wasn't about to waste time trying to track her down or determine if she played any role in what Ridge was up to.

Which left only Ellerbe and Stroh to concern herself with.

From there it was a matter of getting eyes on the targets, determining where they were and who they were meeting with. Once that was complete, she would circle back to Donner with the information, the two together deciding how to proceed.

As far as she knew, they only had to maintain surveillance for a single day, meaning that a constant visual was likely in the cards.

Having spent the previous days at home, trapped inside by the harsh Washington winter and the holiday season, that was more than fine by Packard.

If the pay wasn't so damn enticing, she long ago would have left the post in Donner's employ, life in the private sector a far cry from the joys she'd once experienced traipsing across the globe.

Of course, now fast approaching forty, the time for such things was coming to an end, some thought having to be given to her own future.

That very thing was how she now found herself parked on the curb outside of The Girl Who Bakes Next Door bakery, a small affair tucked just off the major thoroughfares encircling the capitol. Having been fortunate to secure one of the final spots on the block, she sat perched behind the wheel of the battered Honda Civic she kept for such affairs to assist in making her almost completely invisible, her looks providing the rest of any cover she might need.

There was no secret that while she was more than efficient in her duties, the reason Donner had called her was that she resembled a basic soccer mom, her form long and lithe without being muscular, her hair straight and brown. Large eyes and full lips made her pretty, but a round face kept her from being too much so.

In short, she was the ideal person for urban reconnaissance, nobody ever so much as giving her a second glance.

The interior of the Civic was somewhere in the mid-fifties, the heat from the drive over starting to fade as Packard repositioned herself behind the wheel, shifting her weight to one side. Casting glances every few moments into the rearview mirror, she had a full view of the front window of the shop, Ellerbe and Stroh seated across from each other, assorted items strewn on the table between them.

Within the silent confines of the car, the sound of her ringtone erupting sounded several decibels louder than usual, echoing through the space.

No visible reaction could be seen as Packard kept her gaze on the mirror, extending one hand out and squeezing the side of her phone. Not wanting anybody walking by to see her with her hand pressed to her face, she had already set the speaker volume low, knowing the only person that would be calling.

"Packard."

"Donner," came the reply, the background free of noise, giving the impression that he too was probably sitting in a car nearby. "You good?"

"Go ahead," Packard replied.

"What's your status?" Donner asked.

Closing her eyes for a moment, Packard pushed a sigh out through her nose, her boss's insistence on saying things such as that far past the point of being annoying.

With the exception of Ames, none of them had been employed by the military for years.

"I have a visual on two of the three names given, the third being a non-factor."

"You're sure?" Donner inserted.

"Positive," Packard replied. "Records indicate she left months ago, they just never bothered to update their web page."

A grunt was the first response – presumably of approval – before Donner asked, "And the other two?"

"Currently holed up at a bakery not far from their office," Packard said. A handful of additional comments also ran through her mind, ranging the spectrum from stating they looked to be hiding to giving Donner their respective orders, though she refrained.

"You're kidding," Donner muttered, surprise in his tone.

Knowing the question was rhetorical, Packard remained silent, waiting for him to continue.

"Okay," Donner said. "I know it doesn't look like much, but stay on them just the same. If they both go home for the day afterward, you can cut it off, but if they return to the office, remain as close as possible."

"Roger that," Packard said, watching as Stroh repositioned in his chair and cross his legs, looking to be settling in for a while. "Visual only?"

Sighing once, Donner paused for a moment, contemplating the question. "For the time being. I need to swing back with the general here soon, will get further instructions.

"He's going to shit when he hears what I'm staring at right now."

Again the thought of asking for clarification came to mind, though Packard remained silent.

She knew Donner well enough to know he would or wouldn't get to it in his own time.

"Alright," Donner said after several moments, his voice seeming to indicate that he was distracted, sounding much further away than he had just a moment before. "Keep me posted on where we stand, I'll do the same with you."

"Roger that," Packard replied, reaching out and disconnecting the call without another word, the car again falling silent, the world continuing to slip further into darkness around her.

Chapter Twenty-Four

The walk back to the Dirksen Senate Building was even faster than the jaunt to Mulligan's had been, Jackson Ridge almost running most of the way, his polished shoes barely touching the ground with each step before they were up and off again, propelling him forward.

Twice along the route he ignored posted crossing instructions and openly jogged through intersections, pausing just long enough at one point to fish his phone from his pocket, placing the call to Beckwith while resuming his pace, his entire focus on getting back to his office and following up on what Whitner had told him.

While the visit with the man wasn't a total success – a far cry from everything he had hoped to accomplish, in fact – it had managed to serve one key purpose, which was to give him something to keep chipping away at.

Just like Murray and McVey before, nobody had any idea what had really happened with Josh Tarby, but they all knew enough to ensure progress was made.

Given the time strictures he was working under, both from the end of the work day and the end of his very position, that was the best he could hope for.

Even if he had to exhaust every last favor he had accumulated in the process.

Most of the foot traffic around Dirksen was heading in the opposite direction as he passed through a side entrance, pausing just long enough to deposit his phone, keys, and wallet into a plastic bin and walking through the metal detectors. Nodding his thanks to the pair of bored guards on either side, he collected his belongings and again took to jogging, stuffing his things back into pockets as he made for the staircase.

Two minutes later he found himself passing through the front door to his office suite, Ashley standing behind the desk, her coat on, the strap of her bag tossed over a shoulder.

The sight of him appearing so abruptly caused her to visibly flinch, blood rushing to her cheeks, a hand rising to her chest.

"Sorry, Ash," he said, his breath coming in ragged pants, the quick trip back from Mulligan's being the closest thing he had gotten to exercise in quite some time. "Have a good evening."

Taking a moment to collect herself, Ashley put on a smile, her shoulders rising and falling as she matched his breathing pattern.

"Thanks, sir. You, too."

Not having the time or the inclination for small talk, Ridge swung around behind the front desk, looping his scarf up over his head and peering into the bullpen door on the right side of the suite. Seeing nothing but a quartet of empty desks, he paced back across the open space between them and entered his office to find Beckwith standing in front of his desk, both hands clasped before her.

Held between the middle and index finger of her right hand was a scrap of paper, the white square a bright contrast to the dark green suit she wore.

"Hey, Susie," Ridge said, shrugging out of his coat and tossing it at the coatrack, the momentum knocking it back against the wall before swinging forward, the trio of legs wobbling before eventually settling down even.

"Sir," Beckwith said simply.

"Were you able to get what I asked for?" Ridge said, stopping a few steps past the rack and patting himself down. Feeling the bulge of his phone deep in his front pants pocket, he resumed his walk, moving behind his desk, the scrap of paper Beckwith had been holding waiting there for him.

"Thank you," Ridge said. "Not too much trouble, I hope?"

"None at all, sir," she replied. "I hope you don't mind, I told Ashley she could head home."

"Of course," Ridge replied, knowing what Beckwith was alluding to, already having the same thought when he walked in a few moments before.

As clear a role as Ashley played throughout the day, providing a smiling visage and unfailing courtesy to a host of things that sprang up, she wouldn't be of much use with whatever the coming night might hold.

Not that he would ever dream of involving a twenty-four-year-old girl in any of it to begin with.

"Any word from Marian and Kyle?" Ridge asked.

"They checked in a little bit ago," Beckwith said. "Apparently traffic was especially treacherous, so things took longer than expected, but Ms. Tarby is now all settled in and resting comfortably."

"Good," Ridge replied, pulling his chair back a few inches and settling down into the seat. "Anything else around here?"

Assuming her usual position, her lips pursed before her, Beckwith said, "Well, there was another call from Senator-elect Hodges."

Feeling the same pang of anger that usually accompanied the man's name, Ridge allowed his acrimony to flash over his features, waving his hand across his body, dismissing the man and the topic altogether.

"Eighteen hours," he said, "then the sniveling punk can have the place."

"That's what I told him, sir," Beckwith said, turning and beginning to retreat from the room. "Not in those words exactly, of course."

Ignoring the barb, Ridge watched her go, waiting until she was just a step from exiting before adding, "And not a minute earlier."

Pausing just over the threshold, Beckwith turned back and grasped the doorknob. "I told him that as well, sir."

Without waiting for further comment, she pulled the door shut, the sound echoing once through the room before silence flooded in. Allowing it wash over him, Ridge rested his elbows on either arm of the chair, using the tips of his fingers to knead his temples in small concentric circles.

The day was supposed to have been a victory lap, or as close to one as a man that was being unceremoniously dumped on his behind could have.

The morning was supposed to be a photo op, followed by a nice lunch with colleagues, and an afternoon of glad-handing and reminiscing. From there, he would take the staff out for a nice meal, everybody smiling and pretending they weren't on the cusp of unemployment, before coming back the next day for a few perfunctory exercises and another farewell meal.

A couple of days to close his affairs in Washington, and then he was headed back to Wyoming, where he would hunt and fish and occasionally charge exorbitant fees for speaking engagements and consulting gigs.

Instead, he was sitting behind his desk well after quitting time, already feeling the effects of working harder than he had in a long time.

Feeling the concentrated events of the day rise like bile in the back of his throat, Ridge let his hands fall away, his palms slapping heavily against his thighs. Opening his eyes, he blinked away the flashing lights that appeared before them, his vision eventually settling onto the scrap of paper waiting for his attention.

"Christ," he muttered, raising his bottom a few inches from his seat and sliding his phone from his pocket, the device getting extended use on a day when he had almost left it at home.

Flipping it open, he punched in the digits Beckwith had provided, leaning back in his chair and listening as ringing was replaced by the sound of a song Ridge had never heard before, only the use of a slide guitar and the occasional twang in the singer's voice letting him know it was supposed to be country.

Just one more thing that had changed immensely in the time since he first took office.

"Golding," a voice with a similar drawl responded after several seconds, the sound of loud and persistent wind pushing through the mouthpiece.

Leaning up in his seat, Ridge said, "Uh, yeah, yes, is this Harold Golding with CID?"

All traces of the previous southern accent fell away as the man replied, "It is. Who is this?"

"This is Senator Jackson Ridge from Wyoming, former Chair of the Senate Armed Services Committee."

For a moment there was no response, nothing but the sound of the wind.

"Hello? Golding?" Ridge asked.

"I'll call you back in five," Golding replied, his tone indicating all business. "907 area code."

Just as fast as the call had started it was over, the line cutting out, the sound of the wind dying away.

It took a moment for Ridge to realize the conversation was over before slowly pulling the phone away from his face. Flipping it shut, he crossed his right leg over his left, staring off, still trying to make sense of everything that was going on around him.

All he wanted was to determine what had happened to Josh Tarby, a task that should have been as simple as pulling his file and reading the narrative.

What had ensued instead seemed like something he would read late at night from the pages of Tom Clancy.

Still locked on that thought, his focus on the desktop, his phone began to ring in his hand. Without glancing at the screen, he flipped it open and brought it back to his cheek, blinking rapidly to pull himself back to fully aware.

"Ridge."

"I thought you should know, you're being followed."

The voice in no way matched Golding's, Ridge's eyebrows rising as he jerked the phone away and stared down at the screen, a wave of palpitations rising through his chest as he stared at what he saw on the caller ID.

Whitner.

"Black SUV, bogus plates," Whitner said. "Followed you to Mulligan's, pulled away right after you left."

Chapter Twenty-Five

Jackson Ridge was standing along the back wall of his office, his shoulder flush against the heavy maroon curtains lining either side of the picture window behind him. With his body perpendicular to the outside of the building, he peered out into the darkness, trying to imagine who might be out there, lurking, watching.

The call from Whitner had him shook, a fact he was not proud to admit, the feeling filling him with disgust, both at himself and the situation.

There was a time – which he would like to believe wasn't all that long ago – when there was no way he would have been so foolish, so consumed with his thoughts that he forgot who he was or what he was doing. Now, he had allowed himself to become preoccupied, solely focused on some sort of hero's quest that was making him foolhardy, rushing forward headlong.

At the same time, he couldn't help but feel like this was also a validation of sorts for what he was doing. He had no way of knowing who it was that had taken it upon themselves to follow him for a quick run to the corner bar, but clearly, his asking questions had rattled somebody to the point that they felt it necessary to do so.

Which only solidified his desire to keep going, even if he needed to be a little more careful about things.

There was no way Murray would have tipped anybody about what he was doing, even less McVey, who let it be known that he didn't want to be associated in any way.

Double that for Whitner, who made a career out of being invisible, and had even gone the extra length of alerting him as to what was going on.

Who that left as the leak in the chain, Ridge had no idea. He also knew that given the time constraints he was under, there were only so many things he could deal with at a given moment.

Which might be exactly what whoever was out there wanted, to slow him down just enough so that the clock ran out before he got where he needed to be.

The thoughts were all swirling in his head, one shifting mass of ideas and concerns, when the phone on his desk began to buzz. For several moments he merely left it there, the sound barely penetrating his consciousness, his thoughts on the call from Whitner and what it might represent.

Just as fast, what he was doing right before it came in sprang back to mind, the name Harold Golding flitting across the front of his psyche.

Pushing himself away from the wall, Ridge covered the ground to the desk in two quick bounds, snapping the phone up, this time checking the caller ID and seeing the 907 area code he'd been alerted to look for.

"Ridge," he said, remaining standing as he accepted the call.

"You have no idea how long I've been waiting for you to give me a call."

Much like the last line in their previous conversation, any trace of an accent was gone from Golding's voice, his tone a mixture of exhaustion and bitterness.

"Me?" Ridge gasped, his eyes growing a bit wider.

"Not *you* you," Golding corrected, "but somebody from your committee, or Washington, or hell, just somebody in general."

Feeling his heart rate rise a bit, Ridge slowly rotated in place and lowered himself against his desk, the top fitting just beneath his hips. Crossing his left arm over his chest, he rested his right elbow atop it and said, "So you know what this is about?"

"Afghanistan," Golding replied, very much a statement and not a question.

"So you saw the news, too?" Ridge asked.

"The news?" Golding replied, his voice betraying a hint of confusion. "No, that I don't know anything about. What I do know is that was the damn screwiest situation I ever handled, and it's the reason I'm standing up here in twenty-two hours a day of darkness freezing my ass off."

Again raising his gaze to the windows behind him, Ridge attempted to look out into the gloom, almost imagining somebody standing there with a sound bubble, trying to hear every word that was being exchanged.

In reality, all he could see was his own reflection and the office around him, the darkness outside turning the place into a fish bowl.

"Start at the beginning, tell me everything," Ridge said.

Pushing himself up from the desk, he went to the window on his right and jerked the curtains shut, the rollers making a loud noise as they slid into place. Moving straight across, he went to each successive window in turn, doing the same.

A small measure for sure, but at the very least it would keep anybody from having a direct visual.

As he did so, a long sigh could be heard, followed by a pause, the man collecting himself before launching forward with his narrative. When he finally did speak, the words came out fast, as if prepared a long time before, just waiting for any opportunity to release them.

"I'm assuming that you calling me like this," Golding said, "after hours in D.C. and all, means that you've been digging at this for a while."

Notwithstanding the fact that it had only been a number of hours, the number of conversations and favors that had been exchanged on the topic was already becoming quite exhaustive.

"Yes."

"So then you also probably know how the investigative process works, how I ended up on the case," Golding said.

Resuming his place against the front of his desk, Ridge said, "The first part yes, but not the rest. I'm aware of CID and the role they play.

"No offense, but I had never heard your name until about an hour ago."

"None taken," Golding replied, "because there would be no reason for you to. I was a civilian investigator with the CID, brought onboard after twenty years as an MP.

"They wanted me to stay in, keep climbing the ladder when I got out, but as a Carolina boy, the prospect of coming home and working out of Virginia was too appealing to pass up."

Just days from returning to Wyoming, Ridge knew the feeling well.

"I bet."

"Worked right down the road there from you," Golding said, bypassing the comment. "Was housed at the Marine Corps Base at Quantico, sharing space and the occasional resource with the boys in blue."

It had been a while since Ridge had heard the reference, knowing that he was alluding to the FBI, the organization that was headquartered on the same grounds as the base, a joint operation that provided mutual support, to say nothing of the occasional friction.

"Okay," Ridge said, the full background not really necessary, though he wanted no part of derailing the story, hoping Golding would be getting to the pertinent portions sooner rather than later.

"Being based there," Golding continued, "meant that most of the time I was in Virginia working cold cases or putting meat on the bones of open investigations, but from time to time we did get pulled out into the field."

"For instances like Afghanistan," Ridge inserted.

"Exactly," Golding replied, "for things that rose above the pay scale of the general MPs."

"And that's what happened over there?" Ridge asked.

For the first time since he began talking, Golding paused, long enough that Ridge was almost sorry he'd asked anything, his last intention being to interrupt the flow of information, especially just as it was on the cusp of becoming pertinent.

Wincing slightly, folds of skin appearing around his eyes, he found himself holding his breath, waiting for Golding to continue.

When he did – almost a full minute later – a hint of the earlier bitterness was back.

"I'll tell you right up front, I don't know what the hell happened over there," Golding said, "but here's what went down.

"On April 14th of last year, the incident in question took place. The scale back was just getting under way and a lot of supplies were starting to flow out of the city, meaning that the usual convoy routes were now running twice a day, the real big ticket items moving out under the cover of darkness.

"The idea was that any insurgents that might be watching may feel extra emboldened, knowing that there was a ton of goods moving through, this being their last chance to get their hands on them."

His thoughts thousands of miles away, Ridge nodded. While on the surface whatever was leaving would seem to be the same exact things that had previously entered, in most cases their condition a little worse for the wear, he had discounted the timeframe.

Just as he was now doing things that he wouldn't normally while faced with a looming deadline, it bore to reason the enemies in Afghanistan would feel the same way.

"The night runs had started only a week earlier, and up to that point everything had been going fine, not even a shot fired," Golding said. "But on that night..."

"All hell broke loose," Ridge murmured.

"And then some," Golding replied. "Eighteen miles outside of Kabul, almost exactly between the city and the airfield, in a spot where there was no earthly reason for it to have occurred."

Feeling his eyes narrow again, Ridge asked, "What do you mean?"

"I mean, I'm sure you've read information briefings on the Armed Services Committee, are familiar with Afghanistan being a rugged, mountainous terrain."

"Sure," Ridge replied.

"So then you know what that kind of country normally looks like. Narrow passes, winding roads, you name it, this route had it all."

"Which is why the convoy was armed to begin with," Ridge said.

"Well, they're all armed, but the ones going in and out of the city were heavily armed," Golding said. "And with good reason. There was rock solid data telling them that hostiles were holed up in those spots.

"Our guys had seen them on more than one occasion. Ground support had even had a few skirmishes with them."

Grunting softly, Ridge felt himself nodding, visually confirming what he was being told. Earlier in the day, he had looked at the map, seeing the very route Golding was now speaking of, having examined it a dozen times or more in his previous work on the committee, the winding red line of the road now standing out in his mind.

"Okay," he nudged.

"Despite all that," Golding said, "none of those places is where it went down. Instead, it happened right out in the open, on a flat patch of ground with no cover for miles."

"You're shitting me," Ridge said, the words out and gone before he even realized it, the look of confusion that had started around his eyes now grown to encompass all of his features.

"Nope," Golding said. "And let me tell you, this isn't like Iraq, where they could have dug some hides into the soft sand and holed up. That ground is hard and rocky.

"The amount of time it would have taken them to get into position...well, somebody would have noticed. Like I said, they'd been running through there twice a day."

"Right," Ridge said, releasing his left hand from over his torso and bringing it to his forehead, for the first time realizing that he was warm, his skin damp to the touch.

Thinking on what had been shared for a moment, superimposing it onto the data he already had, Ridge said, "So this was a late night run that got hit?"

"It was," Golding said. "Two forty-eight in the morning, local time."

"Damn," Ridge said.

"Yeah," Golding agreed, his voice lowered to match Ridge's.

Again the two men fell silent for a moment, chewing on things, before Ridge asked, "So what was taken?"

"I don't know," Golding said.

"You don't know?" Ridge said, his voice rising just as fast as it had faded, his facial expression matching it in kind.

"I don't know," Golding repeated. "In fact, what I just shared with you is everything I do know, because fewer than thirty-six hours after arriving in Afghanistan, we were jerked off the case and sent back home.

"Week later, I was shipped up here."

Standing alone in his office, Ridge's jaw fell, his face hanging, so much packed into the last few sentences he didn't know where to begin, how to best unfurl the information he'd just been handed.

"I'm sorry, what?"

"Yeah," Golding replied, dragging the word out, the previous bitterness back in full. "They took me out of Virginia, flew me to the other side of the world, had me there basically long enough to see the site, to collect a couple of vague accounts of what happened, and then brought me back."

"And right after?" Ridge asked.

"Yep."

"Were you expecting a transfer? Your time at Quantico coming to an end?" Ridge prodded.

"No," Golding answered, "and that's not even how it works. I'm a civilian, I don't have enlistment terms."

"And I didn't realize the CID would even have a presence in Alaska," Ridge added.

"We don't," Golding said, "or at least we didn't."

To that he added nothing more, the insinuation clear. Whatever he had been doing in the mountains a week earlier was something that nobody wanted to be delved into too deeply, his newest outpost being an obvious hiding place, somewhere to stash him indefinitely.

"If they wanted you out of the way," Ridge said, "why not just fire you? Why go to all that trouble?"

To that a sigh was the first response, the sound drawn out several seconds, the weight behind them clear.

"Senator, I have asked myself that question a hundred times a day, and the only thing I can figure is because it was easier for them to keep tabs on me this way.

"If they'd fired me, they knew I'd have stayed in the area. That's where I'm from, where my friends and family are. This way, they could ship me off to Siberia here, know exactly where I was and what I was doing all the time."

Though he wasn't sure why, Ridge almost felt the need to apologize to the man, even if he had never actually met him.

The situation that was being described was abhorrent, it now clear that Clara Tarby was far from the only person that had gotten a raw deal in the proceedings.

"Who is *they*?" Ridge asked.

"Good question," Golding answered. "I would assume somebody either on-site there in Afghanistan or pretty high up back here, someone that would stand to get a black eye from whatever I found."

"Which was what?" Ridge asked. "Why were they so afraid of you being there?"

Once more there was a sigh, this time the bitterness having receded, simple exhaustion taking its place.

"I don't know," Golding said. "I don't know what they thought I'd find, why they sent me there if they were so scared of me finding it."

Respecting, acknowledging, even empathizing, with the plight the man was situated in, Ridge tried to force himself not to focus on Golding himself, to keep his sights on the goal of ferreting out what had happened that night, on what so many people seemed intent to keep hidden.

"Mr. Golding, does the name Josh Tarby mean anything to you?" he asked.

For a moment there was no response, as if the man was checking a mental database, before replying, "Only insomuch as I know he was one of the deceased. Beyond that, like I said, I didn't have a lot of time to dig on this one."

"Right," Ridge said, nodding, feeling like the conversation was coming to a close having revealed so much, but ultimately leaving infinitely more questions than when he had started.

Again he rifled through the previous conversations of the day, a snippet of something McVey had said to him springing to mind.

"I was told earlier that CID often works with counterintelligence on cases where they think something fishy might be going on," he said, realizing the explanation was far from exact, but knowing Golding would recognize where he was going just the same. "Did anything like that happen here?"

This time the pause was more than a full minute, so long that Ridge thought he might have lost the call, was about to ask if Golding was still there, when the man replied, "Give me an hour. I'll call you back."

Chapter Twenty-Six

The interior of the townhouse General Arnold Ames lived in was quiet, void of life, the space in near darkness as he entered. Stepping in through the side entrance from the garage, he passed directly into the kitchen, the area open, with marble countertops and a matching island positioned in the middle.

Tossing his keys and his briefcase, the sack with his uneaten lunch, all atop the island, he stepped directly through, moving by muscle memory, not turning on a single light as he passed.

Moving into the hallway, he shrugged off his coat and opened a small closet, hanging the garment on a hanger and returning it to place, the few sparse items inside all arranged with uniform precision.

To the casual observer, there was no indication of the day he had had, his face the same measure of impassive it always was, his features stony.

What those same individuals would not know, though, was the tempest of thoughts and worries roiling beneath them, things that had started the moment Leopold Donner first called him, had stretched back much further than that if he really wanted to think about it.

When the opportunity had first presented itself, it seemed like a good idea, maybe even the *only* idea, something that would serve both his interests and the country's in tandem.

In the time since, that impression had begun to change, a combination of shifting societal pressures and expectations, a new regime about to take power on the Hill.

For a long time, Ames had known his days were coming to an end, though never had he realized how fast that eventuality would come to bear. Now, his only hope was to hang on long enough that he could see things through to an ending he dictated, instead of being cast aside like so many others he had encountered over the years.

And doing that meant shutting down whatever it was Jackson Ridge thought he was up to.

Shutting the door quietly behind him, Ames moved down the hallway and onto the staircase, his footfalls silent against the carpet stairs. One by one he slowly ascended them, ignoring the tightness in his right knee, his mind far too preoccupied to be bothered with a bit of tenderness in the joint.

Coming out on the second floor, he hooked a right and entered the master bedroom, his cellphone beginning to buzz on his hip as he walked directly past his bed and stood before the doublewide window along the wall, the illuminated spire of the Capitol framed perfectly within it.

"Ames," he said, answering the phone.

"Donner," came the reply, per usual going through the motions of pausing long enough to make sure both sides were clear and free to talk.

"Go ahead," Ames said, his jaw tightening slightly at the unnecessary gesture, on the younger man's insistence on doing things as if he were a character in a spy novel.

"Checking in," Donner replied.

"And?" Ames snapped, agitation growing a bit higher within.

"And things have gotten worse," Donner said, delivering the information with no voice inflection at all, as if he were discussing the weather or a local sports score.

"How much worse?" Ames asked.

For a moment there was no response, Ames able to visualize Donner doing the same thing with his face that he always did, scrunching it slightly as if contemplating an answer.

"I just got back to the Capitol a few minutes ago after tailing Ridge on a little errand," Donner said.

Keeping his focus on the horizon, the lights of the city springing up at random intervals, igniting everything in a hue of unnatural color, Ames said, "An errand to where?"

"Not where, who," Donner replied.

There he stopped again, almost seeming to be enjoying the moment, making Ames drag the information out of him one little bit at a time.

"Who, dammit?" Ames snapped, his tone letting it be known that he was sick of the cat-and-mouse.

The situation they were in was huge, with the potential to become cataclysmic to both of them. It was hardly the time for Donner to be getting off on the tiny bit of leverage he might have at the moment.

"Terry Whitner."

With his mouth still open, his face twisted up with anger, it took a moment for the name to register with Ames, another for the enormity of what he'd just been told to sink in. As it did, the look on his face slowly receded, his heart rate climbing in kind.

Though, again, there was absolutely no visual response at all for anybody that might have been watching.

"You sure?"

A smirk was the first response, followed by, "Positive. Trust me, that's one face you don't forget."

To that Ames had no response, knowing that Donner was right. Whitner was somebody they had both only encountered a time or two before, the type of person that every government needed on the books, that everybody who ever ran across him wished they had never met.

Ames also knew that if Ridge was calling on the man, he was digging deep into whatever political capital he had left, mortgaging everything he had accrued in the previous thirty-six years for this one last stab at getting something done.

The fact that it was coming at the possible expense of Ames was something he could not abide, whether Terry Whitner was involved or not.

"Any idea what they discussed?" Ames asked.

"Ha!" Donner replied, spitting the word out free of any mirth at all. "It was a complete fluke that I even happened to hear where he was headed, standing in the man's front lobby as he exited.

"If I had tried to set foot in the place, he would have spotted me a mile away."

To that Ames said nothing, wondering how and why Donner had been reckless enough to enter the man's office, but much more concerned with a host of other things that precluded him from going into it.

"Good thing, too," Donner added, "because Whitner would have nailed my ass to the wall."

"Did he see you?" Ames asked.

"No," Donner replied. "I was parked down the block, barely in sight of the place. Was waiting it out, letting Ridge head back the opposite way, when I just happened to spot Whitner exiting."

"Any idea where he went after?" Ames asked.

"No," Donner said. "Hell no. Not a chance I was even attempting to tail that guy."

Grunting in agreement, knowing that the man was probably correct, Ames turned away from the window. Striding back past the bed, he moved by the first closet, half-full of civilian attire, and on to the second. Jerking it open, he stared at the even row of military dress, the olive greens all pressed and ready to be worn.

Selecting the first one in order, he laid it down on the bed before going back, his attention raised to the shelf up high, the line of caps placed there.

"Where are you now?" Ames asked.

"Sitting outside his office building," Donner said. "The old fart must be getting twitchy because he just closed the curtains to his office, but I know he's there. Same for the rest of his staff."

"You sure?" Ames asked.

"Positive," Donner replied. "Orders?"

With the phone pressed tight against his face, Ames stared down at the dress uniform, the time for him to play a more active role having arrived.

"Sit tight. I'm on my way."

Chapter Twenty-Seven

The chairs had remained in position in front of Jackson Ridge's desk all day, there being no point in moving them back and forth, the people filling them a revolving door of characters foreign and familiar.

For the second time on the day, the trio of Beckwith, Ellerbe, and Stroh sat in front of the senator, all in the same position they had been hours earlier.

Of the three, only Beckwith looked the same as she did then, her face up and attentive, her clothes free of a wrinkle, the day planner still clutched on her lap. To either side, Ellerbe and Stroh looked spent despite the early hour, both making it clear they were ready to be off the clock whenever Ridge gave them the green light to go.

Seeing that, knowing the looks they wore, the vibe they were trying in earnest to give off, Ridge had no intention of doing such anytime soon, the conversations he had had since their last meeting only serving to heighten the anxiety within.

"Did you get Ms. Tarby settled in?" he asked, opening the debriefing.

For a moment there was no response, both of his aides staring down at their waists, before Ellerbe raised her gaze and said, "Yes. She seemed somewhat embarrassed by the place, but she eventually accepted it, thanked us for the gesture."

"Embarrassed?" Ridge asked, a crease forming between his brows, the response not what he had expected in the slightest.

"Yeah," Stroh inserted. "Said repeatedly she didn't need all that, even went as far as to point out she couldn't afford such a spread."

"Afford?" Ridge gasped, unable to hide his surprise at the word. "Did you tell her-"

"Of course," Ellerbe said, "which only seemed to make her a bit more self-conscious."

"But she was okay when you left?"

"She was," Stroh said.

"Walked us to the door, thanked us for everything," Ellerbe added.

Nodding once, Ridge pictured the woman that had sat in one of these very chairs earlier in the day, the look of anguish on her face. If anybody deserved a comfortable place and a nice meal for the evening, it was her.

Whatever discomfort she felt about the arrangement was almost sure to dissipate soon enough.

"Good," Ridge said, pressing his lips tight and nodding once. "Thank you both for doing that."

To that neither verbally responded, Stroh matching his nod, Ellerbe offering a smile.

Falling silent for a moment, Ridge shifted his attention to the afternoon he had had, to the meeting with Murray that had kicked things off and all that had transpired since. Opening his mouth once, twice, to begin speaking, he paused, debating how to best approach things, if he even should at all.

Thus far, everything that had transpired of any real import had done so by his hand. His two young charges had helped secure Ms. Tarby, Beckwith had tracked down a couple of phone numbers, but there was nothing any of them had done that really had anything to do with the situation that occurred in Afghanistan.

With each passing moment, it was becoming clearer that something nefarious had taken place, the kind of thing that people were desperate to keep quiet, so much so they had even shipped Harold Golding all the way to Alaska.

To think those very same people wouldn't perhaps come after the people sitting in the room for that reason as well would be a blunder he could not abide.

This quest, this final day, was on him. It was a question that had first been posed his direction, any hope or expectation of relief being aimed at the Senator from Wyoming, not the poor souls that had the misfortune of working for him.

"I am sorry today went later than anticipated," Ridge said, sounding the words out slowly, his gaze shifted to the side before glancing up to take each of them in. "And that I won't be able to join you, but if you don't mind, I would like to buy you all dinner.

"Anywhere you'd like, anything you'd like. Susie, you have my personal cards, please put it on there."

The words, the directive, seemed to be far from what any of the three expected, all looking up in unison, Ellerbe and Stroh void of expression, Beckwith's mouth parting just slightly.

"Sir?"

Waving a hand before him, Ridge said, "I know it's terrible I can't come too, but as you all know, I'm still trying to tie something up, so I should stick around.

"Tomorrow we'll all grab a quick bite before we go, I promise."

Again there was no response, the group sitting in stunned silence, gaping back at him.

"Really," he said, forcing a smile into place, "go get yourselves a nice steak and bottle of wine. You've all more than earned it."

Chapter Twenty-Eight

No matter how many people might be tucked away inside the suite, the front door closed with the departure of Ashley each evening at six, the end of official business hours. From that point forward, whoever was inside could work with abandon, not needing to be concerned with who might be stopping by.

On the final day of Jackson Ridge's tenure, the front door stayed open a bit later than usual but was still closed for the night by half past the hour when Ashley was allowed to leave.

Hidden behind the closed gate, his staff begrudgingly doing his bidding and exiting for dinner, Ridge sat at his desk, the ringer on his cell phone turned up high, the device sitting square before him. Reclined in his seat, he tried in vain to push the events of the day to the side for a moment, realizing it was the first time he had been alone inside the suite in years.

Starting to his right, he made a slow sweep of the room, taking in the décor, examining each of the pieces of taxidermy that covered the walls.

While it was true that every last one had been taken by his own hand, the truth was, the newest one to the collection had been added more than a decade before. When he had first taken office, he had spent as much if not more time back home in Wyoming, making up official business when he could, purchasing cheap fares on whatever airline he could find otherwise.

After growing up on a ranch, the bustle of the city seemed like something from a foreign planet, life too busy, the general demeanor too aggressive.

Somewhere along the line, that balance had begun to tip. The trip became long, the flights expensive. Bit by bit he bought into the city life, finding that he rather enjoyed eating at restaurants that served more than just steak and potatoes, didn't mind fighting the crowds to watch local sporting events.

He even got used to putting on a suit each morning, an eventuality he'd have never thought possible.

A lifetime bachelor, once his parents passed at the start of this term, it was as if he had no reason to go back at all, hiring a caretaker to look after the ranch and retreating to his Washington home full-time.

Which, when he got down to it, was probably what landed him in the situation he was in.

People – especially those in places like Wyoming – believed in a representative democracy, which also meant they needed to feel like they were being represented.

Pretty difficult to convince anybody that was the case from two thousand miles away.

Moving in an unending ebb and flow through his mind, one thought leading to another, Ridge never heard the small knock at the front door, nor did he register the moan of the hinges as it swung up and quietly closed again.

Stopped halfway through his examination of the room, making it as far as a stuffed grouse just taking off in flight before his eyes glazed, Ridge didn't even realize he had a visitor until they appeared in his doorway, a tall man with square shoulders that nearly blotted out the light from the front office behind him.

Believing he was alone, Ridge's flinched noticeably, his head jerking to the side, his shoulders rocking back a few inches. Feeling his heart rate rise, his first thought was to again admonish Susie for entering so silently before stopping, the person standing before him most certainly not his Chief of Staff.

"Good evening," the man said, his voice firm but low, "I didn't mean to startle you."

Pushing himself up from his seat, Ridge said, "I'm sorry General, I thought I was alone."

Opening his mouth as if he might apologize as well, the man instead seized on the words that had been said, taking a step forward into the room.

"So, you know who I am?"

Easing himself to the side, a clear path opening up between the two of them, Ridge replied, "No, but I've seen enough uniforms sit before my committee to recognize the bars of a general when I see them."

Moving forward, he extended his hand and said, "Senator Jackson Ridge, it's an honor to have you here, sir."

Returning the shake, his grip even more firm than his voice, the man said, "General Arnold Ames, I wonder if you might have a few minutes to talk."

"Certainly," Ridge said, extending a hand to the line of chairs that had grown misshapen over the course of the day. "Please, have a seat."

Circling back around to his own chair, Ridge settled down into it, Ames doing the same across from him, his posture impossibly upright, his hat balanced across his knee.

"You're probably wondering what brings me by this evening," Ames began, his focus locked straight ahead, his gaze on Ridge and nothing else.

Considering the question a moment, Ridge replied, "Actually, I was trying to place your face. I've seen a lot of brass sit before the committee before, but I don't believe you've ever testified."

"No," Ames said, "never have. In fact, despite working just across the river, this is only the second time I've ever been inside one of these buildings before."

Although the words were clearly meant to be deliberately vague, Ridge seized on the enormous creases that existed between them, extracting much more from the unspoken than what was clearly stated.

That meant the man worked at the Pentagon, and given the insignia he wore, it likely meant he was very high in the pecking order. The fact that he had attained such a post and been in such close proximity without having any presence on the Hill also denoted he was likely attached to something designed not to get a lot of public exposure.

With each bit of information that rose to the surface, the previous surprise Ridge had felt about the unexpected visit seemed to fade away.

In its place came the realization that this was definitely not a farewell of any kind.

"You're here about Josh Tarby," Ridge said, pushing right past what could have been a drawn-out back-and-forth and cutting right to it, the day, the last two months, even the last thirty-six years, prohibiting him from keeping up the banter any longer than necessary.

To that there was only a slight flicker of the man's features, his gaze still intent as his eyes bore into Ridge.

"Tarby specifically? No, but you're not far off."

Grunting softly, Ridge raised his head an inch or so, letting it be known that he understood, was pondering his response.

For years he had sat up high in his committee seat and stared down at men such as Ames, having seen how they worked, how they positioned themselves, the subtle tactics they used to gain the upper hand in various situations.

Already he could see them at play across from him, everything from the choice to arrive in full dress uniform to the seat he had chosen to the fact that he probably couldn't even tell Ridge the color of the curtains just a few feet to either side of him.

"Meaning?" Ridge asked.

"Meaning, I know about the visit you had from Clara Tarby this morning, and I can give you my word that the answer is an unequivocal yes."

Again, Ridge recognized that the man was speaking in code.

After the day he had, that wasn't quite going to be enough.

"Yes, to which part exactly?" Ridge asked.

"Yes, the young man's death was worth it," Ames replied.

"Worth it to whom?" Ridge replied, the cadence between them picking up, a charged undercurrent growing more pronounced with each traded jab.

"To anybody that might be asking," Ames replied. "To his mother, and to his country."

Another handful of quick retorts all sprang instantly to mind, though Ridge bit them back, as much to let the General's words hang in the air as to try and dispel any of the tension between them.

There was no point in even pretending that was a possibility, the tone clear from the outset.

Having spent decades sitting in committee hearings, Ridge had also developed a few tricks for dealing with men such as Ames, the biggest being to use their own ego against them.

That meant employing the full use of silence, knowing the man would not be able to sit long without feeling the need to fill it, to assert why he was present and what he wanted out of the exchange.

"And now having told you that, I am here to ask that you cease any further inquiry into the matter."

Giving no reaction, sitting completely motionless, Ridge could feel a small ripple through his stomach and nothing more. In just one sentence, Ames had managed to explain why everything about the Tarby situation seemed to be so much more difficult than it needed to be, why he was exhausting every favor he had looking into it.

And at the same time, he had inadvertently handed Ridge an entirely new angle to pursue.

"May I ask why that is?" Ridge said.

"You may," Ames said, "so long as you understand why I respectfully cannot answer."

Again with speaking in code, Ridge took the answer to mean that it fell under the auspices of being classified, was the sort of thing that was still either ongoing or far too sensitive to be shared.

Damned if he was going to be pushed off that easily.

"I'm not a military inquiry board, have no interest in bringing anybody down," he replied. "I am simply trying to give a constituent closure, use the last day I have in this office for a bit of good."

For only the second time throughout the conversation, Ridge saw a small pulse of something move across Ames's face, disappearing just as fast, replaced by the same wooden exterior he most likely always wore. What it meant, what comment was just beneath the system, aching to be released, he could only guess at, though it wasn't hard to surmise it was most likely at his expense.

A fact that only managed to heighten the growing disdain he had for the man, this meeting just one more piece in a day-long puzzle that didn't make sense.

"And I hope that my being here has provided that, both for you and Ms. Tarby," Ames replied.

Just as with every other sentence that he had made, the words were intentionally vanilla, though there was clear meaning attached to each one.

Ridge was being administered an ultimatum.

Something he had never responded all that well to in his life.

Rising slowly from his seat, hearing the springs moan beneath him, Ridge extended his hand across the desk.

"Thank you, General, for stopping by. That does provide a great deal of relief to me, and I'm sure it will to Clara Tarby as well."

Chapter Twenty-Nine

With the sun hours past faded, any residual glow rising over the city was of the halogen and fluorescent variety, completely void of any warmth. Just days into the new year, that put the temperature a degree or two below freezing, every breath exiting Leopold Donner in a white plume, the edges of his nostrils beginning to harden.

Resting on the far right end of a metal bench, the seat positioned at an angle so he could see both the corner office of Jackson Ridge and the exit immediately beneath it, he was still wearing the suit, a topcoat on over it, his thinning hair exposed to the cold.

With his hands buried deep in the pockets of the coat, one was wrapped around the plastic casing of his cellphone, the other curled into a tight fist to stave off frostbite.

Seated in that position, he kept his focus trained straight ahead, not so much as even glancing over as a second figure appeared, taking up the far end of the bench, her footfalls silent as she approached.

In his periphery, he could see she was dressed in a long brown coat with a matching hat, appearing to be nothing more than a Midwestern tourist out for a stroll, viewing the Capitol all lit up for the night.

"Packard," Donner said, keeping his voice low but conversational.

"Sir," Packard replied, folding the leather gloves she wore atop her thighs. "What have we got?"

Raising his eyebrows slightly, Donner tilted the top of his head an inch to the side. "A lot."

Beside him, Packard remained silent, no more in the mood for evasiveness than she ever was.

"Starting with the fact that none other than the general is currently in the building as we speak."

Breaking protocol for maybe the first time ever, Donner could sense her swing her gaze to him, a quick glance over confirming it, adding the aghast look on her face to the mix.

"I'm sorry, he's doing what?"

"Yup," Donner said, shrugging his eyebrows once before turning to look back at Dirksen. "Wasn't exactly my idea, but it's not like I was consulted."

That part of the story was underplaying things tremendously, Donner having gone to great lengths to attempt to dissuade Ames from stepping inside, though his cohort was not to be dissuaded.

Whether or not it was the right call they would likely know soon enough, noon on the morrow not able to come fast enough.

"The point of his visit being?" Packard asked.

"Not sure, exactly," Donner said. "Like I said, I wasn't consulted.

"If I were to guess, though, judging by the full dress uniform he was wearing when he walked in, I think the idea was to throw around his weight a little, get the senator to stand down from what he was doing."

A quick smirk sent Packard's head back a half inch beside him, her hair brushing against the tops of her shoulders. "I can't imagine anybody taking well to that. I think he'd have a better chance of making a vanity play."

"Right," Donner said, risking another glance over, "but I can't imagine him taking well to that, either."

This time there was no response, Packard staring intently at the building beside him.

"Okay," she eventually said, "what else?"

Pausing a moment to take inventory of the seemingly benign question, Donner sorted through the various events of the afternoon in his head.

"Ridge has been busy this afternoon," Donner said. "After calling out to the Archives for Tarby's files, he then had a little meeting with Terry Whitner."

"Terry Whitner," Packard replied, a small twinge of disbelief appearing. "As in-"

"Very same," Donner said. "That's what brought the general out this chilly evening as well."

On the street nearby an errant car horn could be heard, the general ebb and flow of traffic audible. Along the footpath they were seated on the last few stragglers from the work day hurried toward home, their bodies bundled tight as they moved for the train station across the lawn.

"Wow," Packard whispered. "That would do it."

"Agreed," Donner said, jutting his chin out an inch toward the building. "They're currently in there behind closed curtains as we speak."

"Hmm," Packard replied, already moving past the surprise of his previous statement. "And the plan thereafter?"

"Depends on how it goes," Donner replied. "Same standard signal, which is why I'm currently sitting here."

"Ah," Packard replied.

"And your end?" Donner asked.

"Ellerbe, Stroh, and a third woman I recognized from the file as Susan Beckwith all just made a dinner run, reentered the building a few minutes ago from the South entrance."

Nodding, Donner had already figured as much, knowing that most of the heavy lifting that was being done on this project was being performed by Ridge himself.

Whether that was just how a situation like this needed to play or the man was actually trying to protect his staff, Donner could only speculate on, not that it much changed his approach.

"Anything remarkable there?" Donner asked.

"Nothing," Packard said. "After our previous check-in, they eventually returned to the office, weren't inside very long before everybody took off again."

Acknowledging the comment in silence, Donner thought on the new information a bit longer, his head bobbing slightly, the data only conforming to the thought he had just a moment before.

Ridge seemed to be handling things, his staff more or less milling around, waiting in case they were needed, watching the clock.

Just as they all were.

Eighty yards away, the side entrance to the building opened, the sound of the door swallowed up by the ambient noise of the city. For a moment, a flare of bright light could be seen before blinking out, the door swinging back closed.

Through it had passed only a single individual, dressed in complete olive green, his body framed by the overhead security glow above the door. Pausing there, he made a point of standing with his hat tucked under his arm, swinging his gaze in one wide arc before stepping forward.

From that point on he made no effort to look in either direction, cutting a diagonal path away from the building, disappearing from sight within ninety seconds.

"I guess we have our orders," Donner whispered softly, the outcome of the meeting not surprising him in the slightest, only confirming his reasoning for not thinking it was a good idea to begin with.

"Mhm," Packard agreed.

"You know the next step, right?" Donner asked.

"Mhm," Packard replied, rising from the bench and stealing away without another sound, walking in the opposite direction as Ames.

For a moment Donner considered calling out to her to be careful, especially with the possible inclusion of Terry Whitner, but ultimately thought better of it. Joselyn Packard was a pro, that being the reason he had called her. Any attempt at calling out to her would only offend.

Instead, he remained quiet, sitting and staring at the building, counting off seconds in his head, waiting to see how Ridge might react to what happened next.

Chapter Thirty

Less than a minute after General Ames had left, Ridge heard the front door open again, the hinges giving a low moan, the sound more than enough to pass through the charged silence of the office. The instant the sound found his ears, Ridge was back on his feet, still feeling the ire from the meeting a moment before, ready for a second go-round with his unexpected and uninvited visitor.

Unlike the previous visit though, the man didn't steel forward in silence, presenting himself in the senator's doorway, a disapproving look on his face.

Instead, the door opening was punctuated by the sounds of plastic sacks crinkling and muffled voices, it taking less than a second for the sources of them to be recognized, Ridge's stance relaxing considerably.

"Sir?" Susan Beckwith asked, appearing first in the entry to his office, seeing him standing behind his desk.

"Hey, Susie," Ridge replied, his voice coming out with a sigh.

"Were you expecting someone else?" Beckwith asked.

Behind her, Ellerbe and Stroh both appeared as well, the former carrying a clear plastic sack, the contents visible as a stack of sandwiches wrapped in white paper. To the side was Stroh, a cardboard pallet in hand, four cups of equal height balanced atop it.

"Actually, yes," Ridge said, his shoulders slumping slightly. "I thought you folks were going to dinner."

"They don't call it fast food for nothing, sir," Beckwith replied, her mouth again flickering just slightly, going the unneeded step of alerting him she was making an attempt at humor.

Just as she always did.

"May we enter?"

Feeling his body slump a bit more, not realizing how amped the previous meeting had made him until it started to seep from his body, Ridge waved a hand inside, forcing a smile into place.

"Yes, of course, of course. Get in here."

Falling back into his chair, he watched as the group filed inside, a questioning look on Beckwith's face, his two aides oblivious as they paused halfway across the room, glancing between his desk and the single round table off to the side.

"Anywhere you like," Ridge said, "if we make a mess, Hodges can worry about it tomorrow."

This time there was no need to explain the joke, Ellerbe and Stroh both smiling wide as they resumed their seats before him, Beckwith doing the same in the middle.

The sound of paper and cellophane was loud for several moments as his two young colleagues went about distributing food, the smell of meat and melted cheese permeating the air.

"Steak and cheese," Ellerbe said, sliding it a few inches toward the senator but no further, allowing him to accept or reject it on his own. "We didn't know what you might want, but figured..."

"A safe bet for sure," Ridge said, leaning forward and grasping the sandwich, the wrapping warm to the touch.

Almost eight hours had passed since his abrupt departure from the caucus luncheon, though the time in-between had been so frantic he had barely noticed, his body not once mentioning that it was short of fuel until the smell of the food before him found his nostrils.

Only then did the rest of his inner workings move into action, everything clamoring at once for the promised nourishment.

Across from him, Stroh placed plain white cups before each of them, not bothering to explain what was inside, the ladies beside him balancing their own sandwiches across their thighs and beginning to unwrap, the scents in the room growing stronger with each passing moment.

"So, about this expected visitor," Beckwith began, placing it out there as if an innocuous statement, Ridge knowing full well it was an inquiry that wasn't quite dressed up as such.

Not responding for a moment, Ridge peeled back the paper on his sandwich as well, grilled meat and mushrooms staring up at him, a healthy slathering of cheese holding it all together, not a vegetable to be seen anywhere.

Exactly the type of balance he would have at every meal if he could get away with it.

"No, the man was definitely not expected," Ridge replied. "Though when I heard the door open again, I thought he might be coming back for round two."

To that Beckwith paused, the cut end of her sandwich halfway to her mouth, a single eyebrow raised.

"He being one General Arnold Ames," Ridge said, "more or less here to ask – or rather, *tell* – me to stop looking into the Tarby matter."

Without making it the last few inches, the sandwich slowly went back into place, Ellerbe and Stroh each slowing their respective chewing, all three staring in rapt silence, the number of questions each was thinking apparent on their features.

Ignoring the alluring aroma wafting up from the sandwich, Ridge rattled off the details of the previous meeting, omitting nothing from the thin and disjointed dialogue, sprinkling it liberally with his interpretations, both of the man and what it was he was trying to accomplish.

When he was done, all three had stopped eating, processing what he'd said.

Seeing his opening, Ridge dove straight into his sandwich, tearing away a hulking bite and attempting to chew through bulging cheeks.

"What do you think it means?" Beckwith finally asked, the first to venture to break the silence.

Working the mass of food around in his mouth, Ridge waited until he could swallow before saying, "I think it means that my phone calls today are starting to make a few people sweat."

Without stating that that part was understood, Beckwith said, "Which begs the question, was he here as a representative of the army, or as an individual with something to lose that felt you were getting too close?"

Not enough time had passed for Ridge to have gotten that far in his assessment, the surprise of Ames showing up unannounced, the anger at his condescending demeanor, both taking the top spot in his mind since the meeting ended. Pushing them each to the side, he focused on what Beckwith had asked, rolling it around.

The surprise late night visit by a single general didn't seem to be something that would spring from an official source. The military might be many, many things, but subtle certainly wasn't one of them.

If something he was doing had landed on their radar, was rankling feathers high up the chain of command, they would have been calling all afternoon, would have sent over every ranking official they could think of, filling his office with as much brass as possible and trying to instill the fear of God into him.

What had happened instead made him think that this was much lower in prestige, perhaps even as far down as to be something that concerned only Ames and possibly a small handful of associated personal interests.

Even at that, though, his showing up made little sense. Prior to twenty minutes before, Ridge had never heard of the man. For him to risk showing up, giving his name and face, especially if he was involved in something nefarious, moved well past bold into territory that was completely foolish.

The fact that nothing Ridge had done thus far would seem to warrant such action only made it that much more bizarre.

The thoughts still sat at the front of his mind, the senator trying to wrestle them into position, to determine the best way of articulating them, when beside him his personal cell phone began to vibrate, the buzzing causing the device to rotate slightly atop the desk.

Glancing down to it, he saw the 907 area code staring up at him, the name Harold Golding flashing to the front of his mind.

"You all keep eating. I'll be back."

Chapter Thirty-One

Casting a glance to the front door of the office, almost expecting it to swing open again, for Arnold Ames to appear a second time, Ridge stepped from his office into the adjoining bullpen. Walking into the far corner, he leaned his body against the front edge of the unoccupied desk and folded his arms across his chest, bringing the phone to his face.

"Jackson Ridge."

The sound of the wind rushing outside was the first sound to find him again, just as it had been in their previous conversation, before the noise died away and the genial twang of Harold Golding came over the line.

"Senator, Harold Golding calling you back from Alaska."

"Yeah, I can hear that," Ridge replied.

"Oh, sorry," Golding muttered, falling silent for a moment as the background noise died away. "That better?"

"Much," Ridge replied. "Thanks for getting back to me."

"Sorry for ending the previous call so shortly, but after you asked about the counterintelligence angle, I needed to do some digging."

Feeling his grip on the phone tighten just slightly, Ridge pressed it a bit tighter to his face, saying nothing.

"You were right," Golding said, "generally on cases that warrant it, CID and counterintelligence do work together."

"But that didn't happen here?" Ridge said, piecing together what he was being told.

"No," Golding said, "not because it wouldn't necessarily call for it, but because they yanked me before the investigation ever had a chance to get that far."

Just as with their previous conversation, Ridge could hear some of the warmth fade from Golding's voice, replaced instead by the bitterness that could only be felt by a man currently in the throes of an Alaskan winter.

"And I'm pretty sure I already know the answer to this, but I'll ask anyway-"

"Damned peculiar," Golding said, sensing what the senator was going to ask and beating him to it. "Which is why I made a phone call to a buddy of mine over at CI."

Outside, the sound of the office telephone springing to life could be heard, the noise especially pronounced in the late evening quiet. At the first ring, Ridge could feel a ripple pass through his system, a tiny unexpected jolt to the senses.

Leveraging himself up from the side of the desk, he strode across the bullpen to the door and grasped the side of it, Beckwith appearing in the mirroring doorway, a napkin to her lips as she strode for the phone.

Swinging the door closed behind him, Ridge walked back to his post in the corner, the smooth desktop a complete contrast to the other three around the room.

"So they were brought in," Ridge said.

"That I don't know," Golding said. "My contact there wasn't involved in it but was going to take a look around and see what he could uncover. I hope you don't mind, but I gave him this number. He should be calling soon, whether he finds something or not."

"Thank you," Ridge said, "I appreciate the help."

"Sorry I couldn't do more, sir," Golding replied.

"Not at all, this has been a big aid," Ridge said, "I promise you."

To that, there was a pause, a moment that seemed to trend a bit toward awkward, before Golding added, "Listen, senator, I know this is your last night and all, but if you do happen to unravel what happened over there..."

"Of course," Ridge said, "I'll keep you posted every step of the way."

Again there was a pause before Golding said, "Well, I would appreciate it, but that's actually not what I meant..."

Letting his voice trail off, Ridge stabbed blindly for a moment, attempting to put together whatever Golding was hinting at, before things fell into place, his eyes snapping wide.

"Oh! Yes, if I find anything that might be able to circle you back to the mainland, I'll be sure to do everything I can to see it gets in the right hands."

At the door, a tiny knock sounded out, followed by the door opening just a few inches, the face of Susan Beckwith appearing.

"Thank you, sir," Golding said. "I'd appreciate it."

"Thank you," Ridge replied, ending the call there by snapping the phone shut, turning his attention toward the door.

With his focus aimed her way, Beckwith took his stance as an invitation, pushing the door open and stepping inside, her hands folded in front of her waist.

"Sorry to interrupt, sir."

Sensing her shift from just a few moments earlier, Ridge felt his brow come together.

"What's wrong, Susie?"

"That was the Hilton on the phone, sir. There's been an accident with Clara Tarby."

Chapter Thirty-Two

The car was big and spacious, much larger than a traditional taxi, though not quite a minivan in scale. With two rear seats facing each other, Ridge and Beckwith were able to sit together in the far back, Ellerbe and Stroh staring at them, all eight knees so close they were almost touching.

The previous genial mood in the office was long extinguished, none of the four having finished their meal, everybody leaving in a rush once news of Clara Tarby had arrived.

The first details to come in to Beckwith were thin at best, the front desk at the Hilton calling to say they had received a call from one of the guests that they heard noises coming from Tarby's room. A few minutes later, they had sent somebody upstairs to check on her and they had returned later to find her face down on the bed, alive but just barely, and unresponsive.

Paramedics had arrived within minutes and transported her to George Washington Medical Center, the front desk realizing only after the fact that the room had been registered to Ridge's office.

What had happened to Tarby they had not a clue, her room void of any evidence of a struggle or foul play, no visible marks or blood on the body.

Three times in succession Ridge had pressed Beckwith for the details of the phone call, his Chief of Staff relaying the exact same tale each time, her tone not once changing. Many times more he replayed it in his mind, trying to make himself believe that it was nothing but a fluke, that it didn't have anything to do with the conversation he had earlier with General Ames.

For as hard as he tried though, not once was he successful in pushing the thought aside, the evidence too overwhelming for him to truly believe.

Ten hours earlier, a sturdy Wyoming woman had walked into his office. A bit frazzled emotionally for sure, she was in fine physical condition, there to ask him a simple question.

In the course of investigating that question, he had poked a few hornet nests, culminating in a visit from a ranking military leader that he had never heard of, the man more or less telling him to walk away, being none too subtle in the process.

True to his nature, Ridge had more or less told the man to kiss his ass.

Now he was in a car on the way to GW to see to the original woman's health.

Never before had he believed in coincidence, a single one being far greater than he would ever put stock into, this being significantly more than that.

With his hands in his lap, Ridge alternated between curling his fingers into fists and squeezing tight, feeling the tension run from his wrists up to his shoulders, and slowly releasing them. Taking a few breaths, he'd let his nerves calm, his breathing slow, before repeating the process, every imaginable form of wrath possible traversing through his system.

Shifting his gaze to the window, he watched as government buildings filed by, their white marble exteriors aglow from orange sodium lights, only a few intrepid tourists still braving the cold, coffee cups and elongated sticks for taking self-portraits in hand.

With his jaw clamped shut, he set the tone for the rest of the car, a stilted silence settling in, each person finding a different direction to stare, alone with their thoughts.

The total ride from Dirksen to GW was just at three miles, the stop-and-go series of lights between the two stretching the drive to twelve minutes. By the time they arrived, Ridge could feel his nerves pulled as taut as guitar strings, tossing a twenty into the space between Ellerbe and Stroh's shoulders and stepping out into the night air.

A moment later, he reached the main entrance and passed through the automated doors, not once turning to see if his colleagues were still with him, trusting they would have been able to keep pace. Striding across the front lobby, he ignored the myriad of people huddled along the walls and went for the main desk, pressing his hips flush against it, his hands resting on either side.

"We're here to see Clara Tarby, please. She was just brought over from the Hilton."

Behind the desk, a young woman with brown hair pulled back into a ponytail and thick framed glasses went to work on a desktop computer, the full-sized keyboard ringing out with each stroke. Without glancing from the screen, she continued working and asked, "Family?"

"As close as she has in D.C.," Ridge replied.

Frowning slightly, the woman continued on the keyboard before stopping, her lips barely moving as she read from the screen in front of her.

"I'm sorry, but right now Ms. Tarby appears to be in surgery," the young woman read before pulling her attention away to look up at him. "Would you like directions down to the waiting area?"

"Please."

Rising halfway out of her seat, she extended an arm out to her right and said, "Follow this hallway down until you see the blue signs for the emergency surgery ward, which will be on the left. Take that hallway all the way to the end, the waiting area will be off to the side."

Shifting to follow her outstretched hand, Ridge repeated, "This hallway, take a left, follow all the way to the end. Thanks, got it."

"Mhm," the young woman replied, sinking back into her seat as Ridge turned to find the rest of his staff there and waiting.

"They said she's-"

"We heard," Beckwith said.

Nodding, Ridge motioned in that direction with the top of his head and said, "You folks go on down, I need to make a quick call and then I'll be right behind you."

True to form, Beckwith arched a silent eyebrow at him as Ellerbe and Stroh exchanged a quick glance. For a moment not one person moved, each remaining rooted in place, before Beckwith said, "Come on guys, let's make sure somebody is there when Ms. Tarby gets out of surgery."

Scads of thoughts passed through Ridge's head as he watched them slowly shuffle off, Beckwith leading the procession, Ellerbe following with her gaze aimed down, Stroh meeting his eye and nodding slightly before going along as well.

Positioned in the middle of the lobby, Ridge made no effort to move, even less to hide the disdain he felt, both at where he was and what he had potentially brought upon Clara Tarby. Waiting until his team disappeared from sight, he pulled his phone from his pocket and retreated back out the front door, the night air having dropped another few degrees, the wind whipping at his exposed ears, pushing down his throat and into his lungs.

Walking until he was well out of earshot from the entrance, he extracted his phone and pulled up the last number in his log, calling it and pressing the phone back to his face.

It was answered after only a single ring.

"Harold Golding."

"Hey, Mr. Golding, Senator Ridge here, sorry to bother you, just had one more quick question."

"Shoot," Golding said, the wind again rushing in behind him, loud in Ridge's ear.

"Does the name Arnold Ames mean anything to you?" Ridge asked, leaving off the man's title, making it intentionally vague so as to not influence the answer in any way.

"Ames?" Golding asked. "You mean General Ames, from Afghanistan?"

Chapter Thirty-Three

Leopold Donner hadn't bothered to follow Jackson Ridge and his staff as they dashed away from the Dirksen Senate Building. Knowing exactly where they were going, that Packard was already on-site there playing the role of a grieving mother or wife so she could keep tabs on everything, there was no need.

Besides, they had already seen his face earlier in the day. Given the circumstances, it didn't seem likely that they would remember him – at least not enough to put together a definitive identification – but there existed no reason to even take the chance.

Especially not knowing what else the night ahead might hold.

Instead, he waited until they were gone before peeling away from the bench and returning to his car. Hiding behind the tinted windows of the back seat, he changed out of the suit and returned to something more resourceful, not going as far as his preferred tactical attire, but wearing something that allowed him a bit more ease of movement coupled with the ability to blend in.

Not to mention ample room for carrying along some of his most beloved toys, should the need arise.

Once the suit was stripped away, he hung it carefully back onto the hanger and returned it to the back in the event it may again be needed, hoping more than anything that it wouldn't. From there he climbed behind the wheel and exited the parking garage, pulling away into the thin evening traffic.

Cutting his teeth in far-flung locales across the globe, Donner had never been one for urban environments. Most of his training was centered on working in the elements, jungles, mountains, even desert being his preferred mediums.

After moving over into the private sector, a migration toward urban environments had started to develop, a trend that had started slow and begrudgingly, picking up speed with each passing year.

While it used to be that he didn't feel truly alive unless he was hidden away beneath a ghillie suit, peering through a scope at a target that never knew he existed, those feelings had shifted with time. Now he couldn't help but relish the feeling that seemed to be surging through him as he stole down Constitution Avenue, as if he were a predator slipping out into the night, the city rife with potential prey.

Given that so few of the enemies he now faced possessed anywhere near the same skill level as himself, he had grown to appreciate the added challenge that the city possessed, the constant cameras and lights keeping him sharp and focused.

For most of the day, the situation with Ridge had been more of an observational post, but the recent escalation meant that was about to change, a fact that Donner couldn't help but admit excited him to the core.

Seated high in the front seat of the SUV, both hands gripping the steering wheel, veins bulging along the backs of his hands, forearm hairs standing upright, he drew in deep breaths, the adrenaline that was starting to flow as intoxicating as any narcotic could ever be.

Clear up to the point that his phone began to ring, the artificial intrusion pulling him from the moment, putting a scowl onto his face.

A look that only deepened as he glanced at the caller ID and saw who it was that had disturbed him.

"Donner."

"Is it done?" Ames asked without preamble.

Pressing his lips tight for a moment, Donner extended a middle finger at the phone, squeezing the remainder of his fist so tight it quivered, before releasing the tension in his hand.

"It is," Donner replied, not even particularly feeling like lobbing a smart comment at the general, the time for sarcasm having passed. "Ridge and his team went screaming toward the hospital a little while ago."

On the other end there was something resembling a grunt, no other words passing over.

Seeing an opening, Donner asked, "I take it the meeting didn't go especially well?"

In response there was an unintelligible sound before Ames replied, "There's always more than one way to achieve an objective."

Rolling his eyes, Donner made a face, shifting his focus back to the traffic around him. Nestled

280

into the time frame that marked the transition from late evening into night, the city was fast winding down for the day, catching a needed rest before starting well before dawn again in the morning.

Outside, the lights of storefronts were beginning to dim, the predominant color moving toward the filmy orange glow of streetlights. In front of him, a loose cluster of taillights could also be seen, final stragglers making their way home.

Seeing and inventorying the sights before him, little managed to actually register with Donner, his attention still aimed at the man opposite him on the line.

While many had accused Donner at times in recent years of taking the job too seriously, of handling things as if he were still in the service, Ames had the far greater annoyance of being someone that envisioned himself an elder statesman. As a lifetime military man, he had come to let his rank define him, somebody that thought the world viewed him through the same narrow constraints of his professional hierarchy.

Part of that meant he was always doling out unwanted platitudes like the one he'd just dropped, empty words that were meant to sound wise or sage or some such similar nonsense.

"So he told you to piss off," Donner asked, filling in what Ames would have said if he spoke common English.

The long silence that followed managed to tell him that not only was he right, but that he had struck a nerve.

"Do we have eyes on Ridge now?" Ames eventually asked, completely ignoring the comment, further confirming Donner's supposition.

"We do," Donner said, leaving it at that, it fast becoming clear that it would be in both men's best interests to end the call quickly.

"Stay on top of it," Ames said. "If he's going to do something now, it'll be soon."

The same look of derision rose to Donner's face as he again wagged a middle finger at the phone before reaching out to end the call without another word.

Chapter Thirty-Four

Jackson Ridge was the first to hit his feet the moment the doors to the surgical suite opened, a middle-aged man with hound dog eyes that seemed to indicate he had been on shift for the better part of three days shuffling through. Dressed in dark blue scrubs with a New England Patriots scrub cap, he made it just a few feet inside the door before stopping and raising his voice slightly.

"Clara Tarby?"

Taking two quick steps forward, sensing his staff doing the same behind him, Ridge closed the gap to just a couple of feet before stopping.

"She's with us."

Eyes going wide for a moment, the doctor looked to Ridge before glancing to those behind him, eventually letting it go with only a nod.

283

"Were any of you with Ms. Tarby this evening?"

The question seemed to come in from afar, surprising Ridge for a moment. His jaw sagging slightly, he turned to look at Ellerbe and Stroh, the pair appearing just as surprised as him by the question.

"Um, we were," Ellerbe managed, shifting her gaze to Stroh and back again.

"What time was that?" the doctor asked.

"Maybe..." she began, her voice trailing away.

"Five or so?" Stroh said, his tone and expression both letting it be known that there was a great deal of uncertainty in the response.

Pressing his lips tight, the doctor nodded, processing the information. "But nothing since then?"

"No," Ridge said, jumping back into the conversation. "Can you tell us what happened? Is she okay?"

Raising his left hand, the doctor used his fingernails to dig at his scalp, the movement leaving misshapen warbles in the cotton cap atop his head.

"Ms. Tarby presented this evening with a fractured larynx," the doctor said. "We were able to go in and get it stabilized, but I won't lie, it's still a pretty delicate situation. She's mighty lucky it wasn't crushed completely."

Ridge didn't need the doctor to further explain what would have happened if it had been, knowing that there would have been no way to breathe, that Tarby would have sat in her hotel room and suffocated to death.

The very same hotel room that he had arranged for her.

"Thank you, Doctor," Ridge said. "Can we see her?"

The same expression as before crossed the man's face as he shook his head to either side. "No, I'm afraid right now she is still in post-op, which is where she'll stay until we can move her.

"Whether that will end up being intensive care or the general ward, we don't yet know. The next twelve hours will go a long way in determining how hard the recovery will be for her."

"But she will recover?" Beckwith asked, the sound of her voice drawing Ridge's attention to the side.

Just as fast, he snapped it back forward, waiting for a response.

"She will," the doctor said, "but this is one of the worst injuries a person can have, especially one of her age. She's going to have to basically learn to speak again, something that can be as painful mentally as physically."

Allowing his eyes to slide shut for a moment, Ridge slowly exhaled through his nose, the news just one more on an already bulging heap that had been accumulating for most of the day.

"Any idea what might have caused this?" Beckwith asked, Ridge snapping his eyes back open, the moment of dread passing, frustration flooding in behind it.

"Given what I saw in there?" he asked. "The only possible way to cause that kind of damage would be a direct blow, though what that may have been I don't know."

It was clear from the statement and the man's posture that there was some speculation he wanted to add, decorum and a strong desire to be on his way both holding him back.

Sensing that, Ridge thrust his hand out and said, "Thank you, Doctor. Please keep up posted, somebody will be here all night."

Only nodding in response, the doctor returned the shake before disappearing back into the surgical ward, the swinging doors swallowing him up.

Remaining rooted in place, Ridge went through the entire conversation again in his mind, running it start to finish in quick time, as if watching a movie in fast forward. Picking out certain words and phrases, his jaw clenched and his gaze hardened as he stared at the doors the doctor had just fled through.

The symbolism of the event was too much to be ignored.

Clara Tarby had come to him seeking answers about her son, an inquiry that had caused him to start making phone calls, kicking through the leaves to see what he could flush out. Ten hours later she was alone in a hotel room and received a sharp blow that broke her larynx, effectively rendering her voice box useless, making it so it would be a long time before she was able to talk again.

It didn't take a skilled investigator to get from A to B to C.

The bigger question that remained was who had been the one to call in her injury, it most likely being the perpetrator, the attacker wanting Tarby's body to be found, a clear message to be sent.

Handfuls of possible answers existed, though at the moment most were nothing more than educated guesses, something Ridge had been doing all day long.

It was time to start getting something concrete.

Fueled by a renewed flush of wrath, he turned on a heel, his staff still standing three across, waiting for his response.

"You three stay here," he said simply. "I'll be back."

Her lips parting slightly, a charge of concern passing over her features, Beckwith asked, "Where are you going?"

Glancing to the wall, the placard affixed to it forbidding the use of cellular devices, Ridge said, "I need to make some calls."

Chapter Thirty-Five

Two minutes after leaving his team in muted silence in the surgical ward waiting room, Jackson Ridge stepped back through the front doors of the George Washington Medical Center. A loud rush of metal gates sliding open and the overhead heaters kicking to life sprang up in his ears as he walked by, falling away just as fast as the cold night air clutched at every inch of exposed skin.

The day had been cold – certainly not the worst he'd seen, but chillier than his aging body would like – but the evening ahead promised to be even worse, the temperatures clearly below freezing, bits of snowmelt on the sidewalk already turning to ice.

Evening had also turned to night in the short time they'd been inside, most of the movement of human life having died away, replaced by errant sounds. Lining the sidewalk were a couple of vagabonds buried beneath mounds of trash and blankets, not even bothering to look up as he marched past, assuming his previous post along the wall, his back to the building.

Scrolling through his cellphone roster, he found a listing — Pete McManley — and dialed it, the time never once crossing his mind as he pressed the ringing device to his ear.

Five rings later, just short of going to voicemail, it was picked up.

"Senator Ridge," the man said, his voice booming, Ridge almost envisioning the red-cheeked smile on the man's fleshy face. "Long time."

"It has been," Ridge agreed, "which makes the reason I'm calling now all the more difficult."

Over the line, the sound of chair legs sliding across a wooden floor could be heard, followed by lumbering steps covering the same surface. Remaining silent, Ridge waited almost half a minute for the marching to die away before McManley came back on the line.

"Okay, sorry, we were just finishing dinner and I needed to step away."

Feeling the skin around his eyes tighten into a wince, Ridge sucked in a sharp breath of air. "Which again makes this even more difficult."

"Nonsense," McManley replied. "Though shouldn't you be off at a farewell soiree or something right now? Milking my taxpayer dime for the last time?"

Under any other circumstances, Ridge would have laughed – if not genuinely than at least granting his friend the gesture of a fake guffaw – knowing that it was said in good humor, free of any malice whatsoever.

Given all that was occurring, though, he just couldn't bring himself to do it.

"Listen, Pete," Ridge said, "I hate like hell doing this, knowing you're home with your family and all, but I need a favor that I probably don't have coming."

Instantly the mirth faded from McManley's voice, replacing the good-natured friend with the man Ridge had first met, now a sergeant with the Capitol police.

"What's going on, senator?"

"Right now I have a constituent from Wyoming staying in the city as a personal guest," he began.

"I see," McManley said, unease plain.

"Not like that," Ridge said, knowing what the cold opening must have sounded like, especially given the recent spate of legislative infidelities. "This woman's son was recently killed in Afghanistan and my office is trying to help her track down some answers."

The reply was intentionally vague, Ridge knowing that the man was a retired veteran himself, that the story would resonate better than anything else he could have said.

"Okay," McManley said, prompting him onward.

"And we have reason to believe that this search gave cause to her being attacked a little bit ago," Ridge said, skipping a lot of details, both for the sake of time and shock value. "She was just rolled out of surgery at GW. I'm here now."

A moment passed, McManley saying nothing, before finally muttering, "Jesus."

"Exactly," Ridge said, "and it's going to be a while before she's out of the woods. I know this is probably outside of your jurisdiction, but can I get a security detail down here to stand outside her door for a day or two?"

"Absolutely," McManley said, the sound of movement over the line, Ridge able to envision the man already springing into action. "As a personal request from a ranking senator, doesn't matter that it's a few blocks outside our usual area. We can have someone there within the hour."

"Thank you," Ridge said, a tiny pulse of relief passing through him before giving way, his mind already moving ahead to the next task on his list.

"How about you?" McManley asked. "You good? Or should we send someone to ride with you as well?"

"Right now I think I'm good, but can I reserve the right to change my mind?"

"I'll be around all night."

Chapter Thirty-Six

Joselyn Packard was sitting fifteen feet away when the surgeon walked out from the double doors demarcated by the double stripe of red paint on the floor, the barrier meant to keep worried family members and the general public at bay. Positioned at the far end of a center row of chairs, she was seated perpendicular to the impromptu gathering that took place with the doctor, using the convex mirror in the corner of the ceiling to watch everything that played out.

From where she was seated, she couldn't hear a word that was being said, though she didn't really to.

She already knew exactly what would be said.

The ruse was so simple it couldn't even be considered one, walking directly up to the door of

294

Clara Tarby and knocking twice. Tapping into both the facts that Tarby would be a trusting sort and that she would be a ranch woman unaccustomed to how things actually worked at a place like the D.C. Hilton, she had followed the knock by announcing that she was with building maintenance and needed to check a potential problem with the shower faucets.

The door opened without opposition.

The blow was done courtesy of her right hand, a simple knife edge chop that landed just beneath Tarby's mandible. On contact, she could feel the soft tissue crumple beneath her pressure, the woman's eyes bulging as she fell to the floor, hands flailing as she pawed for air.

Less than a minute after arriving Packard exited the suite, showing no signs of tension or even hurry as she calmly walked into the stairwell on the far end of the hall.

By the time she emerged back into camera view twelve floors later, the blond wig she had worn was removed and placed back in her bag, ditto for the pair of non-prescription frames covering her face.

Any preliminary camera shots that saw her entering or exiting would be worthless, any memory Tarby might have erased by the shock of the moment or subject to disbelief by a lack of evidence to substantiate it.

As with most things during the evening, a task that in some circumstances could have been enjoyable but was instead rendered boring by the complete lack of skill or even awareness of those she was up against.

Even now, as she sat in the waiting room thumbing through an old copy of *Redbook* - a publication she didn't know was still being produced – the world was completely oblivious to her presence. Returned to her natural mid-thirties state, she was just as anonymous as any other person in the waiting area, keeping her long brown coat on to block out any view of her clothes or the athletic form they hugged.

Alternating glances between the book and the mirror, she watched as the small gathering spoke for a few moments before the doctor retreated back behind the doors. In his absence, Ridge and his team had another small huddle before he strode away, leaving the other three behind, nobody saying much or seeming to know what to do.

Keeping her seat, Packard remained another four minutes, long enough to ensure that Ridge had not merely stepped off into the john before rising. Giving one last look into the mirror, she saw that her two charges, Ellerbe and Stroh, had both settled back into their previous seats, leaning toward each other as they spoke in hushed whispers.

Easily identified as the team left behind to stand vigil for Tarby.

The fourth member of the team, Beckwith, had waited until just two minutes after Ridge's departure before following suit, she also bypassing the restroom and disappearing down the main hallway.

"I'll be damned," Packard whispered, a tiny flicker of something bordering on respect passing through her mind, as she turned and shuffled away as well, careful not to draw any attention. Trudging just a few feet at a time, she allowed the bulky coat to swirl around her, making it back to the main lobby in time to see Ridge and Beckwith standing on the sidewalk outside.

Going back and forth in conversation, they seemed to be debating something, their faces both drawn up tight, falling just short of hostile as they spoke.

A moment later, a polished black car appeared on the curb, Ridge opening the backseat for Beckwith before piling in behind her.

Just as fast as they had arrived an hour earlier, they were gone.

No longer needing to keep up the ploy she'd been using, Packard cast aside the begrudging gait and strode across the lobby, her body responding in kind, happy to be moving at full speed again. Reaching into her pocket, she extracted her phone and pressed the first speed dial, turning north out of the building and walking fast, the glowing spire of the Washington Monument peeking out between the buildings ahead.

"Go for Donner."

"Packard," she said.

"Go for Donner," he repeated, the phrase every bit as bracing as most of what came out of the man's mouth seemed to be these days.

"Ridge and Beckwith just left the hospital, presumably headed back to the office."

A low whistle was the first response, followed by Donner saying, "I'll be damned."

To that, she only nodded, not about to confess that it was the same thing she had said just moments before.

"Where are you?" she asked.

"Mobile," Donner said. "Will circle back to Dirksen as we speak, be in position when they arrive."

"Roger that," Packard said. "Orders?"

"Anything of note going on at the hospital?" Donner asked.

"No," Packard replied. "They left the underlings to hold down the fort, but there's nothing there. The closest thing to drama with them is whether or not they hook up at the end of the night."

A bit far afield for Packard, the hope was that it would relay the extreme tedium of being attached to Ellerbe and Stroh, allowing her to rotate over onto something a bit more challenging.

Or at the very least, something different.

"Circle back," Donner said, granting her wish, the information received with no visible reaction at all. "I'll attempt to get eyes on Ridge, speak with the general.

"Stay flexible, we've only got fourteen hours or so until this goes away."

"Roger that."

Chapter Thirty-Seven

In no way did Jackson Ridge want Susan Beckwith going to the office with him. He barely wanted to return himself, preferring to fall off the radar, to finish doing what he knew he had to, free from someplace that would make his whereabouts so obvious, but at least there he knew there would be constant security, somebody always around to keep anybody from doing something too foolish.

Having her return presented an entirely different set of circumstances, though, forcing him to split his attention for the rest of the night.

"Look, Susie," he said, his face aimed her direction as he leaned across the backseat, cutting the space between them to just a few inches so his lowered voice could be heard. "Don't think I'm not appreciative, because I am, for everything you've done today and over the years. This one, though, you need to let go.

"Please, I'm asking you, go back to the hospital and wait with Ellerbe and Stroh. Pete McManley promised me personally there would be guards arriving from Capitol Police any moment, and that they would stay there for as long as it took."

"As long as it took to what?" Beckwith countered, a rare hint of defiance appearing in her voice.

Opening his mouth to respond, Ridge closed it and leaned back, shifting his focus to stare out the window, the Washington Mall slowly crawling by on their left. As they moved forward, the assorted buildings of the Smithsonian passed by, their varied styles and architectures each containing the world's greatest collection of antiquities and artifacts, as hodgepodge as they may be.

In each of the buildings, only a few lights were visible, a random individual or two walking between them, though for the most part, the city was settling in for the night.

Just as Ridge wished he was.

At this point there was no use trying to recount the various ways he had envisioned the evening playing out, even less entertaining the many things he would prefer to be doing. In their stead was only a steely resolution that he would push forward with this until a conclusion was reached, whatever it may be.

A path made all the more certain by what had just happened to Clara Tarby.

Having known him as long and as well as perhaps any person on the planet, Beckwith was aware that there was no way he would be pulling back. For as surprising as it was to see her step out into the cold beside him, to have her respectfully but firmly point out he would not be returning without her, Ridge realized it shouldn't have been.

Just because this rose to a new level of danger that his time in office had never seen before did not mean his most faithful colleague would not continue the unwavering dedication she had always displayed.

Last day or not.

"Can you get me whoever it was you spoke to the Hilton?" Ridge asked instead, conceding the defeat by changing course, any previous charge gone from his voice. Making no effort to mask the resignation taking its place, he shifted his attention to Beckwith, meeting her gaze for just a moment.

Matching it, she held the look an extra second or two, responding to his unspoken statement with her own, before sliding a smartphone from her bag and tapping away at the touchscreen.

A moment later she extended it his way, the sound of ringing already audible in the interior of the car.

"Excuse me, can you turn down the blower for a minute?" Ridge asked, leaning forward between the seats a few inches until the driver did as requested, the noise falling away, taking a good chunk of the warm air with it.

"Thank you," he said, counting out rings in his head as he returned to his spot in the rear, his back flush against the leather seat.

"Good evening, Washington D.C. Hilton, this is Nona, how may I help you?"

Covering the bottom half of the phone, Ridge mouthed *who do I ask for?* to Beckwith.

"Raethel Hue," Beckwith responded, her voice only nominally louder than his.

Making a face at the moniker, Ridge removed his hand from the bottom of the phone and said, "Yes, may I speak to Raethel Hue, please?"

"I'm sorry sir," Nona replied, "but Mr. Hue is currently tied up. May I take a message?"

Expecting as much, Ridge said, "This is Senator Jackson Ridge, he called my office earlier this evening about a guest of mine that is staying there that very nearly lost her life."

While there was much more he could have added, both to add weight to the story, and to further expound upon what it was that he wanted, Ridge left it there, trusting that the girl would be able to piece together what he was telling her and track down the man in question.

Just as he thought it might, the tactic worked.

"Oh, Senator Ridge," the girl said, acting as if he were a friend that she had simply not recognized after a long time apart, "give me just a minute here, I think I should be able to track him down for you."

Without waiting for confirmation, she immediately sent the call over to hold, elevator music spitting an off-key rendition of an old jazz tune into his ear.

As he sat and waited, Ridge watched as the Capitol building rolled by on his right, tomorrow being the last time he would ever visit there in any official capacity. In less than three weeks it would be completely done up, every free square inch packed with humanity for the inauguration, though for the time being it looked almost desolate, a striking profile against a darkened sky.

"Raethel Hue," a man with an accent that sounded somewhere between New Zealander and South African said, yanking Ridge's attention away from the view outside.

"Good evening, this is Jackson Ridge."

"Good evening, Senator. Please allow me to say that we are all very sorry here for what happened to your guest, and do hope she is okay."

"Thank you, she is," Ridge said, brushing right past the comment. "The reason I'm calling is to inquire as to who is handling the investigation into the incident."

A long pause followed. "The investigation, sir?"

Judging by the shift in tone, it was clear there was some discomfort on the opposite end of the line.

"It was merely an accident," he said. "No authorities were ever phoned, we merely reached out to your office because it was listed as the emergency contact on the registration form."

"Hmm," Ridge said, attempting in vain to mask the displeasure he felt at the information.

"Is there reason to believe that something might have been done deliberately to Ms. Tarby?" Hue asked.

"Her surgeon sure seemed to think so," Ridge replied.

Even as he said the words, he knew his tone, his approach, everything about the call, was a bit unfair, though that didn't stop him from proceeding in the slightest.

Right now, he had neither the time nor the inclination to be playing nice.

"Oh my," Hue said. "Thank you for letting know. I shall reach out immediately."

The car pulled to a stop, the familiar gray stone building rising up alongside it, though Ridge made no effort to climb out. Instead, he merely sat and stared, letting his gaze go glassy as he processed things.

"Actually, I'll call it in for you," he eventually said. "There's reason to believe this may be connected to something else, so it might be best to have some continuity in place."

Chapter Thirty-Eight

"That wasn't exactly what the doctor said, you know," Beckwith said, standing shoulder-to-shoulder in the elevator beside Ridge as the two ascended. Almost all of the few times he ever chose to ride over taking the stairs was when he was with her, knowing she suffered from a knee ailment that should have been treated ages ago, though she refused to ever take the requisite time off for the procedure.

Hopefully, now that their tenure was coming to a close, she would be able to do so.

"I'm aware," Ridge said, "but it got Hue moving in the direction we wanted."

"And that direction was?"

Debating the question a moment, Ridge watched the lighted numbers above the door count off the floors, waiting until they reached their destination and a ding sounded out before responding.

"Allowing him to let McManley and his guys have the first crack," Ridge said.

Under normal circumstances, he wouldn't mind allowing the Metro Police to do their job, as the crime did occur off the ground of the capitol. Though plenty in the city liked to deride the local force, he had never had any complaints with their performance, the task of guarding one of the most visited places in the country far from enviable.

The fact that it also happened to house the largest concentration of political power in the world had to push it into something closely resembling a nightmare.

Given the truncated timetable he was working with, and the personal responsibility he felt for what had happened to Clara Tarby, he preferred to have the Capitol crew handle it, knowing they could do things faster, and more importantly, get information back to him much quicker.

If that meant things devolved into a jurisdictional pissing match in the days to come, so be it.

As if sensing all of that, knowing it even before her boss said a word, Beckwith said only, "Hmm."

Increasing her pace a half-step, she pulled ahead of Ridge and opened the outer door to the office, pushing it open and stepping aside so he could enter.

For a moment he began to do just that, barely crossing the threshold before pulling back, self-awareness and preservation both kicking in, a renewed bit of adrenaline bolting through his system.

"Stay here," he said over his shoulder, hoping that for maybe the first time ever Beckwith would just accept his directive. Without waiting for her to respond, or even giving her a moment to do so, he strode across the front sitting area and around the desk.

Seeing no one, he ducked into the bullpen, checking under each desk and in the supply closet, before crossing over into his own office and doing the same, even going as far as to check the enormous folds of the curtains hanging in front of each window.

Two minutes after entering, content that they were in fact alone, he crossed back out to the front part of the office and said, "Okay, Susie. We're good here."

Remaining there, he watched as she entered, arching an eyebrow as she did so, the twist of her lips showing she thought he was being a bit paranoid, though she wasn't about to comment on it.

Given where they had just come from, he couldn't bring himself to much care even if she had.

"So what's the plan now?" Beckwith asked, walking as far as the front desk before depositing the stack of items she'd been holding pressed to her chest upon it.

Most of the ride over from the hospital had been spent on that very question, though Ridge still didn't have a clear heading. His most immediate steps after leaving were to call the Hilton and to get McManley looking into things, the report from the doctor about Tarby receiving a direct blow to the throat too much to ignore.

While an argument could be made that she might have fallen, may have landed awkwardly and happened to smash into a counter ledge or the corner of a coffee table, the far more likely culprit was that somebody had entered her room and done it to her.

Especially in such close proximity to the visit Ridge had just received from General Ames.

"Ames," Ridge said, the name popping to mind, his psyche seizing on it, purpose flooding in just as fast.

"Ames?" Beckwith asked.

"Ames," Ridge repeated, already starting to drift toward his door. "I need to find out more about who this guy is and what his interest is in all this. No way he just happened to show up here tonight out of coincidence."

Leaving Beckwith where she stood, Ridge strode straight for his desk, intent on beginning to shake the contact tree again, not particularly caring what time it was or who he pissed off in the coming hours.

Just three steps into the room, though, his phone began to buzz, again pushing him in a new direction he had not yet considered.

Chapter Thirty-Nine

Spending all but his brief time in the military split between Wyoming and Washington, D.C., Jackson Ridge knew each of the corresponding area codes for those areas, as well as a handful of others for the surroundings of each. Staring down at the odd configuration appearing on his screen, he had no idea where the 614 prefix was assigned to, his face screwing up slightly in confusion.

Just as fast it passed, knowing that the call in some way had to be connected, even if he as yet had no idea in what way or from where.

"Jackson Ridge."

Unlike the previous calls, there was not a hint of background noise as a deep and graveled voice said, "This is Al Bumppo from Army

Counterintelligence calling for Senator Ridge, please."

"This is Ridge," he repeated, realizing that he had stopped walking halfway across the room and beginning again. Leaving his coat on, he traversed around his desk and fell into his chair, the leather seat wheezing beneath his weight.

"Good evening, Senator, I apologize for calling so late, but Harold Golding reached out and asked me to contact you."

Hearing the name Golding, a small tingle passed through Ridge, his body perking up, for the first time realizing what the purpose of the call might be.

"That's alright," Ridge said. "Appreciate you getting back to me."

"Of course," Bumppo replied. "So listen, Hal gave me a quick overview of what was going on here. I understand you're looking into the convoy ambush that took place last April?"

"That's right," Ridge said, giving a quick overview of the situation and why he was looking into, choosing for the time being to leave out the name Tarby in any way.

"Ahh," Bumppo answered when he was finished, adding, "yeah, that would do it."

Not sure how to respond, or even if he should, Ridge remained silent, allowing the man on the other end of the line to push ahead whenever he was ready.

Which turned out to be just a few seconds later.

"Well, as I'm sure Hal told you," Bumppo began, "this case was a doozy from the outset. You should know right up front there are things about it neither one of us understand, so I won't even pretend to try.

"That okay by you?"

"It is," Ridge said, "I appreciate anything you may have on that night."

Which was true, a few scant facts being far more beneficial than a boatload of unfounded conjecture. So often people felt the need to over deliver when speaking to a man in Ridge's position, a predisposition that more than once had turned into far more trouble than it was worth.

"Okay," Bumppo replied. "I know you were Chair of the Senate Armed Services Committee for a while, but I should probably start by asking how much you know about the investigative process in the army?"

Surprised at being addressed so early in the conversation with a direct question, Ridge felt his jaw sag a bit, taking a moment to find his voice.

"Only really what Golding shared with me earlier, that his division worked felonies, often partnering with you guys when the charges rose to a certain level."

"Exactly," Bumppo said, "with two key things there being the most important.

"First, we almost always *partner* with the CID guys, meaning that usually, it's me and one or more of their guys going through things together, sharing information back and forth."

"Complete transparency?" Ridge inserted.

"Always," Bumppo said. "Think of it like a joint task force, only on a much smaller scale. Heck, sometimes we'd even fly in and out together, stay in the same room, depending on the place."

Hearing the words, the inflection placed on certain ones, Ridge nodded, already working to piece together what Bumppo was telling him.

"But that didn't happen here?" he asked.

"Nope," Bumppo said, "and I mean *none* of it happened here. I didn't even see Hal on this case, had no idea he was the one working it until much later, let alone share any information."

Without consciously realizing it, Ridge pushed a long, low whistle out, his mind seizing on the peculiarities he was hearing.

"And that's odd?" he asked.

"First time in thirty years for me," Bumppo said, "same for Hal as well."

"Any idea why?" Ridge asked.

Feeling his temperature start to rise slightly, he leaned forward in his seat. Starting with his left arm, he peeled off the heavy overcoat he was wearing before switching the phone to his opposite cheek and doing the same with the right side.

Free of the garment, he felt ten degrees cooler, leaving it bunched up behind him as he resumed his stance against the chair back.

"Are we off the record here?" Bumppo asked.

"Very," Ridge assured him.

"My best guess was, they had to bring us both in - Hal, because it would clearly rise to the level of a felony, and me, because it fell under the auspices of terrorism – but they never had any real intention of this being an investigation.

"They already had a narrative sewn up and buttoned down before either of us ever arrived."

"Which was?" Ridge asked.

"Which was that it was a clear ambush, nothing that hasn't happened before, unfortunately, will probably happen again," Bumppo said, hints of sadness, weariness, in his tone.

Nodding once, Ridge remained quiet for a moment, considering what was being said.

If the story that was already in place long before they arrived was true, it would go a long way to explaining why the respective investigators were shuffled through the process. As Bumppo mentioned, as sad as it was to admit, things like ambushes did occur in hostile environments, especially on clear supply lines.

What it didn't answer was why they had been brought in in the first place.

"Tell me," Ridge said, "if it was such a clear case of an ambush, why did they fly you guys in? Shouldn't the local MPs, or even the crews there on the ground, have just cleaned up what they could and moved on?"

Knowing full well that the question sounded a bit callous, Ridge hoped that he would be forgiven, everything about what he was now facing forcing a bit of political correctness into the background.

"Because they had to," Bumppo said. "That's standard procedure whenever there are that many guns that are seized like that."

For maybe the fifth time already on the evening, Ridge felt his adrenaline surge, the feeling threatening to overcome his faculties, pushing his body into a higher state, every limb starting to tingle. So strong was the sensation that it pulled him to his feet, the phone gripped tight.

This was the first time he had heard such a thing, his search starting to move forward.

"Guns?" he asked.

"Oh yeah," Bumppo said, his tone seeming to indicate he grasped what Ridge was currently experiencing, the senator almost envisioning a smile on the man's face. "And pardon my language, but a whole shitload of them at that."

Warning flags and flashing lights began to go off in Ridge's mind, some things falling instantly into place, others seeming to fit less now than they had just moments before.

"Which meant you had to be on hand to make sure everything was on the level," Ridge asked.

"In theory," Bumppo replied, "but like I said, they shuffled us through there so damn fast, all they really got was a rubber stamp saying we'd been on the ground and asked a few questions."

"So there was no report?" Ridge asked. "Nothing concrete that could be returned to later?"

"Not really," Bumppo said, "I had just made my first small break when I was told that was good and sent packing."

Shaking his head, a bitter taste rising to his tongue, Ridge said, "Straight back where you'd come from."

"Nope," Bumppo said. "I didn't get it as bad as Hal, but let me tell you, central Ohio in the wintertime isn't exactly an enviable post either."

Feeling his eyebrows rise slightly, Ridge said, "You got relocated immediately after getting back home?"

"Sure did," Bumppo said. "Hadn't been in Virginia long either, had no reason to think I'd be moving on soon, but that's how it goes sometimes."

"Any idea why?" Ridge asked.

To that, there was a long sigh before Bumppo said, "Again, long after the fact I figured out it must have had something to do with whatever happened over there in Afghanistan, but why it would be bad enough to send my ass out this way..."

Letting his voice trail off, it became clear the question was rhetorical, the man still searching for some reasonable way to answer it, even though both men knew the likely outcome was simply that he had been somewhere he shouldn't, witnessed more than he was supposed to.

"Can I ask you what it was you'd just found?" Ridge asked. "Right before they sent you back?"

Lowering his voice just slightly, Bumppo said, "They were so hell bent that this thing was an ambush that they already had the case closed by the time I got there, right?"

"Right," Ridge said, silently urging the man forward, unable to shake the feeling that whatever he was about to hear would be huge.

"Then can you explain why only three of the ten trucks in the convoy were hit?" Bumppo asked. "Or how they just so happened to be the only three out of the whole group carrying weapons?"

Chapter Forty

Leopold Donner was still in the front seat of his SUV, the automobile a nondescript black sort, the same as a thousand others roaming the streets of downtown D.C. With all but the front windshield tinted dark, the only difference between it and most on the streets was that the plates weren't government issue, a fact that very few people ever made it as far as noticing.

Not that they were registered to Donner either, the name on the paperwork someone that was said to work for his employer, a person with their own payroll account and even desk in a corner somewhere should somebody ever feel the need to come looking.

Of course, in the event that ever happened, they would be sitting at that desk for an awfully long time waiting for its owner to surface, the person assigned to it a complete figment, the very same person that was named on all paperwork for the organization.

Despite having such a level of security protecting the car he was in, Donner knew there was only so far he could push his luck, making two revolutions of Dirksen before pulling back.

During the light of day, traffic would be thick enough that nobody would notice him, never piecing together that it was the same person making repeated trips should they ever look twice his direction.

With the clock now nudging past midnight, though, the streets all but deserted, it would be hard for them to do anything but notice him as he made repeated right-hand turns.

Easing away from the tight tangle of one-way streets twisting through the congressional office buildings, Donner drove three blocks over, easing into street parking in front of a small strip mall just down from the Eastern Market. Housing five businesses in total, four of them stood dark and quiet while the fifth, a combination mini-mart and liquor store, threw garish neon light out into the night, a steady trickle of people entering and exiting.

Grabbing up his cell phone from the middle console, Donner left the engine running and turned down the heater before dialing Ames, the time of night not once entering his mind.

Judging by the fact that it was snatched up after a single ring, the general wasn't much for sleep either.

"What have you got?"

Per usual, a smart barb crossed through Leopold's mind, a quick comment meant to get under the skin, though he managed to shove it aside.

There would be plenty of time for such things once noon arrived, even he knowing they were in the midst of something that precluded a bit of playful banter.

"I just made two passes by Dirksen," Donner said. "I saw Ridge and his Chief of Staff enter the building, though they still have the curtains pulled, so I have no visual beyond that."

"But you're sure they are there?" Ames asked.

"I haven't seen them exit," Donner said. "Can't imagine them coming back at such an hour just to turn around and leave again."

He didn't bother adding that he had no idea where they would possibly go, the notion that Ridge would suddenly just decide to retire home for the night so absurd it didn't warrant voicing.

An indecipherable sound somewhat approximating a grunt was Ames's only response, quiet settling in over the line, Donner waiting for the old man to process things in his own time.

Which, he couldn't help but notice, was becoming slower with each passing day.

"And the woman?" Ames asked.

"She hasn't left either," Donner said. "She being his Chief of Staff-"

"Not *that* woman," Ames snapped, his tone sharp, causing Donner to raise his middle finger again to the phone, his features taut as he stared at it, wishing nothing more than that the condescending prick was there to receive it in person.

Moments such as these were fast becoming the problem with working in the private sector. Men such as Ames were too accustomed to the military life, being able to say and do whatever they pleased with impunity, the existing structure meaning that they were always obeyed without question.

For people like him that had been inside for so long, it became impossible to separate that from the rest of the world, truly believing that everybody should snap to their word like nineteen-year-old enlistees.

Something Donner had not been in a long, long time.

"She's out of surgery," Donner said, relaying what Packard had given him. "Packard is on-site there now with the two junior members of Ridge's staff."

"So she's alive and well?" Ames asked.

Again Donner felt his face contort at the inanity of the question, at the fact that it was an odd thing for a man with so little regard for those around him to even be asking.

"She's alive," Donner said. "We didn't get a full report or anything, but judging by the fact that Ridge left and his staff remained..."

He didn't bother filling in the rest, hoping what little common sense the general may possess could do that for him.

"Hmm," Ames replied. "Anything else?"

"Packard said a team from Capitol Police just arrived," Donner said.

"Is that a problem?" Ames asked.

"No," Donner said. "If it was, they would have already arrested her. She's sitting there in plain sight."

"So it's purely precautionary," Ames reasoned.

"Seems to be," Donner said.

Another few moments passed, the general continuing to put things together in his mind, plotting in silence.

On the other end of the line, Donner couldn't help but feel his ire rising. All afternoon and now evening, they had done little more than monitor, Ames hoping his face or even what happened to Tarby would be enough to make the situation go away.

What he couldn't seem to grasp was that wasn't going to happen. Ridge now had his fingers sunk into something, an event they would all like to keep buried, and he wasn't likely to just suddenly stop.

Not unless he was made to.

"My orders?"

Chapter Forty-One

The information was scribbled down on a notepad in front of Jackson Ridge, everything Al Bumppo had just told him transcribed as fast as he could. Jotted down the moment the conversation ended, he had scratched out each detail, not wanting to forget a single thing, the resulting mash of blue ink on the page looking closer to a Rorschach Test than an actual collection of information.

Not that Ridge thought he would actually need it, the new data seared into his mind, bringing with it a whole host of new questions, ideas and considerations that needed to be entertained.

With them came the realization that his time was continuing to dwindle, the clock moving well into the new day.

His final day.

His thoughts and focus still on what Bumppo had said, what it might mean, how it might tie back to Josh Tarby, Ridge had to force himself to try and push the information aside for a moment. When that didn't work, he took the additional step of literally doing so, reaching out and shoving the list to the side.

He had to slow down, to continue taking one thing at a time.

Before the call from Bumppo, he had entered his office set on looking into General Arnold Ames. Prior to that, he had been interrupted by the call from the Hilton, the visit from the man now hours earlier, Ridge still needing to get in there, to determine exactly what the man's angle was.

Reaching for his cell phone, Ridge flipped it open and checked the indicator in the corner, seeing he was already down to just two bars of battery life remaining. After using the device more in the previous ten hours than he had in as many years, he was amazed it was still functioning.

The thing had been on staff longer than all of his employees save Beckwith, after all.

To his knowledge, the sole charger for it was at home on the kitchen counter, the act of plugging it in each night one of pure rote habit and nothing more. If there even was a suitable spare anywhere nearby, he had no clue, an eventuality that could become problematic.

As with most things with the situation he was in, he just had to hope it didn't get that far.

Thumbing his way back into his address book, Ridge scrolled until he found the name he was looking for and pressed send. Rising from his seat, he grabbed the wadded up coat from it and walked to the side of the room, tossing the garment toward the rack, not caring enough to follow and pick it up when it missed and crumpled to the floor.

Instead, his focus was on the ringing in his ear, on the crotchety voice that answered after a handful of tones.

"Christ, man, you know what time it is?" Sebastian Murray asked.

"I know, Sea Bass, but this is important."

"Isn't it always?" Murray groaned, letting out a pained sound, the spring of a bed creaking beneath him just audible. "What's up?"

Knowing that Murray probably wasn't completely over the late call, Ridge didn't bother launching into another apology, knowing it would only slow their conversation down, both sides wanting to get on with things as quickly as possible.

"Arnold Ames," Ridge said. "Ever heard of him?"

"Who?" Murray responded instantly, answering Ridge's question with one of his own.

"General Arnold Ames," Ridge said, adding the man's title. "Army."

Another exhausted sound somewhere between a sigh and a grunt slid out over the line, followed by more bed creaking and two feet hitting a hardwood floor.

"Ames," Murray repeated, saying the name three times in total. "Nope, name doesn't ring a bell. Should it?"

"No clue," Ridge said. "Before tonight, I hadn't heard of the man either."

"Before..." Murray said, his voice falling away as he connected what Ridge was telling him. "Was he overseeing things in Afghanistan at the time?"

"Don't know about that either," Ridge said. "I just know that a few hours ago he showed up here in full dress attire and tried to scare me off the hunt."

He didn't bother adding the part about Clara Tarby being assaulted just minutes after, the timing too much to be coincidental, but the severity of the attack being too much to lob at a ranking general without definitive proof.

"Subtle," Murray said.

"As a gun," Ridge replied.

"Alright, give me a few minutes," Murray said, the words coming out with one last grunt. "Let me see who I can now wake up and piss off for you."

"I appreciate it."

Chapter Forty-Two

Sea Bass was going to get back to him. Clara Tarby was out of surgery, Ellerbe and Stroh there to report any new developments. Harold Golding and Al Bumppo had both shared their experiences attempting to look into whatever had happened in Afghanistan, each having been pulled off before they could really accomplish much, their collective attitude trending hard toward bitterness, both having been sent bouncing around the country the moment they returned.

Looking down at the notes from his conversation with Bumppo, Ridge stood behind his desk, attempting to sort things out in his mind, to put things into a logical progression.

If not to determine what had happened to Josh Tarby, then at least to figure out what his next step was in attempting to do so.

Extending a hand down toward the desk, Ridge tapped his fingertips against the polished top of it, drumming them faster and faster, the sound a perfect soundtrack for the way he felt. Remaining in that position for several moments, trying in vain to parse out his next steps, he broke the tension of the moment by snapping his hand back and falling into his seat.

Landing hard, he allowed his momentum to push him to the rear edge of the plastic mat beneath him, the wheels catching as they shifted to the carpet, stopping him instantly. Resting his elbows on the pads of the chairs, he laced his fingers before him, nervous energy pulsating through his body.

Raising his left arm, he shoved back his sleeve and checked the time, the clock now marching steadily on toward one.

He had been awake for twenty hours and counting, his heart rate surging for most of it, the chance of sleep any time in the next twelve hours dismal at best.

He had to slow things down, had to purge some of the anxiety within so he could breathe and think and analyze what he needed to.

When that worked only slightly, he shifted to what might help instead.

His first thought was to step over to the window, to shove it upward and allow the cold night air to swirl around him. Hopefully, the icy chill would manage to lower his body temperature, to calm his nerves enough that he could take one thing at a time, to keep moving in an ordered and logical progression.

Just as fast he pushed the thought aside, his gaze flitting across the curtains pulled closed around the room. Most likely anybody that might still be tailing him had given up - if not from the cold then from the obviousness of sitting out there staring up at his window at such an hour – but he couldn't take that chance.

Instead, his focus wandered to the folded up remains of the sandwich he had started a few hours earlier, making it no more than a few bites in before having to stop and rush to the hospital to see to Clara Tarby.

Almost as if on cue, his stomach let out the slightest rumble, a not-so-subtle hint that he was running on reserve energy, adrenaline only able to carry him so far before basic physiology won out.

Extending the heels of his boots out before him, Ridge pressed the rear edge into the plastic, using his quads to pull himself forward. Retracing the same path he had rolled just moments before, he returned to the edge of the desk and grabbed up the sandwich, the wadded paper rustling as he placed it into his lap and began to unfold it.

"Please tell me you aren't seriously considering eating that?" Beckwith said, the sound of her voice unexpected, extra loud in the solitude of the office.

Not even realizing she had entered, Ridge's head snapped up, his eyes widening as a jolt of surprise rocketed through his chest. In its wake, he could feel his heart pounding, his breathing increase.

"Damn it, Susie, how many times..." he began before letting go of the same admonishment he had made a thousand times before. "Make some noise, will you?"

Assuming the same posture she always did, Beckwith stopped behind the chair she had used a few different times throughout the day and said, "My apologies, sir. Now, please tell me you aren't actually going to eat that."

Glancing down to his lap, Ridge realized that the sandwich was still sitting half-open across his thighs, bits of meat and bread peeking out at him.

"I was certainly thinking about it. Why?"

"And I was thinking that thing has been sitting out for more than four hours now," Beckwith said. "There's no way that can be healthy."

Opening his mouth to respond, Ridge paused before any sound could be heard. Pressing his lips together, he felt his mouth curl up into a smile.

"And you really think some hard bread and meat is the biggest threat to my health right now?"

To that there was no response for a moment, Beckwith simply staring at him, trying her best to give a disapproving glare, before she too succumbed to a smile. As she did so, she stepped around the chair and lowered herself into it, unloading the items in her arms onto the seat beside her.

"No, I suppose it isn't," she said, her voice betraying one of the few hints of weariness he had heard in all their years together.

"Ha!" Ridge let out, the sound completely reflexive, gone before he even knew it, a fact that only made them both smile more. "At least she's honest, folks."

Allowing the good humor to settle for a moment, one of the few happy times in a day that was supposed to be chock full of them, Ridge remained reclined in his seat, his attention drifting down to his lap, the sandwich no longer seeming nearly as appealing as it had before.

"Ask you something?" he asked, the mirth of before gone, his voice back to neutral.

Across from him, Beckwith had also returned to her usual state, staring back intently at him, waiting for him to ask without providing a verbal command to do so.

"Do you think I'm crazy for doing this?"

In the previous ten hours, hundreds of thoughts had pushed their way through Ridge's mind, almost all of them connected to the Tarby family, or General Ames, or a supply convoy in the desert months before. Very few had actually been about the task he was performing, about whether or not the ends could ever justify the means that were underway.

"Do I think-" Beckwith began to repeat, the words clearly phrased into a question.

"Yeah," Ridge said, jumping in, cutting her off. "With all of this. The calls, the favors, the sitting here at one in the morning on my last night in office, my whole staff still awake and strewn across the city."

"None of us mind," Beckwith said. "You know that."

"Not exactly the point in all that I was looking for clarification on," Ridge replied, arching an eyebrow.

Matching the look, Beckwith pursed her lips and said, "I know that, I was just saying, you don't need to worry about us."

"And I know that," Ridge said, "but it doesn't mean it isn't part of a situation that has gotten far more out of hand than I ever envisioned."

"You?" Beckwith replied. "How do you think I feel? Had we done a better job of vetting our guests this morning, this never would have happened."

Seeing a flash of confusion cross Ridge's features, his brows coming together, she continued, "She was supposed to have asked something about national parks, say thanks and be on her way. If she had..."

Again her voice fell away, not needing to state the obvious, Ridge knowing where it was going.

To a degree, she was right. Not about her failing to vet properly - that single piece he had not once considered – but to the fact that had Clara Tarby only played by the rules, they would all be sleeping comfortably right now, herself included.

"Did you see the state of that woman when she sat down in front of me?" Ridge asked, bypassing Beckwith's statement and picking up a new parallel track. "The look on her face, her physical appearance, the anguish when she spoke."

Boring his gaze into Beckwith, he held the position a moment before looking away, "I just...she deserved to at least know what happened to her son."

He didn't bother adding that she was also right, that he had spearheaded the effort to send those troops over, that the fate of Josh Tarby was at least partially tied to a decision he had made.

Not that he especially needed to, Beckwith almost always having a way of understanding such things.

"I agree," Beckwith said softly. "Which is why the answer to your question is no. I don't think you're crazy for pursuing this at all."

Chapter Forty-Three

"Jesus, have you stepped in it now."

The words were delivered free of inflection, very much a statement and not a question. For a moment, Ridge allowed his face to relay the confusion he felt, pulling the phone away from his face, using the caller ID to identify the voice on the line, the tone familiar, but only just quite.

Murray.

"Sea Bass?" Ridge asked. "Where are you? Why do you sound so different?"

"Don't worry about where I am," Murray snapped, the words clipped and curt. "And the reason I'm talking like this is so nobody can hear me."

The same look still strewn across his features, Ridge pulled the phone away from his face, covering the receiver with his other hand.

"Susie, I'm sorry, can you excuse us for a moment?"

Offering only a curt nod, Beckwith collected her things from the neighboring chair and stood, pausing for an instant as if she might say something before letting it go with a nod and turning for the door.

A moment later she exited, closing it behind her.

"Why can't you let anybody hear you?" Ridge asked. "What the heck did you stumble into?"

"*I* didn't stumble into a damn thing," Murray said, agitation and irritation both plainly obvious in his tone. "You're the one that bumbled haphazardly into a mess and happened to pull me along with you."

Even if the words came out a bit more forceful than intended, the point was no less received, Ridge feeling his stomach contract tight. The very last thing in the world he had wanted was to start pulling innocent bystanders into this labyrinth, his goal simply to provide some long overdue relief to Clara Tarby.

Somehow in the time since, he had managed to put her in the hospital and had Murray on the run, to say nothing of whatever other collateral damage he might have kicked up.

"How bad?" Ridge said simply, hoping that the words and the tone that dripped from them would be sufficient to relay how sorry he really was.

For a moment there was no response, the only sound a long sigh, before Murray replied, "Pretty damn."

Just as with most of the people he'd spoken to over the course of the evening, gone was any trace of the previous venom that had laced his words, replaced instead by deep-seated exhaustion.

"I'm listening," Ridge replied.

For as cold, as callous, as the response might sound, Ridge meant nothing by it, knowing that Murray would understand it as such.

The man had called him back, clearly, because he had information to pass along. The faster Ridge made it possible for him to do so, the better.

"Ever heard of an outfit called Black Water?" Murray asked.

His visage scrunching slightly, Ridge mumbled the words several times in succession.

"I'm guessing you're not talking about the song from the Allman Brothers?"

"The Allman-" Murray started, cutting himself off just as fast, muttering something that Ridge vaguely heard that seemed to include the words *white people music.*

"No," Murray continued, "I am not talking about the song from the Allman Brothers. What I am talking about is the military contracting outfit that was started five years ago and has been popping up with increasing frequency in war zones all over the country.

"You've heard of Black Forest? This is the latest knockoff version."

Snapping himself forward, Ridge placed his backside on the front edge of his chair and reached out, sliding the legal pad and pen back over before him. Drawing two hard lines across the width of the page to demarcate his notes from Bumppo, he wrote the name of the organization in block letters, scrawling a blue box around them.

Not until the name Black Forest had been mentioned did things really click into place for him, the name one that he had encountered with far more frequency than he would have liked over the years.

"Okay," he said, "Black Water, who are they and what do they do?"

"What they do," Murray said, skipping to the back half of the question, "is pretty much what all contracting outfits do, which is whatever needs doing.

"Private security, cleanup details, escort units. These guys are mercenaries for hire, making a quick buck wherever there is turmoil enough to support their particular brand of skills."

"That brand being..." Ridge began, already foreseeing where this was headed.

"The best and brightest our planet has to offer," Murray said. "Soldiers of fortune across the board, all with a healthy swath of patriotism that was later replaced by capitalism."

"Meaning?" Ridge said, fighting to process everything he was hearing, wanting to be careful to parse out this organization from Black Forest and any lingering presuppositions he might have about them.

"Guns for hire," Murray said. "To borrow clichés, they kick ass, take names, and get paid handsomely for it."

Nodding, Ridge continued jotting notes, questions flooding into his mind.

"Alright," he said, scribbling out a final few letters and underlining parts of the previous sentence. "So why do I care about Black Water in particular?"

"Because they were co-founded by none other than your General Arnold Ames."

Poised with his hand held an inch above the legal pad, Ridge stopped writing, his eyebrows rising up his forehead. All air was expelled from his lungs as he stared at the desk, long enough that the various objects all lost focus, swirling into one large mash of colors.

"What?"

A humorless snort was the first response, followed by, "I thought that might get your attention."

Blinking quickly in succession, Ridge returned to the tablet, writing the words in oversized letters across the bottom of the page. Flipping the pen down atop them, he leaned back in his chair and rubbed at this forehead, staring at the notation he'd just made.

"So that little stunt he pulled showing up here in full dress uniform..."

"All for show," Murray said. "I mean, he did technically retire in good standing from the army, and he is still employed down the street at the Pentagon, but he's purely on the civilian side now.

"Traded in his patriotism for the almighty dollar, just like the rest of them."

It was a narrative Ridge had heard many times over the years, happening with increasing frequency as time passed. Soldiers enlisted at an early age and allowed the government to train them up before moving into the private sector and using those skills to make a tremendous amount of money.

Leaders that spent a lifetime in the system that wanted one big payday before walking off into a retirement.

In a way, it wasn't much different from what happened in the very office building he now found himself sitting in, people like Ellerbe and Stroh padding their resumes before shifting to the other side for exorbitant pay raises.

The only difference was that the havoc wrought by people like those employed by Black Water could potentially be a lot more devastating.

"And when you say global?" Ridge said.

"Yep," Murray confirmed, "they currently have people on the books from all over. Couple of South Africans, a few from the Swiss Guard, even a Latvian or two, though how the hell they found those guys is anybody's guess."

Shaking his head slightly, Ridge said, "No color has ever unified the world quite like green."

"Yep," Murray repeated, his cadence beginning to pick up slightly, it becoming clear he needed to wrap things up, to be moving on soon. "So that was all I got on Ames, and I don't know that anything is afoot here, but just the same, I'm going to disappear for a little while."

He didn't have to say the rest of what it was clear he was thinking, Ridge getting the message.

Murray was from that moment on off-limits. Any existing markers – professional or personal – were now considered paid in full.

"Be careful, Sea Bass," Ridge said simply. "Thank you, and let me know when you come back up for air."

For a moment there was no response, as if Murray was contemplating how to best respond, before he said, "I just may do that. In the meantime, keep your phone on.

"There might be a call coming in from the other side of the world that could give you a little help."

Chapter Forty-Four

An hour earlier when he had given Leopold Donner the order to do nothing, Ames had been under the impression that the situation still required monitoring and little more. Jackson Ridge was certainly becoming a bit worrisome, was burning up the phone lines, calling in untold favors that only someone with three-plus decades of experience could have, but that didn't necessarily make him a threat.

The incident that he was looking into was nothing remarkable on the surface. Unfortunate for sure, perhaps even tragic to the outside observer, but it featured nothing that would be grounds for any amount of real concern.

That line of thinking had been with Ames as he sat in the dark, slowly sipping from a glass with three fingers of Glen Livet, alone in the living room of his home. With his back pressed tight against the stiff sofa, his gaze was aimed at the glowing spire of the Capitol Building a short distance away, his mind tracing over how far he'd come – or rather, fallen – in the preceding years.

The decision to move into the private sector was one he had never wanted to make, not that it was ever really up to him. Circumstance and the occasional cruelty of fate had decided to intervene and take that over for him.

For as well compensated as a general in the army was, it seemed amazing how fast the costs of long-term care could chew through a retirement account, the joint ailments of his parents causing him to move into the private sector, knowing that if ever he was going to keep them taken care of or have any hope of retiring the way he would like himself, he needed to take advantage of his last few years of earning potential.

From that was born Black Water, a joint venture with a pair of silent partners, the hope being to capitalize on his own extensive network of contacts to ensure he was first in line for some plum contracts.

And for five years, just that had occurred, even landing him a post inside the Pentagon, allowing for enough water cooler conversation and workplace scuttlebutt to make it possible for him to always be in point position whenever an earning opportunity presented itself.

And earn he did.

So much so that his focus shifted, his grasp on the things that truly mattered slipping to the wayside. With more money coming in than he had ever imagined, in a matter of just years he had been able to afford the brownstone he was currently sitting in, taking up a liking for things such as the scotch he was now drinking, the steak he had had with Donner earlier in the day.

And as such things tended to do, the access to more only increased the longing for more.

Twisting his focus from the white marble aglow in the distance to his own reflection in the picture window, Ames could see the light coming in from the neighborhood outside, the faint hue outlining the right side of his face. Cut from hard lines and ridges, he still looked the part of a man that had dedicated his life to the service, even if his driving force had changed in the ensuing years.

At times, he had allowed himself to fall into bouts of bitterness or self-loathing, even going as far as standing in front of the mirror each morning and questioning his own manhood, wondering what he had become.

Just as fast he had given up on the notion, pushing such things to the side, knowing that nothing good could come from them.

He had made his decisions, had consciously chosen the path he was on. There was no use subjecting himself to self-flagellation in the aftermath.

Now, all there was to do was continue monitoring, waiting for noon to arrive, hoping that Ridge would be shunted to the side by the hands of time, allowing him to continue on that path.

What had happened to Josh Tarby was an accident, was tragic, but it would not be enough to be his undoing. Not now, not after so much time and careful planning.

With that thought in mind, Ames raised the scotch to his lips, intent to take another deep sip, but was stopped with the tumbler halfway there, his phone kicking to life beside him. Pulling his attention to the side, he stared down at the buzzing device, holding the glass in place a moment before slowly lowering it back into position.

Using his opposite hand, he snapped up the phone and pressed it to his face.

"Ames."

"General," a voice said, the tone instantly recognizable.

"Go ahead, Valdez."

"Just thought you should be aware, there's some activity," Valdez said, rattling the information off in quick fashion.

"I know," Ames said. "I figured it was only a matter of time before Ridge started pinging me."

To that there was a long pause, the man falling silent, before saying, "Sir, this traffic isn't from Senator Ridge, and it isn't concerning you."

The creases of Ames's face drew tighter as he left the glass beside him on the couch and stood, taking two steps forward and stopping, close enough to the window to feel the cold air emanating from the glass.

"Continue."

"It's about Black Water, and it's coming from somewhere else," Valdez said. "Can't tell exactly where yet, the back trail is pretty well covered, but I should have it soon."

At the mention of Black Water, Ames felt his body go rigid. Even if the inquiry itself wasn't coming from Ridge, there was no way that somebody else just happened to be digging into them right now.

Not with everything else that had played out over the course of the day.

"Keep on it," Ames said, already having a pretty good idea who might be behind such a thing but wanting to know for sure. "I'll be here all night."

"Yes, sir," Valdez said, the two sides disconnecting.

Lowering the phone just a few inches, Ames scrolled down a couple of spots in his call log, highlighting the one he was looking for and pressing send, bringing it back to his face.

Less than thirty seconds later it was answered, the all-too-familiar voice of Donner appearing over the line.

"Donner."

"Ames."

For a moment neither spoke, allowing each to do whatever they needed to, before Ames said, "I just got a call from Valdez."

"I see," Donner replied. "What's Ridge up there digging into now?"

Expecting such a response, Ames said, "Not Ridge. And whoever it is is now looking into Black Water."

In one of the few times since Ames had met the man, Donner seemed to grasp the enormity of what he was being told, any hint of mirth or sarcasm gone from his voice.

"Has to be connected, right?

"Has to," Ames agreed.

"So now's the time?" Donner asked.

Again shifting his gaze to the glass right before his nose, Ames stared back at his own reflection.

"Yes. Not too crazy, make sure he lives, but make damned sure he's out of action for the next twelve hours or so."

"Roger that."

Chapter Forty-Five

Every impulse was for Jackson Ridge to go back to the windows, to throw open the curtains and stare out into the night, almost defiant as he searched for whoever might be watching. Of that fact he had little doubt, knowing that if somebody was following him earlier to his meeting with Whitner, they would most certainly still be on him now.

As much as he wanted to do that, to let them know that he was not afraid, would not be bullied, the more prudent, self-preservationist side of his brain won out.

Whatever Murray had uncovered had been enough to send him underground for a while, in and of itself sufficient to let Ridge know that this crew was not to be trifled with. Coupled with the fact that he still had Beckwith sitting not twenty feet from where he was, he knew he also couldn't do anything rash that might risk putting her in danger.

Just as he had Clara Tarby.

At least he now knew that Capitol Police was with her, watching over Ellerbe and Stroh as well.

With his hands clasped behind his back, Ridge strode back and forth across the middle of his office, his senses heightened in a way that he hadn't known in years. He was currently working on almost twenty-four hours since rest of any kind, had barely eaten a thing, but his body didn't seem to notice either, instead relying on natural chemicals for energy.

His heart rate had been up for what seemed like hours on end, the cotton undershirt he wore damp with sweat, his mustache a bit itchy from the same lining his upper lip.

Unlocking his fingers, he raised his left arm and checked his watch, running the math in his head.

Ten more hours. That's all he had to go, both to find the conclusion to the story of Josh Tarby, and to keep himself and his team safe.

Resuming his pacing, Ridge played back the previous conversation in his head, running it from the inauspicious start up through the impromptu farewell that Murray had tacked on the end.

Never before had Ridge heard of Black Water, much less encountered them, though he had been around long enough to know of many outfits just like them, to have a pretty clear idea of what it was they did.

The idea was still too fledgling during his own time in the service, the world at large having not yet completely given itself over to unbridled capitalism. In those days, if a person was intent on being a soldier, they did so through the military or as a mercenary in some off-the-grid location, but never did the two sides meet.

And never was either very lucrative.

It wasn't until after Vietnam, when the market became flooded with former soldiers, many of them possessing a very singular, very specific skill set, did such things start to pop up. Returning home to find a country that largely despised them, a job market that felt much the same, private contracting groups were born.

Getting their start by simply offering to do the grunt work that no organization – even one as large and multi-faceted as the military – wanted to do, contractors had taken the toehold and run with it. In just a few short decades they had gone from handholding and toilet scrubbing to a multi-billion dollar industry, making a lot of people extremely wealthy in the process.

So much so that sentiment on them had actually swung back in the opposite direction, many in the military hierarchy feeling they had grown too strong, their bargaining position overly entrenched.

To those on the outside looking in, they appeared to be nothing more than an off-the-books system to allow the military to do whatever they pleased, a hidden arm that could act with impunity, free of oversight or regulation.

Which is exactly what he suspected might have happened with Black Water, even if Murray hadn't gone as far as to say so.

Again raising his wrist to check the time, Ridge found it just a few minutes later than the previous look. Just as he had for much of the previous twelve hours, he needed information, the time of night and depth of subject matter narrowing his options to precious few.

Twice more he made passes in front of the desk, his gaze aimed down at the light tan loops of the carpet before him, the sound of his footsteps swallowed by the very same material.

On the start of the third trip, a thought occurred to him, a single name that would fit both of the parameters he was working with, someone so obvious the only reason he hadn't thought about it sooner was because of the swirling mess that had been the last few hours, a marathon stretch of waiting rooms and phone calls.

Not that the latter was bound to change anytime soon.

Stepping forward between two of the chairs still positioned in front of his desk, Ridge grabbed up his cellphone and flipped it open. Clasping it with both hands before him, he checked the dwindling battery supply before going into his call log and working his way past half a dozen entries.

Moving on by strings of digits he knew to represent Murray and Golding and Bumppo, he found the listing he was looking for, a single name typed in, one of the few that actually had a title saved into his roster.

Staring at it for a moment, he drew in a deep breath, allowing his chest to expand and shoulders to rise and sag, before expelling it slowly, trying to push from his mind how much he really did not want to be making the call.

But, just like with the previous one, there didn't seem to be any other option.

Failing to surprise him even a little, the call was snatched up after only a single ring, no sound at all meeting his ears for the better part of a minute. With his heart hammering, Ridge reached out for the front edge of his desk, leaning his hip against it, bracing himself for support.

Questions pinned just beneath the surface, aching to be released, Ridge forced himself to wait. The fact that the call was even picked up was unexpected, the silence that followed a clear message to let it be known that the act was a courtesy extended out of obligation and nothing more.

When at least the man on the other end did speak, his tone seemed to relay that exact sentiment, the words short and clipped.

"Earlier today when I said I still owed you, I didn't mean for you to be calling it in already."

Drawing in a deep breath, steeling himself in the knowledge that this conversation likely wouldn't go the way he wanted, Ridge said, "I know."

"So then why are you calling me?" Terry Whitner asked.

He didn't bother adding the extreme time on the end of the question, Ridge not sure if that part was implied, or if the man simply hadn't even noticed.

"What do you know about a group called Black Water?" Ridge said, jumping straight to the punch line, hoping that would be enough to get Whitner's attention.

Again silence settled in over the line, almost another full minute passing, before Whitner repeated, "Black Water."

"Yeah," Ridge said, not sure if the statement was an invitation, but snatching at it just the same. "Apparently, they were on the ground in Afghanistan, and I have reason to believe that they may be connected in some way to what happened with Josh Tarby."

Phone pressed tight to his cheek, Ridge leaned forward at the waist, almost willing Whitner to respond, using his body language in an attempt to spur along a response.

Instead, all he heard was, "Don't call this number again," before the line went dead.

Chapter Forty-Six

The digital readout in the top right corner of her phone screen told Marian Ellerbe she was down to her final few gasps of battery, the device being the sole reason she was still awake. In the aftermath of the senator and Susan Beckwith leaving, she had been riding an adrenaline surge, the events of the evening being far past anything she had ever experienced.

Hailing from Jacksonville, which was much closer to a retirement community than a city where actual violence ever occurred, things such as clandestine investigations and hotel room assaults were the stuff of fiction novels, not everyday life.

Certainly not hers, anyway.

When Ellerbe had awakened that morning, she had braced herself for the usual tedium of continuing to wrap things up at the office, her final few lingering tasks having been dragged out much longer than necessary, meant to ensure she had something to do in the final hours of her tenure. After that, she would sit dutifully through the handful of group meals, smiling at the right time, ordering from the cheaper end of the menu, before setting off the next day with the few remaining personal items she still had at the office.

A day later she would fly home, having pushed back her annual holiday visit, knowing she would have the dual benefits of unending time off and cheaper airfare just after the first of the year.

From there, things were still a bit up in the air, a couple of lower-end job offers having trickled through, but nothing that was yet what she was looking for.

Something with a bit more excitement.

The thought almost seemed a cruel irony now, a harsh reminder of how misguided she'd been, her surroundings painting a very stark picture of what a bit more excitement could potentially mean.

Flicking her gaze to the phone in her hand, Ellerbe saw that it was now half-past two in the morning. Beside her, Stroh was out cold, just as he had been for the previous few hours. Prior to that, he had been able to force himself awake every so often to attempt stunted conversation, but even that had eventually fallen away.

At the time, Ellerbe had been glad for the silence, though now she would even take the most of awkward of back and forth just to have some form of distraction.

In the corner, a pair of Capitol Police officers stood leaning against the wall, their backs turned to her, both seeming jovial as they bantered in low voices. By her count, neither had so much as glanced over at the thin crowd filling the waiting area in the better part of an hour, both seeming glad to be in out of the cold.

Shifting her focus back to the phone, looking at the waning battery life, Ellerbe considered going back online, checking Facebook for the hundredth time, hoping for status updates that had stopped coming in hours before. From there she thought on checking up on People.com, or perhaps even scrolling through CNN or Fox News, catching up on what the media was saying about the legislative transitions that were now just hours away.

Pushing both aside, she opted in favor of saving the last few wisps of life the device had left, knowing she would need them to eventually check in with Beckwith, not even sure if Stroh had his phone with him.

"Hey, we're going to make a quick coffee run, be back soon."

The voice was deep and bombastic, much too loud for the small space, jerking Ellerbe's focus up from the phone. Feeling palpitations flutter through her chest, blood rushed to her cheeks as she found one of the two officers standing before her, his bulbous midsection at least four inches closer than the rest of him.

"Oh, okay," Ellerbe managed, not expecting to be engaged in conversation, having no idea why the man felt the need to do so.

Even less why it took two of them to fetch coffee.

"Everything looks good here, but just give a shout if you need us," the man said, his chest plate displaying his last name as Roberts. "We won't be long."

Managing only a nod in response, Ellerbe pressed her lips together, feigning a smile, her hair swinging free on either side of her neck.

Matching the pose, Roberts turned on a heel and strode away, the various items on his belt making a variety of noises as he left, audible long after he turned a corner and disappeared from sight.

Watching until they were gone, Ellerbe could only shake her head, lowering her focus back to the phone. Depressing the button on the side of it, the backlight sprang to life, displaying that only a few minutes had passed.

How long they would be expected to sit and wait she wasn't quite certain, knowing only that at this point, noon could not arrive fast enough.

"Ridiculous, isn't it?"

Much like the previous time, the unexpected voice snapped Ellerbe's attention up, a second flutter rippling through her chest.

Unlike the first though, the voice was much softer, almost gentle, meant to not be overheard.

How the woman had managed to slip into the seat beside her without being noticed, Ellerbe had no idea. Just a moment prior the seat had been unoccupied, the room appearing lifeless.

With straight brown hair and a long coat, the woman looked as fresh as if it were the middle of the day, her face unlined, not bearing the slightest hint of fatigue.

"Cops and their coffee," the woman said, shifting her head to stare down the hall before looking back to Ellerbe. "I mean, they're supposed to be here watching Clara Tarby, making sure you two are safe, and instead all they can do is play grab ass and make a Starbucks run."

With her gaze turned to the empty hall stretched out before them, it took a moment for the words to register with Ellerbe, her lips parting slightly as realization set in. Again reaction passed through her chest, this time seizing her tight, the air becoming short as she slowly shifted her attention to the woman beside her, seeing her anew.

"Who are you?" Ellerbe asked, her voice rising slightly, a natural reaction to the fear and adrenaline surging through her.

Reaching out, the woman placed a hand on her thigh, her fingers digging into the flesh like talons.

"Easy now," she said. "There's no need to get loud, no need to cause a scene."

Speaking from the side of her mouth, she passed her gaze over the waiting area, the scant number of people strewn in various positions, all attempting with varying degrees of success to find sleep.

"This is how this is going to go," the woman said. "You're going to leave your boyfriend to his sleep there, and the two of us are going to take a little walk, just like those useless cops that just waddled away from here."

Fighting to keep herself from crying out, the woman's grip tearing through her leg, Ellerbe bit down hard on her bottom lip, a sheen of moisture appearing over her eyes.

With her opposite hand, the woman peeled back the front flap of her coat and added, "And if you do anything that I don't think is appropriate, you and your friend are going to meet my friend here."

There was no stopping the tear that dripped down from the underside of Ellerbe's right eye, the left quickly following suit, twin trails etched across her cheeks.

"Do you understand?"

Chapter Forty-Seven

The phone was still in Jackson Ridge's hand, the shock of his conversation with Whitner very much on his features. Staring down at the device in his grip, he remained rooted in place in the center of the room, trying to make sense of what just happened, hoping that a clear heading for what came next might present itself.

Hoping more than anything that he had not just committed a terrible faux pas with the one person in D.C. he knew better than to piss off.

Raising the phone back to his ear, Ridge said, "Hello? Hello?" hoping that the clicking sound he had heard so distinctly was anything besides Whitner hanging up, that the man was still there, sour about the late intrusion, but still willing to honor the marker that he had given out.

As he suspected though, there was no response, nothing but dead air over the line.

"Great," Ridge whispered, flipping the phone shut and sliding it over onto his desk. Swiping a hand across his forehead, he wasn't surprised in the least to feel it come back damp, a single pass along the outside of his slacks brushing it away.

Perhaps the move to call Whitner was a bit hasty, but between the dwindling timeframe and number of contacts he had left to lean on, there didn't seem to be much else in the way of options. While he had gotten a great deal closer to his final destination, he couldn't shake the feeling that there was still much more that remained to be uncovered, precious few hours left for him to do so.

"Okay," he whispered, leaving the phone on the desk and resuming his pacing. "What do we know already, and what do we need to figure out?"

Said low enough to ensure Beckwith couldn't hear him, he traveled to and fro over the same walk he had made no less than a million times before. Six steps in either direction, the carpeting soft underfoot, the cavernous room swallowing any whisper of a sound from around him.

It was clear that while he had never heard of Black Water, Terry Whitner certainly had, the response visceral and instantaneous, palpable over the line. Within seconds of mentioning the name, the man had done nothing more than repeat it before cutting the call short.

Whether that was a good or bad thing for his own interests, Ridge had no way of knowing.

Before Whitner, Murray had even gone as far as to think that poking around in Black Water affairs was enough to go offline for a while.

Taken together, Ridge couldn't shake the notion that whoever this organization was, they were a lot higher in the pecking order than the usual military contractor, with some serious clout, and an extreme deference to anything resembling a conscience.

And considering some of the similar organizations he had encountered, that was not a good thing, to say the least.

Also to be considered was the presence of General Arnold Ames, a man whose rank and experience gave the unit at least some semblance of legitimacy, a fact that made whatever he might need to do that much more difficult.

Lost in those thoughts, trying to determine who else he might be able to shake out of bed, to have poke around for more information, Ridge only vaguely became aware of the phone beginning to vibrate on the desk. So used to ignoring it, or the sound of phones ringing, or fax machines kicking to life, or the ping of emails hitting his inbox, the noise didn't manage to penetrate his psyche at first.

Not until what he guessed to be more than a half-dozen tones passed did it manage to pull his attention toward the desk, his focus landing on the small silver object rotating a few inches with each buzz.

The first thought that passed through Ridge's mind was that Whitner had been cut off, that the man was returning his call, as he sprung across the room and grabbed the phone up. Flipping it open, the thought was pushed from his mind as he saw an extraordinarily lengthy list of digits staring back at him, the number much too long to be from a standard U.S. line.

Feeling his brow come together, Ridge accepted the call.

"Jackson Ridge."

The first response through the line was a loud burst of static, the noise followed by what sounded like a long line of traffic in the background, large machines with enormous diesel engines and oversized tires.

"Yeah, this the senator?" a man almost yelled, his pitch raised to be heard over the ruckus nearby.

Wincing, Ridge pulled the phone back a few inches and stared at the receiver in his hand before bringing it back to his face.

"Yes, this is Senator Jackson Ridge. Who is this?"

For a moment, there was no response, the noise in the background somehow growing even louder, before most of the residual sound fell away, the quiet almost jarring.

"Sorry about that," the man said. "I placed the call thinking we were all set over here, then got pulled back out for a second."

Who he was referring to or where they had gotten pulled out to, Ridge could only guess at, hoping that things started becoming clearer fast.

"That's no problem," Ridge said.

"Apologies for the time, too," the man said, "Sebastian gave me the number, said you'd be awake."

Sebastian.

At the mention of Murray, the previous call with Whitner fled from mind, Ridge recalling the final thing Murray had said, that help might be coming in from the other side of the world.

When he'd first said it, Ridge hadn't pretended to have any idea what he was referring to, things just now beginning to make sense.

"Yeah, for sure," Ridge said. "This being my last night in office, needed to wrap some stuff up before handing in my keys."

"And let me tell you," the man replied, "those of us out here on the front line appreciate it. Nice to know the guys calling the shots back home are working just as hard as we are."

A flush of blood traveled to Ridge's face at the unexpected compliment, his temperature rising a few degrees.

"You're quite welcome," Ridge said, feeling as if he were a schoolchild squirming before his teacher, anxious to push on past. "I'm sorry, who did you say I'm speaking with again?"

379

"Oh!" the man said, a bit of dawning in his tone. "That's my bad, I hadn't actually gotten there yet. Master Sergeant Aaron Bills, 103rd Infantry by way of Erie, Pennsylvania."

Having been to Erie on two separate occasions, Ridge pushed aside his first inclination to offer condolences, instead seizing on the first half of the introduction.

"Pleasure to meet with you, Master Sergeant. Thanks for getting back to me."

"Not a problem, sir. Any friend of Bassy's is a friend of mine."

One corner of Ridge's mouth curled up at the mention of Sebastian being called *Bassy*, the moment passing just as fast, his mustache falling back into place.

"Well, I do appreciate it," he said. "Did he happen to tell you what this was about?"

Another sharp crack of what sounded like metal hitting a concrete floor exploded across the line, Ridge again wincing as he jerked the phone back a few inches from his face, holding it there until he heard Bills's voice reappear.

"Sorry about that," Bills said, annoyance plain in his tone. "FNG, again."

One corner of Ridge's mouth drew upward, it being the first time he had heard the unofficial acronym in years, glad to know there was at least some commonality between his time in the service and the present day.

"You'll get that," Ridge said.

"Every time," Bills said, the irritation already pulling back into resignation. "And to answer your question, sort of. Said it had to do with the convoy attack that occurred last April?"

"That it did," Ridge said. "I was wondering what you might be able to tell me about it."

A small sound escaped over the line, as if Bills was beginning to speak before stopping short. For a moment, there was nothing but quiet between them before a door could be heard closing, wood butting up flush against a metal frame.

"Sir, may I ask a question?"

There was no need for the man to continue calling him *sir*, though Ridge knew better than to even bother saying as much, the habit so ingrained in people like Bills it would be worth more hassle to both men that it was even worth.

"By all means," Ridge replied.

"Is this conversation off-the-record? As in, my name will never be mentioned?"

His eyes tightening slightly, Ridge fixed his gaze on the far wall, his attention landing on a painting of the Big Horns at dusk, his mind barely even loading what it was seeing.

"Master Sergeant, I can promise you that this conversation never even took place."

Again there was a slight pause, the man clearly debating how to proceed, before he said, "Would you like to hear what I know? What I suspect? Or what speculation around the base thinks?"

The same tremor that had visited several times to the pit of Ridge's stomach popped up again, this one clutching him tighter than the others before combined.

"Yes."

A quick snort was the first response, followed by, "Okay, this is what I know for a fact. On the night of April 14th, a convoy headed from Kabul to Bagram was ambushed. It happened in the wee hours of the morning, right out in the open, nowhere near any of the traditional choke points."

All of this information Ridge had heard from Al Bumppo, though he nodded to himself, listening keenly. "Okay."

"I also know that of the ten trucks involved, only three were rendered unable to go any further, left behind while the other seven ventured on."

The first part Ridge knew, though never had he given much thought to the fate of the remaining trucks.

"They were just left sitting in the middle of the road?" he asked.

A long sigh could be heard, Ridge almost able to envision the man shaking his head on the other end of the call.

"Yeah, but it wasn't like that. They were still taking heat, and those three were all suffering from engine fires. Whoever hit them knew exactly what they were doing."

"Hmm," Ridge said. "And the other trucks were loaded with supplies and didn't want to risk the same fate."

"Even worse," Bills said, "most of them carried personnel."

Out of pure reflex, Ridge shot a low whistle between his teeth, the sound drawn out several seconds in length.

"And the three trucks?" he asked, already knowing the answer but wanting confirmation.

"Weapons," Bills said. "Which leads me to what I suspect."

Blinking several times in succession, Ridge walked quickly around his desk, flopping down in his chair. Grabbing up the legal pad, he turned to a new page, holding the pen inches above it, ready to begin transcribing.

"Go ahead."

"All three trucks that were hit were carrying weapons," Bills said. "And when I say weapons, I mean everything from small arms to heavy artillery."

"Enough to inflict some serious damage," Ridge added.

"Enough to start your own civil war," Bills said. "Basically, a do-it-yourself armory starter kit."

Unable to stop his head as it shook a few inches to either side, Ridge said, "Damn."

"A fact that I'm pretty sure somebody knew," Bills added. "I mean, how else would they just so happen to pick out the second, fourth, and eighth trucks in a line?"

Scribbling down the numbers, Ridge felt his eyebrows rise. "You're kidding me."

"Nope," Bills said. "And we switch up the order in the convoy every trip. No way anybody gets that lucky on their own, and if they do..."

"I want their picks for the Super Bowl next month," Ridge finished.

"Exactly."

Leaning forward, his elbows resting on the edge of the desk, Ridge circled back through everything he'd just been told, almost picturing the events of April 14th in his mind, seeing the burning trio of trucks positioned out in the open, watching seven sets of red brake lights grow smaller in the distance.

"So you suspect that somebody knew what was going down, set this thing up," Ridge said, prompting Bills for the third portion of his response, the part about base speculation.

"I do," Bills said, "especially considering that was the third time it had happened in less than a month."

The pen in Ridge's hand slid from his fingers, bouncing against the wooden desktop as his mouth dropped open. The bottom fell out of his stomach and his mouth went dry as twice he attempted to speak, neither time being able to find his voice.

"The third time?"

"In less than a month," Bills repeated.

"And the contents?" Ridge asked.

"They varied," Bills said, "but each time at least fifty percent of what was taken was weaponry."

Hearing the words, Ridge's eyes slid closed, the bright office light fading from view. Handfuls of responses came to mind, though only a single one kept resurfacing, pushing all others to the side, refusing to be ignored.

Not once had Bills made mention of it yet, but Ridge couldn't help but ask the question, the two previous phone calls still fresh in his mind.

"And tell me, Master Sergeant, does the name Black Water mean anything to you?"

386

Chapter Forty-Eight

Jackson Ridge felt good. Damn good.

After fourteen hours of digging, he was finally starting to get somewhere. What had started as a scavenger hunt to answer a single question from a constituent, to give a grieving mother some relief, to assuage his own aching ego, had turned into far, far more than that.

Had he known at the beginning that it would have gone as far as it had, there was no telling whether or not he would have continued on the path, though that was well past the point now.

For the first time all night, a truly muddled situation was finally starting to take shape.

Positioned on the far side of the office, his phone still in hand, Ridge found himself staring at the closed curtains before him. His thoughts a hundred other places, his eyes failed to even register the scene before him, his mind replaying the conversation with the Master Sergeant, a handful of others before it.

The sum total of them added up to a great many things – none clearer than the fact that he had expended far more favors than he ever had reason to believe he was owed.

On the morrow he would begin finding those that carried a marker, offering to do whatever he could to square the debt, knowing that the further removed from office he became, the less useful he would be to anybody. Despite that, it was also clear that there were certain things he would never be able to atone for, beginning with the fact that Murray was now on the run, and going on to a host of others.

For the time being though, he had more pressing matters to tend to. The final narrative of Josh Tarby was at last beginning to take shape, he just had a few more things he needed before it all made sense.

From there, decisions about what to do with whatever he found would be made by someone else, people that could expend their own resources ferreting out the ills of Black Water.

All he was concerned with was ensuring Clara Tarby woke up to her first bit of good news in ages.

That singular point, that touchstone to the entire ordeal they had been through, brought things full circle, and the next step becoming obvious in Ridge's mind. Blinking himself back awake, he looked down to the phone still clutched in his hand, the stuffed fowl displayed a few feet before him.

Rotating on the ball of his foot, he went straight back across the office and out into the foyer, his strides elongated, moving fast. He had no idea what time it now was, his body clock impervious to the lack of sleep, endorphins and adrenaline having him feeling the best he had in ages.

"Susie," he called. "Susie!"

Covering the expanse between the two offices in just a few steps, Ridge went for the opposite doorway, pulling up abruptly. Extending both hands and pressing them into the frame one either side, he stopped his forward momentum, his shoulders straining just slightly with exertion before bringing him to a stop.

Confusion was the first sensation to creep through his body, starting on his face and moving south quickly.

In order, it was followed by the bottom dropping out of his stomach, fear flooding through in a quick wave, getting to every nerve ending and muscle fiber in his body.

Last to show was realization, more dampness coating Ridge's skin as he stared at what was before him, his jaw sagging open.

During the conversation with the Master Sergeant, he had been completely consumed. The door to his office had been open, he was aware that Beckwith was around, but his entire focus was on the discussion at hand, his body pacing out of muscle memory alone. If pressed, he would be unable to recall a single visual from the course of the conversation, his mind elsewhere, his senses reliving the tale that he was being told.

Stranded in such a state, he must have failed to hear the front door open, missing the enormous man that was now seated in the bullpen before him.

Resting on the front edge of the free desk in the corner, the man stood with one boot planted on the ground, the other raised, swinging free a few inches above the carpet. Dressed in cargo pants and a black windbreaker, he seemed to be the walking poster child for a contractor advertisement, the look completed by the silenced weapon balanced across his thigh.

Thinning hair sat high atop his head, framing a sloping face that was smirking back at the senator.

"Who are you?" Ridge asked, his throat feeling numb, his voice sounding distorted as it passed into the air.

The question only seemed to heighten the sneer on the man's face, his foot swinging to and fro the only movement of any kind.

"How did you get in here?" Ridge pressed, wondering how anybody that looked the way he did could have possibly made it past security.

Realizing just as quickly that someone that made a living the way he did likely wouldn't be deterred by something as basic as locked doors or rent-a-cops.

The man raised his eyebrows for a moment, dismissing the questions in turn, before saying, "Hell of a conversation you were having in there, Senator. Hope you didn't mind the two of us listening in."

Flicking his gaze to Beckwith still seated at her desk, Ridge saw that her usual ramrod posture seemed to be even more pronounced than usual, her mouth drawn so tight that no bit of her lips could be seen.

"You okay?" Ridge whispered, knowing that the man would hear but wanting to give her the assurance that he was speaking only to her, the two of them the only ones in the room that mattered.

"Yeah, she's fine," the man answered, pulling Ridge's attention back his direction, a scowl on his face. "And you're fine, and I'm fine, thanks for asking."

For the first time, a new feeling started to creep up within Ridge. Fleeing fast was the initial shock of seeing someone sitting in his office, dressed in black, a gun in hand.

Pouring in to take its place was anger, a deep-seated hatred for what the man represented, everything his organization had done that he knew about, the countless other things that were even worse that he had no idea on.

"So then why are you here?" Ridge asked.

As he posed the question, he began to assess the situation around him, keeping his attention aimed into the room, his mind starting to rifle through everything he knew.

Which was all decidedly bad.

There was no weapon in the office, nothing beyond some blunt objects or letter openers that would be crude at best, it illegal to bring firearms into the Capitol office buildings. Making it worse was the fact that he was standing framed in the doorway, Beckwith seated a few feet away, both presided over by a man with a gun and a clear disposition for using it.

"Really?" the man asked, his features bearing a mix of surprise and disgust. "Come now, don't insult either of us."

To that Ridge gave no reaction, waiting, not wanting to offer any bit of information that man might not already possess.

"I mean, did you really think you could spend all day poking through our business and nobody would show up?"

Again Ridge remained silent, staring at the man, making no effort to hide the growing loathing he felt.

Raising his free hand, the man scratched at his scalp, digging his nails in before pulling them back and inspecting them a moment. "It's like this line I heard in a movie once. You knock on the devil's door long enough, eventually, he's going to answer."

Dropping his hand back into place, the man slapped it against his thigh, a leering smile crossing his face. "Well, I'm here."

Chapter Forty-Nine

The interior of the SUV was clean and spacious, the only personal touches that even hinted to the man who owned it or what it was used for being the faint scents of high-end tobacco and gun oil in the air. Had he not lived the life he had, Jackson Ridge might have missed both, recognizing each in an instant, knowing what both most likely represented.

Tucked into the passenger seat, Ridge sat with his right shoulder pressed against the door, his hands secured with zip ties in front of him.

In the backseat, Beckwith was stretched from one side to the other, her wrists and ankles bound, her gaze vacant as she stared up at the ceiling.

"I've seen you before, haven't I?" Ridge asked, glancing over to the driver before aiming his focus back out the front windshield, the first words from anybody in the twenty minutes since they'd left his office.

Coming with the man was not something Ridge had wanted to do, knowing that whatever slim chance they had at survival diminished greatly the moment they left the confines of Dirksen. As such, he had tried in vain to avoid the obvious, saying anything he could think of, making promises he had no way of fulfilling, before the conversation was stopped short by the man doing the one thing Ridge would never have imagined.

Pulling his cell phone from his pocket and showing him a picture of a terrified Marian Ellerbe, her hands bound, a rag wrapped around her head, stuffed between her parted lips.

How the man had managed that, or where he had taken the young girl, Ridge had no idea, both questions going unanswered no matter how many times he asked, the same cocksure smile crossing the man's face as he rose from the desk and pointed to the door.

Unable to object in any way, Ridge had stepped aside, waiting for Beckwith to go first, putting himself between her and their captor.

After that, there was no choice but to be compliant, neither even having the chance to grab their coat before being led down to the parking garage and into the SUV they were now seated in.

A faint smile crossed the man's face, the reflection of it just barely visible in the front windshield, as he rolled his attention over to look at Ridge.

"Half an hour to put it together," he said. "Not the best I've seen, but certainly not the worst. Especially for a man your age."

The last bit was an add-on meant to be nothing more than a barb, Ridge seeing it instantly for what it was, shoving it to the side to instead focus on the less obvious part of the statement.

This was far from the first time the man had done something like this.

"Davenport," Ridge said, trying to recall the brief glimpse of the man standing in his lobby earlier in the day, the event nothing more than a flash, feeling like a different lifetime. "That's what you said, wasn't it?"

In his periphery, he could see the man glance his direction, the look of amusement still in place.

"I'll be damned."

Matching the glance, Ridge said, "But that's not your real name, is it?"

Switching his attention back to face forward, the man continued maneuvering them due west, pushing hard on Highway 66, the dense urban of the city and close suburbs falling away behind them.

In their stead, things began to unpack, bits of grass and open lots starting to appear between buildings. Skyscrapers and office complexes gave way to fast food restaurants and gas stations, most standing dark and empty for the night, a few intrepid places braving the wee hours of the morning in preparation for the morning slog that would soon begin moving in the opposite direction.

"Does it really matter?" the man asked.

A handful of answers sprung to mind as Ridge watched a mini mall slide past, the overhead lights dark, the lot empty. "Just wondering what I should call you."

"Well, that depends on you," the man said. "As terribly corny as it sounds, I can be your best friend or your worst enemy, the choice is entirely up to you."

The man was right, it did sound terribly corny, Ridge fighting hard to keep from rolling his eyes.

"So I play ball, and this all goes away, we all make it home in time for breakfast?"

A small grunt was the man's first reply, his head tilting slightly to the side.

"Breakfast might be a push. Given your terrible habit of calling and looking into things you shouldn't, I would put it closer to lunch."

Rolling his gaze over to Ridge, he added, "You know, something closer to the noon hour."

Ridge had known from the moment he'd seen the man sitting in the bullpen why he was there, but it was the first time he had confirmed as much.

Doing so now could only mean he likely didn't care what was disclosed from this point forward, not believing that either one of them would be around to share a word they heard anyway.

"Black Water?" he asked.

There was no response from the man save his foot pressing down a little harder on the accelerator, the engine bucking slightly, spurring them onward. Overhead, signs began announcing exits for places like Manassas and Fairfax, outposts that Ridge hadn't been to in many years, despite living in such close proximity.

Places that were considered rural.

Where very little good occurred.

Shooting past them, the man continued onward, more than a full minute of silence sliding by, his jaw set as he stared out.

"See now," he eventually said, his voice low, "questions like that are what make me think you're pushing much harder to soon be calling me your worst enemy."

Chapter Fifty

The drive out from D.C. took more than forty-five minutes in total, an effort made easier by the total lack of traffic in the late night hours. Pushing fast, they had left behind the sprawl of the city in about half that, moving on into the Virginia countryside and eventually into West Virginia, where the landscape changed dramatically.

Right at the moment a sign alongside the road welcomed them into Wild and Wonderful West Virginia, the topography changed, the flats and rolling hills of Virginia ceding to steep inclines, the eastern front of the Appalachians rising quickly.

Dense forests pushed in hard from either direction, pine trees rising straight up alongside the roadways, tall enough that they seemed to converge in the sky above, blotting any residual moonlight from view. In its absence, the front lamps of the SUV were the only light source, the white halogen glow seeming especially out of place, illuminating things in an unnatural hue.

Staring out, Jackson Ridge couldn't help but feel his core tighten with each passing moment. He had been concerned since the moment this man first arrived, his cocksure demeanor and cavalier brandishing of the weapon making it clear that he was in control, quite comfortable with whatever might occur.

Had the man been content to simply sit on that spare desk and make sure that the inquiry went no further, that still would have been grounds for worry, Ridge counting seconds down, wanting everything – from the meeting with the man to his investigation to his term in the Senate – to all be over.

The fact that they were now driving along a rural stretch of West Virginia single lane pushed that into an entirely different territory.

As they drove, Ridge couldn't help but try and run through things in his mind, attempting to determine what small bits he might be able to negotiate with, any hope he might have at getting his captor to succumb to reason.

His primary concern was with Beckwith in the backseat, Ellerbe presumably already waiting where they were headed. From the old guard that still believed in things such as chivalry, Ridge couldn't stand the thought of something happening to them, whether it be as basic as catching a few errant punches or as depraved as things he would prefer not to think about.

Whatever happened to them would certainly be on him, their only sin being to have gotten too close, his blind wanting to help Clara Tarby putting others in danger.

"I think I saw a house back there," Ridge said, his voice low, the first comment in more than twenty minutes. "We could drop Susie off there, you and I go on alone."

The same sneer as before crossed the man's face for an instant, wavering for just a moment as a flicker of something resembling respect came into view, before returning to the fore.

"Susie? That's what you call her?" he asked. Pausing a moment, as if considering the name, he shrugged his eyebrows and said, "That's cute, almost quaint."

Checking the rearview mirror, the man said, "Yeah, she looks like a Susie. You ever get with that?"

His mouth sagging slightly, it took a moment for the question to register, for Ridge to compute what he'd been asked.

Once he did, white hot rage bubbled to the service, his hands curling into tight fists, the black plastic ties biting into his skin.

"You son of a bitch," he snarled, his voice still low, but the tone markedly different, "what kind of man are you? Grabbing innocent women and dragging them out into the night?"

Flicking his gaze down to the ties Ridge wore, the man let him see his smile, his eyes meeting the senator's before looking back out through the windshield.

"What kind of man am I?" he asked. "Right now, I'm the man in charge."

Scads of angry replies came to Ridge's mind, vitriol roiling to the surface, threatening to spill from every orifice, though he remained silent, his hands still squeezed tight.

"How's it feel to not be sitting up high behind your committee table telling everybody else what to do for a change?"

Ignoring the comment, Ridge kept his head turned, his gaze aimed outward. With as much concentration as he could muster, he tried to record every detail of the road they were passing on, though there were scant few to be seen.

In their stead was nothing but dense forest, a heavy tree line pushing up tight on either side, the road so desolate there weren't even reflector strips to denote where the center lines or edges were.

"Where are we going?" he asked.

Nearly thirty seconds in silence before the man said, "Now, finally, you ask a worthwhile question."

Easing his foot back off the gas, Ridge felt the SUV slow, coasting forward under its own momentum.

"Though I can't actually answer it," the man said, slowing further and hooking a sharp turn to the right, forcing his way into a gap in the trees so narrow that Ridge would have never even noticed it was there.

"Because we're already here."

Gunning the gas twice, the big engine in the machine responded with a gnashing of gears, the front end bucking as they pushed into the woods. Before them, twin tracks were carved out on the forest floor, muddy ruts offset by grasses standing tall.

As they drove, Ridge could hear them slapping at the undercarriage, the driver paying them no heed as they pushed deeper into the forest.

Above them, any trace of the sky was blotted from view, the headlights the only glow of any kind.

Running straight away from the road at a perpendicular angle, the path continued for what felt like nearly a mile, the forest tight on either side before suddenly falling away. Keeping the pace steady, they emerged into a clearing more than eighty feet in a diameter, only a few stray trees breaking it up, a small cabin standing in the exact center of it.

Parked out front was a matching SUV – this one silver in color – with Washington, D.C. plates and sprays of mud rising from the back tires.

Sidling up beside it, the man jerked the SUV to a stop with a hard press of the brakes, the machine sliding a few inches before stopping all movement.

Shoving the gearshift into park, the man snatched the keys from the ignition and turning to stare at Ridge.

"Well now, here we are. Be a pal and help Susie inside?"

Chapter Fifty-One

The cabin was a simple affair, the kind of thing Jackson Ridge used to have on the outskirts of the family ranch, meant to be suitable for a night or two while out hunting, but not to stay in long term.

Knowing they were currently in West Virginia, he imagined that the place served a very similar purpose, deer and a host of other woodland creature calling the land they were on home.

No more than fifteen feet square, one side of the room was fashioned with a wash basin and small fridge, the freestanding unit humming loudly. Only the back wall was a stone fireplace, a small teepee of wood aglow in the bottom, crackling loudly.

On the opposite side of the room was a futon that would double as a sleeping surface, the back of it pulled upright into a sofa. In the center of the room was a roughhewn table with three matching chairs.

The walls were barren, the surfaces formed by the rounded edges of the logs that formed the structure, any gaps between them filled with faded white daubing, a single window on either side reflecting the scene back onto itself.

Marian Ellerbe was already seated on one side of the futon as they entered, her eyes wide, her visage void of any color. The gag had been removed from her mouth since the photo Ridge had seen was taken, though her hands and feet were both tied to match Beckwith, her mouth sagging as she saw them all pass over the threshold.

Standing beside her, back toward the fireplace, was a woman Ridge would peg around forty, straight brown hair pulled back tight, wearing matching attire as the man that had grabbed them. With an impassive gaze, she watched as they entered, not seeming the least bit surprised by their appearance.

Grunting softly under the weight of Beckwith across his shoulders, Ridge wrestled her across the small expanse of the cabin, his quads burning, his lower back aching. Struggling to move her slight frame, his lungs clawed for air, sweat lining his forehead, streaming down into his eyes, causing them to burn.

"Atta boy," the man mocked, watching as Ridge placed Beckwith's feet to the floor in front of the futon, allowing her to lower herself into position on the seat, just a few inches separating her from Ellerbe. "And here I almost thought the walk would give you a heart attack."

His clothes sweaty and disheveled, his hair a mess, Ridge turned to glare at his captor, the man that had been tormenting him for more than an hour.

"Well, hoped it might anyway," the man said, raising his eyebrows as he looked at the woman in the room, smiling her way.

In response, the woman remained stolid, her thoughts on the man seeming to match Ridge's.

"Take a seat old man," the man said. "Get comfortable. A trek like that can take a lot out of someone."

Not appreciating the continued quips or the flippant attitude the man employed, Ridge remained standing, open hostility on his features.

"Who the hell are you people?"

The man looked to the woman beside him, this time a bit of questioning passing over his features, before he again shrugged with his eyebrows.

"Well, since you've already figured out as much already," he said, "just call us Black Water. I'll be Black, she can be Water."

As he made the introduction, he flipped a finger between he and his partner, delineating which was which, before again gesturing to the futon.

"Sit down, old-timer, no need to get worked up."

"Go to Hell," Ridge snapped back, his concern for the ladies only superseded by the animosity he felt for the man before him. "I am not some damn old fogey you can boss around. I am a United States Senator, and this is my staff. You really think you can just take us into the woods and shoot us because we asked some questions you didn't like?"

With each word that spilled out, Ridge could feel his hatred growing higher, emotions taking over, filling in any gaps his mind might have missed.

Despite whatever the man might have said earlier, it was clear that there was no intention of ever letting them walk free again. Not after everything he had uncovered, not after their captors letting them see their faces and their license plates.

"We are important people, people that will be missed," Ridge continued. "Investigations will be launched-"

"Yeah, yeah," the man said, twirling a hand before him, his voice rising to cut off Ridge. "Investigations, inquiries, law enforcement agencies. We've heard it all and we've seen it all.

"You really think this is our first time? How the hell do you think we got to all of you so easily?"

Not expecting to be interrupted, to have questions posed back in his direction, Ridge paused, unsure what to say, his mouth dry and his bottom jaw sagged open.

Giving the man just the opening he needed to again reveal the silenced 9mm that had been tucked into the rear waistband of his pants. Extending it to arm's length, he held it at shoulder height, the barrel no more than a few feet from Ridge's brow.

"And as I said before, sit your ass down."

No part of Ridge wanted to do that, as much to prove to the man that he didn't have to do a damn thing he said as knowing that once he sat down, it was likely none of the three would ever rise again.

Moving right down the line, the man would pick them off in a row, either leaving them to be found later or dragging them out into the woods to be buried in a shallow, unmarked grave.

A far cry from the hero's internment that was usually bestowed on a man of his position.

Just as much though, Ridge knew that there was no need to rile the man further than necessary, his only hope that time, that discussion, might eventually reveal some tiny crack he would be able to leverage.

He also knew that if he did something rash to instigate the shooting, there would be absolutely nothing left to save Beckwith and Ellerbe, their fates all but sealed.

The floorboards beneath his feet creaked slightly as Ridge took a few steps over and settled down onto the futon beside Beckwith. He thought about trying to offer some words of comfort to the ladies beside him, the situation not allowing it, forcing his attention to his captors as he settled onto the stiff padding, the wooden supports underlying it biting into his tailbone.

"There now," the man said, raising the tip of his weapon toward the ceiling, "was that so difficult?"

The same smile that Ridge so abhorred appeared on the man's face as he shifted to his colleague and said, "And just to be certain that our friend here doesn't get any idea, would you mind binding his feet up as well?"

Just as she had since their arrival, the woman remained completely silent, nodding only in response.

Crossing over to the closest chair, she rooted deep in the side pocket, emerging a moment later with another pair of zip ties, the glossy black plastic flashing as she turned to Ridge, her face void of any emotion.

It was a look she would wear into eternity, the sound of breaking glass and the sight of pink mist exploding from the back of her skull happening in tandem, so fast and unexpected Ridge was unable to react in the slightest.

Chapter Fifty-Two

The next thirty seconds or so moved in starts and stops, as if spliced together from different snippets of the same movie, short bursts offset by momentary breaks.

The first thing to register with Jackson Ridge was the sight of the woman's head snapping back.

Pause.

The hole appearing in the smooth skin of her forehead, followed by a pink spray, blood and bone and brain matter expanding in a fan away from the back of her head.

Break.

The sound of broken glass from the bullet passing through the window above him. The feel of fine particles of it against his neck and scalp, the rush of cold wind passing through.

Gap.

The momentum of the shot lifting the woman into the air, depositing her back on the table. The sturdy construct of it holding her weight as her frame slid across the surface, the top of it wet with her own blood.

Reset.

The sound of her body thumping to the floor, the vibration of the boards as she hit hard, the feeling carrying over to him, passing through the soles of his shoes and up his legs.

The sensation of her impact seemed to be the jolt he needed, his senses and brain finally again synching up, the scene around him transitioning from a poorly constructed movie back into real time.

The man that had tried to pass himself off as Black was the first to react, dropping to a knee. Extending his weapon out at shoulder level, he gripped it in both hands, rotating in a quick arc, jerking the barrel in six-inch increments, eyes wide.

Not once did he bother going to his partner, making no effort to call out or check for signs of life, it immediately clear to all present that she was gone long before she even hit the table, much less the floor.

Second to react was Marian Ellerbe, a low and mournful wail sliding out from deep in her diaphragm. Starting low, it continued for several long seconds, gaining volume before eventually petering out, her gasping breath unable to sustain it.

"Down," Ridge hissed, reaching out with his clasped hands, trying in vain to grab for his colleagues and pull them to the floor. "Get below the windows, cover your head."

Doing the same himself, Ridge dropped to the floor, his kneecap cracking against the exposed planks, a ripple of pain traveling up his thigh and into his core. Stymying any sound that threatened to escape, he continued to claw for Beckwith and Ellerbe.

Side by side, they both slid to the floor, Ellerbe visibly trembling, a host of sounds following suit. Beside her, Beckwith seemed to lose all control of her body, her movements so fluid she seemed to melt to the floor, hitting the ground and curling tight where she lay.

Extending his body atop their huddled mass, Ridge lay across the pair, his manacled hands covering his head.

"Who the hell is that?" the man said, Ridge chancing a glance long enough to see him continuing to rotate, eyes wild. "Who've you got out there?"

Thoughts floated through Ridge's mind in large clumps, starting with attempting the false bravado route, telling the man to stand down, that the place was surrounded, he had alerted the authorities and they had followed him into the woods. Just as fast they cycled through to every possible permutation, ending with the strong desire to tell the man to go to Hell.

Deciding on an option much closer to the middle, Ridge pressed his cheek flat against Beckwith's back, saying nothing, hoping that would be the response to incur the least amount of wrath.

The truth was, he had no idea who was standing outside the cabin, no clue if it was friend or foe, what their motivation might be.

All he knew was that his captors were now a person down and that the man who'd been enjoying his demise all evening was now focused on something other than tormenting him.

"Hey! Ridge!" the man snapped, his voice louder, angrier. "Call your man off!"

Keeping his face pressed flat, Ridge answered, "He's not mine!"

A brief snippet of sound erupted from the man, seeming like it might be the start of a reply, before falling short, the man cutting himself off. Instead, he aimed his face a half-inch toward the ceiling, raising his voice several decibels.

"Whoever is out there – I have Senator Jackson Ridge and his team inside! Stop shooting and step into the cabin with your hands raised or I will kill them all!"

The move was clearly one of desperation, the final gasps of a man trying to play out a losing hand, but Ridge did not for one second doubt the veracity of the statement. Beneath him, he could hear another moan slide from Ellerbe, her body quivering, as Beckwith seemed to wilt a bit more.

"You have until I count to ten!" the man called. "One...two..."

He never made it to three.

The second shot came from the opposite window, Ridge's eyes open, his focus on the man across from him as the bullet entered. With this hands both wrapped around the barrel of the gun, it was a simple task for the round to pass through both wrists, moving through his left and then right as if they weren't even there, twin circles appearing on his light skin.

With them came blood spatter spraying across the barren floor, hanging in the air, the metallic scent of blood so strong it almost caused Ridge to gag.

Just like with the woman, it took a moment for the sounds to match up with the velocity of the round, the bullet through the man's wrists before the breaking glass became audible. Following in order was the man's pained gasps, his face twisting up in agony as the gun slid free, thumping to the floor.

Pulling his arms in tight against his chest, the man drew in deep gasps of air, pulling them in through his teeth, a sucking sound echoing through the cabin.

Remaining that way for several moments, Ridge watched as bright red blood pulsated out from the man's wrists with each beat of his heart, splashing against his chest, staining the black shirt he wore, leaving it shiny, firelight reflecting off it.

Shifting his body just a few inches, Ridge posted his body against the women beneath him, using their forms for purchase, his focus on the weapon lying on the floor between him and the man. Drawing his knees up under him, he shifted his weight, readying himself to dive forward, to grab the weapon and end the man that had violated his office, had taken him and his staff out into the woods, intent on doing Lord knew what.

Feeling that resolve flow through him, Ridge rocked once, twice, against Beckwith's hip, ready to hurtle himself forward.

But he never got the chance.

Instead, any action he might have taken was thwarted by the door swinging open, the wooden gate exploding backward, a shower of splinters and wood shards spraying across the floor.

For a moment there was no movement, nothing but darkness, the door a gaping maw, an entry to whatever lay on the other side.

Just as fast it was filled as Terry Whitner strode into view.

Chapter Fifty-Three

For as many questions as Jackson Ridge had, for all the varied reactions he felt at seeing Terry Whitner walk through the door, his first response had to be seeing to the ladies. Getting them outside, ensuring they were safe, well beyond the horrors of what was sprawled on the floor beside them.

Of what was sure to occur in the coming moments.

Using the leverage of Beckwith's body that just an instant before was to be used to hurl himself at the discarded weapon on the floor, Ridge pushed himself upright. Holding his hands out before him, he ignored the pained whimpers of the man on the floor, hopping twice toward Whitner, his arms extended.

For a moment there was no response, Whitner only staring at him, before reaching into the back pocket of his jeans. Extracting a folding hawksbill blade, he snapped the knife to full extension and ran the blunt edge along the pad of Ridge's thumbs, the metal cold against his skin.

"Just so you know, we're now even."

Not bothering to respond in any way, Ridge let the plastic binding fall to the floor, rubbing his wrists with either hand before accepting the extended handle of the knife. After freeing his ankles, he went to the ladies and carefully worked his way around the tangled mass of their bodies, cutting away all four bindings, Ellerbe twitching as hers were removed, Beckwith giving no response at all.

When he was done, he walked back and returned the knife to Whitner, who accepted it without a word.

"Give me just a minute to get them out?" Ridge asked, the words phrased very much as a question, the response nothing more than a nod.

Waiting for nothing more, Ridge strode back to the futon and grabbed up the faded quilt from the back of it. A relic that had been in place for an untold number of years, the material was coarse and dry, almost brittle to the touch as he draped it over their skin.

"Come on, ladies," he said, his voice just loud enough to be heard over the continued panting of the man on the floor beside them. "Let's get you up and out of here."

Slowly, carefully, he managed to get Ellerbe to her feet first, the girl's face streaked with tears, her body twitching. Once she was standing, Ridge sure to keep her face toward the outer wall, he tugged Beckwith up as well, almost foisting her entire mass from the floor, checking to make sure she could stand under her own power once he got her there.

Only once he was certain they were upright, that there was no chance of losing them again, did he begin to lead them toward the door, Whitner not so much as glancing their way, his focus on the man across the room as Ridge coaxed them out into the night.

In total, he had been inside less than ten minutes, though the world felt noticeably different, somehow even darker and colder than when they had arrived. Staying out a few steps ahead of them, Ridge descended the stairs first, helping them to ground level, before taking them on to the same black SUV they had arrived in.

Standing to the side, he waited as both women slid into the rear seat, each suffering from their own version of shock, their hands clinging to each other as they passed over the leather seat.

Once inside, they huddled close together, the blanket wrapped around them, the vapor of their breath visible each time they exhaled.

"I'll only be a minute," Ridge said, remembering the man pulling the keys from the ignition and pocketing them when they first arrived, knowing he was unable to turn on the engine, to keep them any warmer for the time being.

"Stay strong, girls. We're almost home."

There was no response from either one, both curled up tight in the backseat, Ellerbe's shaking violent enough to cause the bundle they were hidden beneath to tremble.

Not needing to see anymore, the guilt, the remorse, he felt pulsating through him, Ridge slammed the door shut. Setting his jaw, he strode back across the open expanse of ground, gravel crunching beneath his feet, before ascending the three stairs and stepping through the open doorway to the cabin.

Without a door present, the temperature inside had fallen several degrees. In just the few moments he had been gone, Whitner had gotten the man up and into a chair, a tendril of blood snaking down from the man's left nostril a sign that the move wasn't entirely voluntarily.

Just as he had been before, both hands were cradled against his chest, his fingers fighting a losing battle to keep his blood inside. Dark and thick, it oozed through every possible opening, painting his skin red, pulling all color from the man's face.

Standing against the wash basin, Whitner stood with his arms folded, a look of disinterest on his face.

"Was it him in particular or mention of Black Water that got you out here?" Ridge asked, his face tilted a few inches to the side, his gaze leveled on the man in the chair.

Several moments passed without a response, long enough that Ridge flicked his gaze over to Whitner, letting him know that the question was aimed in his direction.

"Both," Whitner eventually said. "Black Water and I have some lingering business. This is the bastard that was following you earlier."

He offered no more than that, though he didn't have to. Any bad blood that existed between the two sides was likely extensive, Whitner not the kind to carry this level of grudge without purpose.

As to the second part, if this man had been tailing Ridge he had likely also seen Whitner, an eventuality that would never be abided.

"Who is he?"

Still wearing the same detached mask as always, Whitner nudged his chin toward the man.

"Ask him."

Not in the mood for games, hyper aware of the ladies and their condition, of the icy car they sat in, Ridge made no effort to bite back his scowl, turning his attention to the man seated in the chair before him.

"Who are you?"

Still pulling in breaths in rapid sequence, shallow and fast, just barely enough to fill his mouth, let alone his lungs, the man stared back in hatred, saying nothing.

"Who do you work for?"

A faint flicker of the same defiant sneer the man had used all evening flashed to his features, the man too weak to keep it in place, but making a valiant attempt just the same.

Seeing it, recalling all the times it had been used on him already, all the untold people it had been deployed on before, Ridge couldn't tamp down the acrimony that swelled within. The hostility, the pure unbridled hatred that he felt for the man and everything he stood for.

Stepping forward, Ridge lifted the silenced 9mm from the floor and extended it at arm's length.

"Last time, who the hell are you?"

Lifting his chin just slightly, the man leveled his focus on Ridge, exhaling loudly, making it quite clear he had no intention of answering.

Jerking the weapon down a few inches, Ridge aimed for the fleshy part of the man's thigh, the same spot he'd been resting the gun just over an hour before.

There was no pause, no lengthy monologue, not even an attempt to let the man plead for mercy, as he jerked back on the trigger, the suppressor on the end doing its job, pulling the sound back to little more than a pop as an orange flicker ignited from the tip.

The front end of the gun bucked just slightly, much less than the hunting equipment he was used to firing, the smell of cordite and smoke instantly finding his nostrils.

Soon after it, the sight of blood splashing down onto the floorboards, the sound of the man gritting his teeth, pushing out a mangled noise, soon joining.

The impact of the shot twisted the man to the side in his seat, his body listing hard to the right. Releasing his grip on his bloody wrists, he wrapped both hands around the leg, blood from his assorted wounds mixing together, painting everything red.

"Again," Ridge said, shifting the tip of the weapon to the opposite leg, "who the hell are you?"

A spool of spittle appeared on the man's lower lip, dripping down between his legs and hitting the floor beneath him, mixing with the blood droplets already painting the boards.

Bent at the waist, the man stayed in that position, slowly raising only his head to glare at Ridge, his forehead sweaty, his eyes glazed.

"His name is Leopold Donner," Whitner said, the sound of his voice breaking the tension of a moment before, pulling Ridge's focus over to the side.

Taking a step forward, Whitner raised a hand, wrapping his fingers around the barrel of the gun.

"And believe me when I say, he isn't getting off that easy."

It took a moment for the words to take hold, for Ridge to grasp what he was being told and to relinquish his grip. Easing the tension in his hands, he allowed Whitner to take the gun, the man meeting his eye and nodding once.

"He works for Black Water, serves as the right-hand man for someone I believe you've already met."

A crease appeared between Ridge's eyes, just as fast falling away, comprehension taking over.

"Ames."

"Ames," Whitner echoed.

Holding the gaze for a moment, Ridge shifted his attention to Donner, to the woman beside him on the floor. "Do I need to do-"

"No," Whitner said. "I got this."

Nodding once, Ridge retreated a step. Reaching out over the table, he grabbed up the keys to the SUV, the metallic tangle cool to the touch, rattling softly.

"Thanks."

Chapter Fifty-Four

General Arnold Ames was still in his dress attire when the knock sounded at the back door. After his visit to the capitol, he hadn't bothered to take it off, knowing that there was a decent chance it would be needed again before the affair was finished.

In most scenarios of the end game, he had envisioned that it would be the other way around, that he would be making a return jaunt, a victory lap to ensure that things were still in place.

How it had ended up going the other way he had no idea, though as he sat with his back pressed against the rigid sofa in his living room, watching as the first hints of dawn appeared on the eastern horizon, he would be lying if he said he was entirely surprised.

Or disappointed.

The reasons Ames had made the transition over were clear enough. A life in the military was a good living – especially for a single man like him, with modest tastes and meager needs – but it was never going to do all the things he needed it to.

Even on a general's wage, two chronically ill parents, his own advancing age, and a host of other financial considerations all meant that things were going to be tight. Never once had he doubted the decision to move over into the private sector, the formation of Black Water being a much-needed reprieve from the front lines, even allowing him to work full-time in the famous structure that for so long had been his goal.

At the time, the plan had been simple enough. With the formation of his new enterprise, he would use his lifetime collection of assets and connections to put things in place before stepping to the side, creating a machine that could run even on its own, bringing in a steady residual income.

Allow him to go hiking, or fishing, or whatever other nonsense men like him were supposed to do in retirement.

As should have been foreseen though, as almost always occurs in similar situations, somewhere along the line things became blurry. The men he hired were cut from a different cloth than the ones he had worked with in the military, the primary motivation financial above all other, their backgrounds multinational.

Within just a few short years, the company transitioned from an on-the-ground assistance firm into full-blown mercenaries, the difference stark.

Through it all, Ames had told himself that it was worth it, that the growing balance of his accounts, that the increased comforts of his parents, justified the means, but there was only so long he could keep up the charade. Whatever integrity he had spent a lifetime building had managed to come down in just a few short years, the events of the past day only confirming how fast and complete his descent had been.

Sitting alone in the darkness, Ames waited past the first knock, knowing who would be on the other side. Raising his glass of Glen Livet, he took one final swig of the liquor, savoring the warm liquid as it slid down his throat, before leaning forward and placing the tumbler on the table before him.

Resting his palms on his thighs, he pushed himself upright, a series of assorted pops and cracks finding his ears. Grabbing the bottom hem of his dress jacket, he pulled it down tight over his midsection, smoothed the front of his pants.

"Come in!" he called, raising his voice, employing the deep resonant bass that he normally saved for his men, the sound booming inside the silent house.

In response, he could hear the hinges on the front door moan slightly, parting just enough for a person to enter, before going back shut. Walking over to stand beside the picture window, Ames turned his shoulder, gazing at the capitol, seeing it lit up one last time, as the sound of dress shoes on hardwood floors grew ever closer.

"It's something, isn't it?" Ames said once the cadence fell away, knowing that his guest had crossed from the exposed wood of the hallway onto the heavy carpeting of the living room.

"It certainly is," Senator Jackson Ridge replied. "I'm going to miss it."

Hearing the hint of sadness that permeated the statement, Ames couldn't help but feel the same way, his features softening slightly as he nodded in agreement.

"So am I."

"Going someplace?" Ridge asked.

To that, Ames felt his face again harden, his eyes narrowing as he turned to face Ridge.

If not for the respective attire each man wore, Ames couldn't help but think that it would be hard to determine at the moment which one was the senator and which one a civilian contractor. While he was in sharp dress, his hair combed, Ridge wore the events of the previous day plainly, his suit rumpled and dirty, his appearance disheveled.

"Don't do that," Ames said. "You've already won."

Shoving his hands into the front pockets of his pants, Ridge lowered his gaze for a moment, seeming to be debating something internally as he sauntered forward, taking up a post on the opposite end of the window.

"Somehow, I don't feel like there were any winners here today," he said. Leaning forward, he pressed his shoulder into the casing encircling the

436

window, the wood moaning just slightly under his weight.

Unable to disagree with the assessment, Ames remained standing upright, resisting the urge to assume a similar position, each man fixing their gaze on the capitol.

"How long do we have?" Ames asked.

"About ten minutes," Ridge replied.

Pressing his lips tight, the general nodded, processing the information.

His first thought was to how much time ten minutes afforded him. Subduing the senator across from him would be no problem, Ames having more than twenty pounds and ten fewer years than his foe, to say nothing of the sidearm strapped to his hip. With just a few quick movements he could have the man down, could have his go-bag in hand, could be in his car and out on the road.

But to what end was the question.

He had no desire to further sully a dazzling career, no interest in being the subject of breaking news, of having himself watched by a stunned nation as he led police on a car chase or was the subject of a manhunt.

Absolutely refused to tarnish his parents or the uniform he wore in such a way.

"Impressive work," Ames said.

Raising his eyebrows slightly, Ridge tilted the top of his head and said, "Well, you guys didn't exactly make it easy."

"My team?" Ames asked. "Dead, I presume?"

"The woman," Ridge said, nodding. "The man – Donner – I presume, as well."

"So you didn't...?"

"No," Ridge said, shaking his head. "Apparently, I wasn't the only one your unit has pissed off over the years."

To that Ames felt surprise creep onto his features, a host of follow-up questions coming to mind, though he let them all pass in silence.

Such was hardly the point now.

"Just you and me now then, is it?" Ames asked.

"Just one soldier talking to another," Ridge replied.

Again Ames could feel a bit of surprise come to his features, the statement quite an overstatement, the couple of years his counterpart spent in Vietnam hardly worthy of being mentioned in the same breath as his career.

Just like before though, he let the sentiment pass, the time for arguing such semantics long past.

"What were you guys doing with the guns?" Ridge asked, his voice gaining a bit of steel as he turned to regard Ames square, opening the volley with more vigor than anticipated.

For an instant Ames considered feigning ignorance, claiming he had no idea what the senator was referring to, before pulling back.

It was clear the man had done his homework. There was no need to insult them both by playing hide-the-ball for the next nine minutes and counting.

"Do you know how many people in Afghanistan hate the Taliban and Al-Qaeda just as much as we do?" Ames replied, answering the question with one of his own.

"Meaning?" Ridge asked.

Ignoring the response, Ames said, "And do you have any idea what happens to most of those weapons once they are cycled out of the country?"

This time Ridge didn't bother responding, fixing his gaze on Ames, waiting in silence.

"They were going to arm the resistance," Ames said. "Helping those already in the country, allowing them to ensure that we never crossed paths with the same insurgents again. Or worse yet, that they never showed up here."

A muscle twitched in Ridge's neck as he nodded, listening to the information. "So you were something of a self-appointed Robin Hood? Stealing from the rich, arming the poor, that sort of thing?"

Venom swelled in the back of Ames's throat, threatening to spill over his tongue, to come pouring out at any moment.

This was the problem with politicians, the same sort of nonsense he had been forced to death with over a lifetime in the service. They saw things through their own particular lens, no matter how narrow the view afforded really was.

To them, life was all about dollars and cents, about being accountable to their constituents and their checkbooks, ignoring the enormous amount of waste that they perpetuated every single day.

"Like I said," Ames replied, "the guns were all set to be decommissioned anyway. You know how big a pain in the ass it is to scrub a weapon that spent years in the sand?"

The question was rhetorical, meant to illustrate a point, not evoke a response, no surprise coming in the least when Ridge failed to give one.

"Your Robin Hood analogy does hold weight in one key area, though," Ames said. "Never did we accept a cent for what we were doing."

A look that seemed to match the way Ames had felt just a moment before flashed across the senator's face, his ridiculous mustache twisting up into a snarl.

"Unless, of course, you count non-financial costs, like the life of Josh Tarby."

Lashing out was the first inclination of Ames, telling the man across from him that such a pointed barb seemed especially rich coming from a man that had played a significant role in the deaths of two of his ranking employees.

Once more he managed to push it aside, drawing in deep breaths of air, aware that their time was fast coming to a close.

"Josh Tarby, while tragic, knew what he was getting into," Ames said.

The scowl on Ridge's face grew more pronounced, his upper lip curling back into a snarl as he stared back at Ames, "Don't give me that line about soldiers signing up for that sort of thing."

"And don't pretend you even knew who he was before yesterday," Ames said. "That if you hadn't gotten embarrassed by the media, you wouldn't be home in bed right now, riding out your last night in Congress the same way you've treaded water for the last six years."

The words were out before Ames even realized it, Ridge's self-righteous posture, his continued jabs, becoming too much, forcing out the sentiments that were pinned deep inside.

Seeing that the words had struck, that Ridge was left with his mouth hanging open, the sneer fading as he searched for a response, Ames continued, "And I wasn't quoting some worn out line about Josh Tarby. He knew what he was getting into because he signed on for it."

Less than five feet away, Ridge seemed to go through a handful of stages, each more pronounced than the one before, attempting to work his way through the information he'd just been given.

"Yeah," Ames said, forcing his voice to remain even. "He sought us out, just like every patrolman for every run we ever hit did. All we had to do was put out the word that we would pay good money for them to look the other way, maybe have to spend a few minutes out in the desert before we came to pick them up, and they came calling."

The summation was a bit of a simplification, but not by much. Basic pay for men in their position was such that it was almost too easy to get them to sign on, some doing so for a pittance that would be laughable if it wasn't so pitiable.

"Bullshit," Ridge spat back in reply.

Expecting the response, Ames knew that would be the reaction, men like Ridge refusing to believe that one of the baser human instincts could ever exist in places like the military.

"Yeah?" Ames countered. "So Tarby didn't come from a single mother in a one-horse town in Wyoming? He didn't have a girlfriend named Sara Yellowhair with his child back home that he felt the need to provide for?"

The words seemed to do exactly what they were intended to, stopping Ridge cold, his face sagging with shock as he stared back, eyes wide.

Nodding once, the words a final small victory, Ames said, "We do background checks just like any other employer, Senator, only we go much, much deeper."

When there was no response, he added, "We have to. If we end up employing the wrong people, a lot of innocent folks end up getting hurt."

Letting his voice fall away, Ames turned his attention back to the window. His final monologue would certainly never be enough to exonerate some of the things he'd done, but hopefully, it would at least clarify, provide some context for the way in which his story was framed moving forward.

In the East, the faint glow became more pronounced as the first sliver of orange light crested the horizon, just starting to peek out above the jagged skyline of the city.

"I guess none of us are going home with our hands clean on this one, are we?" Ridge asked, Ames flicking his gaze over to see he had taken a similar stance.

He didn't bother responding.

There was no need.

Chapter Fifty-Five

The final favor that Jackson Ridge cashed in during his tenure as a United States Senator – and if everything went to plan, his life - was made to Micah McArthur back in Cheyenne. Technically not a favor, since she did still work for him for a few more hours, he had still felt bad about calling and waking her up, the time difference meaning it was just six a.m. where she was.

Repeatedly she had stated over the phone that she was awake and didn't mind, though the yawning and stilted conversation she muddled through seemed to indicate otherwise.

Even more so was the point driven home an hour later when she called back with the information he had requested, the data scribbled down on a slip of paper that was now tucked into his pocket as he strode back through the front entrance of the George Washington Medical Center.

Still dressed in the same suit he'd been wearing for twenty-six hours, muddy water was splattered atop his boots, the hems of his slacks crusted solid. Spots of various fluids – bodily and otherwise – dotted his exterior, and his hair stood in a tangle that no comb could ever hope to contain atop his head.

In dire need of a shower, a shave, and a jolt of liquid caffeine, Ridge ignored every bodily urge that was roiling through him as he walked the same hallway he had just ten hours before. In their stead, he focused on the events of the past day, of everything that had been discovered.

Of the things he wished had remained hidden.

Unable to change any of them, not sure he would even if he could, Ridge stepped into the waiting area at half past nine, the area significantly more populated than on his previous visit. As he appeared, a handful of people glanced his direction, his gaze dancing over them before landing on a trio tucked away in the corner.

In the far seat, the arm of her chair flush against the wall, sat Ellerbe, a gray wool blanket pulled over her as she leaned to the left, the top of her head resting against the plain wallpaper. Unlike the last time he had seen her, she appeared to be at ease, her lips moving just slightly as she rested, her eyes closed.

Beside her sat Kyle Stroh, very much awake, leaning forward with his elbows on his knees, his fingers laced together, hanging down between them. Staring directly at the floor, his tie had been removed, his shirt opened at the collar and the sleeves rolled up, a look on his face that seemed to intimate he was currently fighting a losing battle with remorse and self-loathing.

Neither of which were his to bear, though Ridge couldn't begin to shake the feeling that it would be a long time before the young man believed that, if ever.

Sitting third in the row was Susan Beckwith, her back tight against the chair, her head upright, attention aimed forward, with her eyes closed.

The last time Ridge had seen her or Ellerbe was when he dropped them off at GWMC after leaving the cabin, both in a clear state of shock, neither saying anything, even as they pulled up and he helped them unload.

Remembering back to his own first encounter with death, it had struck him how ill-prepared for the total sensory onslaught it had presented. While there were certainly ways to prepare the body for the sight of blood, it was always the smell of it, the sound of bullet entry, that stuck most with a person.

His first time had not been greatly different than the reactions that the two women had exhibited, the only likely explanation for their current state being that they were sedated, released back to their post in the waiting room.

In just a few minutes, Ridge would return for all of them. He would take them back to the office, have one final briefing, try in some small way to express the regret and sorrow he felt for involving any of them.

For the time being though, he had one more thing to tend to first.

Leaving his team in the corner, Ridge walked to the counter lining the side wall, the desk that had sat dark on his previous visit now manned by a young woman in lavender scrub pants and a matching print top, her thin black hair pulled into a ponytail behind her head.

"Good morning," she said, her tone nor her features seeming to match the words.

"Morning," Ridge said, digging into his back pocket and extracting his wallet.

Hating like hell to play the angle – even if only for one last time – but wanting even less to go through the rigmarole that usually accompanied such things, he extracted a business card and held it toward the girl.

"I'm terribly sorry for showing up unannounced, but Senator Jackson Ridge here to see Ms. Clara Tarby."

The girl's mood seemed to sour as she looked from the card to Ridge, examining the disheveled state of him, a look of disbelief on her face.

"Please," Ridge said. "She's a constituent of mine, doesn't have any family in the area."

Examining the card for another moment, she eventually shrugged, adding an eye roll that seemed to say *whatever* without requiring her to actually make a sound. Reaching under her desk, she pressed a button, a clicking sound echoing out from the wooden door behind her, the mechanized latch holding it in place released.

"Room eighteen, just down the hall," the girl said, her voice letting it be known that he had about as many seconds to make his way through before she changed her mind.

Stuffing the card back into his pocket, Ridge murmured his thanks and slid around the desk, passing through the door without so much as a glance over his shoulder.

The instant he stepped through, an abrupt change was evident, the subdued colors and carpets of the waiting room giving way to white tile and bright light. Open air rooms lined either side of the hall, separated from each other by floor-to-ceiling curtains held in place by small hooks latched to metal tracks.

Gone were the groups of family and well-wishers, their eyes bleary, waning attention aimed at televisions along the ceiling or handheld electronic devices. In their stead were scads of hospital staff, all dressed in scrubs or white coats, most of them awake and energized, ready for the start of a new day.

Unlike the surgeon that Ridge had spoken to the night before, none of the people looked to be pulling extended duty, buzzing past as if he wasn't even standing there.

The heels of his boots clicked softly against the tile floor as Ridge rolled forward onto his toes, stretching out his strides, flicking his gaze to either side, watching the numbers to the patient rooms rise.

Fifty feet down the hall, more than halfway to the end of it, he found the one he was looking for and stepped inside, the curtain pulled almost all the way shut, the lights dimmed.

It was hard for Ridge to recognize Clara Tarby at first, the woman free of her enormous coat, her hair left free to fall on either side of her head, splashed against the pillow beneath her. Beneath it, her entire throat was wrapped tight in gauze, a bevy of IV's connected to her left arm, a series of bags hanging from a metal stanchion beside her.

Lining the back wall was the standard array of machines and monitors, each making small sounds as they performed their task, none seeming to interrupt her sleep in the slightest.

Sliding forward a few feet so as to avoid making any sound against the floor, Ridge pushed his hands into his pockets, feeling his card in one side, the note with the information from McArthur in the other.

"Good morning, Ms. Tarby," Ridge whispered, knowing before he arrived she would likely be sleeping off the surgery, that even if she wasn't awake, there was no way she would be able to speak to him.

"Let me just start by saying how very, truly, sorry I am. When I offered to move you to the Hilton, I could have never imagined..."

For more than an hour, Ridge had been trying to find the right words, contemplating the best way to approach Tarby, to best summarize everything he had found.

Even as he stood by her side though, he was at a loss, the right words evading him.

"I don't want to disturb your rest," he whispered, "and I will be back later today, and tomorrow, and every day after for as long as it takes until you are better, but I thought it was important to come by this morning.

"You came to me yesterday and asked me a question, as your senator, and I needed to come back and answer it in much the same way."

Pausing for a moment, Ridge looked back over his shoulder to the outside hallway, seeing a pair of orderlies pass by, nobody even seeming to realize he was there.

Despite that, he felt himself lean forward at the waist, removing his hands from his pockets and placing them on his knees, using them to brace himself as he lowered his face just a few inches from hers.

"Yes," he whispered, his voice just barely audible. "Your son's death was worth it."

Fixed in that position, his mouth half open, Ridge paused. There was so much more he could share, so many things that he had learned about the incident in Afghanistan, about Josh's role in it, about his motivation for doing so, but he chose not to.

There would be time for that in the near future, long hours of sitting by Tarby's side and allowing her to scrawl out every question she had, doing everything he could to respond, perhaps even going as far as to track down Sara Yellowhair so that the two women could meet.

Now was most definitely not that time, though.

Pushing himself back to full height, Ridge remained rooted in place a moment, watching as a faint flicker tugged at the corner of Tarby's eye. As it did so, a single bit of moisture managed to leak out, streaking sideways down her face, before disappearing into the tangle of hair that lay spread atop her pillow.

Epilogue

Marian Ellerbe and Kyle Stroh had both gone directly home from the hospital, Ridge even asking the Capitol police to drive them there personally, allowing a slight insinuation that the two cops had failed to do the one small thing they were tasked with the night before to coerce them into providing the escort free of complaint.

More than once he had tried the same approach with Susan Beckwith, the woman having recovered from her bout with shock, and the ensuing medication, her usual staid demeanor back in place, dismissing the idea as quickly as he suggested it.

Knowing better than to argue, that it would end no differently than their previous trip away from the hospital, Ridge had hailed a cab to take them back to Dirksen, the two now seated in his office, assuming the same stance they had a day before, just as they had a thousand others before that.

"So," Ridge said, extending his feet out and placing them on the corner of the desk, folding them at the ankle, "what do we have on the agenda for today?"

Allowing the corner of her mouth to curl up slightly at his attempt at mirth, Beckwith just as fast let it fall back into place, all business to the end.

"Well, I would say it looks to be pretty uneventful, but the last time I said as much seemed to jinx us."

Ridge's first reaction was to smirk, a movement that pushed the top of his head back several inches, a small sound escaping with it.

An instant later the look vanished, the events of the last day rushing back to him in a thick fog, so much having transpired, large parts of it bucking comprehension, even now as he sat and pondered on it.

"Susie," he said, his voice low, "I cannot begin to thank you enough for everything you've done these past twelve years."

Across from him, Beckwith seemed to go rigid, veins and muscles standing out, striated beneath the skin of her neck.

"Nor can I tell you how very sorry I am for these last twenty-four hours. If I had had any idea..."

Beckwith's nostrils flared just slightly as she sat and stared at him, processing what he had told her, a small part forming between her lips as she took it in.

"I'm sorry too, sir. I can't help but believe that this was somewhat my fault for not properly screening Ms. Tarby-"

"Nonsense," Ridge said, waving a hand to cut her off, "if there was any fault at all in this, it rests with Black Water and nobody else."

Even though Ridge had spent the cab ride over filling Beckwith in on everything that had transpired with Ames that morning, it still wasn't clear if either one believed what he'd just said.

"I'm just glad we were able to get to the bottom of things before time ran out."

Moving slowly, Beckwith reached up, pinching the bridge of her nose between her thumb and forefinger. Holding the pose for a moment, she drew in a deep breath, seeming to be debating something, before lowering it back into place and staring straight at Ridge.

"What you did here was a good thing, Jack."

Feeling his eyebrows rise slightly, noting it was the first time she had ever used his first name, Ridge remained silent.

"It was the kind of thing that the man I signed up to work for would do, a completely selfless odyssey to help someone else, a right proper use of power, the kind of thing a lot of people in these buildings could stand to show more often.

"The sort of thing I hope Willis Hodges understands before he steps into the office because he has some mighty big shoes to fill if he ever wants to be considered in the discussion of great Wyoming leaders."

His lips parting slightly, his eyes bulging at the unexpected outpouring, Ridge sat silent for a moment.

She was right, just as Ames had been before her. He had been coasting the last few years, had gotten complacent, and a hungry constituency had made him pay for it.

But just the same, it had also provided him with one last chance to make amends.

"It was a hell of a last day, wasn't it?" he asked.

"Yes, sir, it was," Beckwith agreed.

Nodding slightly, Ridge raised his left arm up from the desk and pushed back the sleeve of his shirt, checking the face of his watch.

"Eleven-thirty," he said, releasing his grip on the shirtsleeve and lowering his hand back into place. "What do you think? Is it getting to be that time?"

For a moment there was no response, Beckwith staring straight at him, her features impassive, completely void of a reaction.

Just as quickly, a faint smile crossed her lips, the right side of her face scrunching slightly.

"The Constitution says we have until noon. Let's let that bastard wait while we enjoy every last second of it."

About the Author

Dustin Stevens is the author of more than 25 novels, 18 of them having become #1 Amazon bestsellers, including *The Debt* and the Hawk Tate and Zoo Crew series. *The Boat Man*, the first release in the best-selling Reed & Billie series, was recently named the 2016 Indie Award winner for E-Book fiction.

He also writes thrillers and assorted other stories under the pseudonym T.R. Kohler, his first novel released in 2017, entitled *Shoot to Wound*.

A member of the Mystery Writers of America and Thriller Writers International, he resides in Honolulu, Hawaii.